MY HUSBAND'S WIFE

BOOKS BY CARLA KOVACH

What She Did

Find Me

The Houseshare

On a Quiet Street

DETECTIVE GINA HARTE SERIES

The Next Girl

Her Final Hour

Her Pretty Bones

The Liar's House

Her Dark Heart

Her Last Mistake

Their Silent Graves

The Broken Ones

One Left Behind

Her Dying Wish

One Girl Missing

Her Deadly Promise

Their Cold Hearts

Her Hidden Shadow

Meet Me at Marmaris Castle
Whispers Beneath the Pines
To Let
Flame

MY HUSBAND'S WIFE

CARLA KOVACH

bookouture

Published by Bookouture in 2025

An imprint of Storyfire Ltd.
Carmelite House
50 Victoria Embankment
London EC4Y 0DZ

www.bookouture.com

The authorised representative in the EEA is Hachette Ireland
8 Castlecourt Centre
Dublin 15 D15 XTP3
Ireland
(email: info@hbgi.ie)

Copyright © Carla Kovach, 2025

Carla Kovach has asserted her right to be identified as the author of this work.

All rights reserved. No part of this publication may be reproduced, stored in any retrieval system, or transmitted, in any form or by any means, electronic, mechanical, photocopying, recording or otherwise, without the prior written permission of the publishers.

ISBN: 978-1-83618-740-0
eBook ISBN: 978-1-83618-739-4

This book is a work of fiction. Names, characters, businesses, organizations, places and events other than those clearly in the public domain, are either the product of the author's imagination or are used fictitiously. Any resemblance to actual persons, living or dead, events or locales is entirely coincidental.

To those who are grieving over the loss of someone dear to them.

PROLOGUE

It's positive. He's waiting at the other side of the toilet door for me to reveal the big news. Finally, I'm going to be a mother. That's all I've ever wanted. I dreamed I'd have two, or maybe even three, but this precious baby will likely be my only one. I place my hand on my stomach, and I know that my little one is barely more than a few cells, but I already love him or her more than anything. Nothing else in the world matters more than my little bean.

He knocks again. 'Well? Don't keep me in suspense.'

I slowly open the door and pass him the pregnancy stick. 'We're having a baby.' I can't feel any more love in my heart in this moment. My life is beyond perfect. The people close to me think we've rushed into this but when you know it's the real thing, you know.

He picks me up, kissing my face and my neck, then he spins me around until I'm nauseous – but in a good way. When I eventually manage to release myself from his arms, he heads to the kitchen and puts some music on, returning with two champagne flutes. One for him with bubbly in it and another for me containing orange juice. We clink glasses. 'To us,' he says, his gaze lovingly meeting mine.

I look away from him and swallow. Why when I love him so much am I lying so badly? I can't ever tell him that the baby isn't his. I grab his hand and rest it on my stomach. 'To us and our little life inside me.'

ONE

EVA

I always thought that once you'd found your one true love, there could never be another. How wrong was I? My heart is singing. As I tick off the jobs on my to-do list, I do it with a slight dance. Not only have I found the man I'm spending the rest of my life with, my ten-year-old son, Caiden, loves him to bits. I tape up the last packing box, then I write *Shed* on the cardboard.

Our West Highland terrier looks up at me and whines, his white fringe partly curled over his eyes. 'Big day today, Freddie,' I say. He wags his tail. I take a photo of him next to the box and post it to Instagram with the caption 'new beginnings' underneath.

My phone buzzes and I open the message.

Zach: I'm missing you like crazy. This place is amazing but it's empty without you. Can't wait for you to get here. I love you so much. X

I can't wait to move into our seaside house in Combe Martin with my son and new husband. I think of all the work that Zach has done. Over the past two months, he's transformed it into a home.

I packed the mostly eaten box of chocolates that I came home with yesterday. I'd been excited to finish working my notice and leave Malvern behind, though I'm going to miss my colleagues and I'll miss Mum.

The removal people are due any minute so I take a quick walk around the house. I catch Caiden sleeping on the sofa with his mouth open. I navigate the sea of boxes to kiss him on the forehead, and he stirs.

'The removal people are on their way.'

He rubs his eyes and cuddles Doggo under his arm. The old stuffed dog that his father and I bought him as a baby looks like it's been washed up after a storm, and its one amber eye is scratched to bits, but it always melts my heart that he loves Doggo so much. At just turned ten, he's still my little boy. I gently hug him and inhale his apple-scented shampoo and the slight smell of biscuit where he dunked a chocolate digestive for too long then laughed as the soggy biscuit slid down his chin.

The more I look at him, the more I see his father. The way his nose looks slightly long on his face is identical to Hugo's. My stomach sinks at the thought of what I'm leaving behind. Caiden has grown up in Malvern. He went walking up the hills with his father; they fished in local lakes and went birdwatching together. I worry that I'm taking Caiden away from his memories and that he'll forget how wonderful his father was. A shiver runs through me. There are things I want to leave behind, things that haunt me at night but I can't think about them now. I breathe in and then out to quell the anxiety bubbling inside me.

Hugo has been dead for five years. I swallow as I think back to the accident. I call it an accident but the official verdict was death by suicide. Things weren't always perfect between us and I feel churned up inside as I think of the arguments we had. He lied for me, covered for my shortfalls and he was always there. I have this memory of this faraway look that used to spread across his face. Hugo knew all my secrets but I always had the feeling I knew none of his.

'Love you, Mummy. It's all going to be fine,' Caiden says in a way beyond his years.

My heart melts like it always does when he tells me he loves me.

'Love you too, son.'

It's actually happening. I'm leaving all this behind and the past will stay in the past. I am happy, really I am, but there's a tear in the fabric of my happiness when I think of Hugo. He wouldn't want me to remain unhappy until I die. I know he loved me and he adored Caiden. Scrolling through my phone, I find the photo of Caiden when he was only three, on the beach at Combe Martin in Devon. We alternated our holidays between there and the Scottish Highlands even before Caiden was born, and we wanted to share our love of these places with our little boy. The joy on Caiden's face as he built sandcastles with his plastic spade never fails to make me smile. I put my phone down and check for the removal van out of the window, but it's not quite eight in the morning.

I think of Zach, who is waiting for us to arrive. When Zach had asked, 'If you could choose to live anywhere in the world, where would it be? We can go anywhere?' I didn't hesitate in saying Combe Martin because it was a place he loves too.

Soon the cold March mornings will be replaced by summer, and all I can picture is our new life and our sea view. A niggle makes my stomach nervously flutter. I wonder if it's wise to go back to a place that holds so many good memories of my dead husband – but I love it. I love the rockpools, the cute cafés and the pub on the beach. The sheltered cove feels like it's hugging its visitors, and I'd love to walk the South West Coast Path with Freddie. What I do know is I can't stay in the area where my husband died. Swallowing hard, guilt washes through me again so I swallow it down and send Zach a quick reply.

> *I love you so much too, and I can't wait to start our new life together. See you soon. XXX*

A whirlwind of activity follows and the removal people have come and taken all our worldly possessions in a lorry. I lock the front door to the cottage that has been our home for a year and I post the keys.

I get into the car and glance in the rearview mirror. Caiden has a bit of jam stuck to one side of his face. I pretend to scrub my face and he laughs as he wipes it off. Freddie is secured so we're ready to go.

'What are the flowers for?' Caiden asks.

'I thought we could go and visit your dad's tree one more time, before we leave.'

He nods, not taking too much notice of what I say. It hurts me to think how little he probably remembers of Hugo. My phone beeps. It's Mum.

> *Have a safe journey and give Caiden a kiss from Nanna. I'll come and visit soon. Call me when you get there. Love to you all. X*

As I drive along the steep road down the hillside, I try not to cry. I'll miss my mum most of all. We said our temporary goodbyes last night over dinner, and she promised she'd visit soon. She's been my rock since Hugo's death. I take a deep breath. It's not like we're moving to Australia; it's a three-hour drive to our new home. Mum used to drive coaches to the Highlands in Scotland before she retired. Driving to Combe Martin will be a walk in the park for her, and I kept reminding her that I'll be coming to visit all the time.

. . .

As we reach our old house in Malvern that Caiden and I shared with Hugo, I pull over.

'Can I stay in the car with Freddie?'

'I'd really like you to come with me. I think we should both leave these flowers for Dad, don't you?'

'Of course, Mum. I'll come with you. Shall I put Freddie's lead on?'

'Yes, please.'

Above us, a sheet of grey cloud is pierced by a golden ray of sun. It bounces off the car window, almost blinding me, as I open the back door to release Freddie and Caiden safely onto the path. My son presses his lips together as he looks at the Victorian house we called home for nearly nine years of his life. It stands proudly, double fronted and three-storeys high – solid and imposing on the panoramic landscape behind it. The curtains I made for the upstairs windows are still hanging up. I almost see the ghost of Hugo holding Caiden as a baby, bouncing him up and down while pointing at the birds nesting in the tree opposite.

Hugo and I moved in three months after we got married. The tall ceilings, original tiled hall and the dining room that fitted a ten-seater table in it overwhelmed me. Growing up, it was just Mum and me, living in our small apartment in Redditch right opposite Grandma's bungalow. Meeting and marrying Hugo felt like a dream. Soon after I found out I was pregnant, we danced around the living room, ecstatic with the news.

Here I go again, living in the past. I feel my chest getting tighter and my breathing quicken. Being back here does that to me. While playing with my wedding ring, I count and breathe slowly to quell my anxiety. As my heart rate returns to normal, I open the passenger door and grab the bunch of daisies off the seat.

'Come on, Mum. We've got a long drive ahead.'

The new owner comes to the window. She rocks a tiny baby in her arms while pointing at a raven sitting on the stone wall that divides the drive and the road. She turns my way, her features hardening as she pulls the curtains closed.

I follow my son to Hugo's apple tree, the one we planted on the edge of what was our land, when we moved in. The wall that separated the car parking space from the sheer drop below was never rebuilt. My heart bags and blood thuds through my ears as I think of our old car being driven through those bricks, straight over the steep ledge. The weathered tape that someone from the council had tied across the gap has been there for years now. I should have fixed the wall before I moved out, but money had been tight back then. Hugo had a life insurance policy in place to cover the outstanding mortgage on his death, but there wasn't much left in the way of savings. I always thought we had more but it seemed we didn't have a buffer.

Freddie drags Caiden to the tree and pees. 'Freddie, that's Daddy's tree.' Caiden gently pulls Freddie over to a patch of grass.

I smile and sit opposite the base of the tree. Placing the flowers against the bark, I take in the messages that Caiden and I have carved into the wood over the years. *Hugo's tree... Sadly missed... Love you to bits...* With my help, Caiden had scratched a smiley face into the bark. Beneath the earth, I'd buried a brief letter to Hugo, asking why – just why. I told him I loved him over and over again. He really left a hole in my heart; but now I've met someone who has filled that void, though it feels disloyal being at the tree while I'm so happy. I'll always bring Caiden here when we visit Mum, but I am saying my final goodbye to sadness and mourning. I owe it to Zach to find closure and concentrate on us. He's a good man who deserves all of me. It's not that he isn't understanding, he is. He's known loss too; that's why we are such a perfect fit.

'I will never forget you, Hugo.' I pull my first wedding ring from my pocket and the mini gardening spade from my bag. Digging up the earth around the tree, I drop my ring into the mud before refilling the hole and placing a grey stone on top. There's a slight lump in the earth where I buried my letter. It looks disturbed so I shovel some of the mud away, and when I dig a little deeper, I find my letter has gone. Someone has taken it. It saddens me that someone would do such a thing.

I glance at the edge of the drop and my stomach lurches. Caiden is getting closer to the drop as Freddie pulls him in every direction. I want to shout at him to get back, but if I alarm him, he might fall over the edge.

My knees turn jelly-like as I get up and creep up behind my son. I snatch him in my arms, drawing him close. 'Don't you ever do that again, Caiden,' I shout.

He stares at me, wide-eyed, like I'm crazy. It's been a long time since someone has looked at me like that. Guilt immediately washes over me. Caiden has every right to look at me in that way; he just doesn't know why.

'I was just looking at the fields and trees. I wasn't near the edge, I promise.'

'You were, I saw you.' One pull from Freddie and he'd have been at the bottom of the hill, dead amongst the treetops below. The sheer drop sends my stomach whirling. The miles of green fields ahead of us, interspersed with roads and houses, make me lightheaded. I place Caiden down then I pull him even further away from the dangerous drop. A raven lands in Hugo's tree and croaks, sending shivers through me. It's as if Hugo is there, watching over me and reminding me of my past failings.

'Are you angry, Mum?'

'You scared me. Your dad lost his life here, you know that. I don't want to lose you, too, do you understand?' I see from his reddening face that he thinks I'm telling him off, but I'm not. I have nightmares of what happened to his father and I couldn't bear anything like that to happen to my son. In my mind, I picture Hugo going over that edge in his car and it haunts the hell out of me.

He bites his bottom lip and nods in his usual exaggerated way. 'I'm sorry.' He pauses and stares at the flowers. 'Bye, bye, Daddy.' He smiles. 'Can we go now?'

'Yes, I'd like that.' I grab the mini spade and throw it in my bag.

As we get into the car, I feel lighter now that we're leaving the old for the new, and I can't wait to get to Combe Martin. I turn the radio up and 'Happy' by Pharrell Williams plays. Caiden shouts 'happy' every time Pharrell sings the word, and right now, apart from my son standing too close to a steep edge while we were by the tree, I am happy and nothing can take that away from me; from us.

I should be able to leave the past behind, but all I can think of is Hugo going over that edge. Guilt threatens to overwhelm me. Hugo also took my secret with him, one so big, if my son found out what I did, he'd never forgive me.

TWO

After a few rain showers, I'm finally driving through the quaint narrow streets of Combe Martin. We had to stop five times so that either Caiden or Freddie could pee but we've made it.

I received a message two hours ago telling me that the removal lorry had arrived and all our belongings were being unloaded. Taking the snake-like roads slowly, I can't help but notice the white-rendered houses with touches of blue that scream seaside. I almost let out a shriek of excitement when I give way to let a car pass through a tight gap. There is the cutest little shop with seashells in the window. We're going to be so happy here. Caiden yawns as he wakes from his brief slumber, and Freddie starts barking.

'Mum, I can see the sea,' Caiden yells as he rubs the sleep from his eyes.

'Yay, we're here. You played on that beach when you were even smaller than you are now, and we were even here when you were in my tummy.'

'I'm not small. I'm ten.'

Yes, still small, I'd like to say to him, but he thinks he's grown up now because he makes sandwiches and cupcakes.

'Do you remember the time you filled your bucket with seaweed and poured it over me when I was sunbathing? I screamed so loud, a man walking close by thought I'd been hurt. We never laughed so much.'

Caiden's brows are furrowed. We have lots of photos but I worry that Caiden will have forgotten how it felt to hug his dad. Could he still hear his dad's voice in his head, or have those memories gone? 'I think so,' he replies, deep in thought.

After the car has passed, I carry on driving. I don't think Caiden really remembers that holiday. It was a hot August day when Caiden was four. Later that same day, we'd had an early dinner at the beach pub. Caiden had fallen asleep in Hugo's arms and I just blurted out what I'd been thinking. 'I really want another baby.' Hugo couldn't contain his excitement. We made plans, we were happy and after several months of trying for a baby with no success, he was gone.

I take a couple of deep breaths. This move is meant to be our new start, so why can't I stop thinking about the past since visiting Hugo's tree? Maybe it's because I came to live here. I shake those thoughts of the past away. Our new house awaits us.

The closer we get, the more excited I am. The happy, nervous butterflies in my tummy begin to flutter. A couple with a child walk up the steps from the beach, raincoats flapping in the breeze. A quick glance to my left tells me that no one else is on the sand, nor are they walking around the rockpools that frame the far end of the beach. The huge cliff and hills behind the beach make me shudder a little. I always end up living on hills and Hugo died on a hill, but I find them breathtakingly beautiful. What happened to Hugo was tragic, nothing more.

I drive around the bend and continue for half a mile until I come to our new home. I pull up behind the lorry and smile as I watch Zach carrying boxes. My new husband, Zach. I feel a little dizzy when I say that in my head as it's been such a whirlwind.

Before I get the chance to grab my phone, Caiden is already out of the car and Freddie barks in my ear. The gate is open so I leash Freddie before I let him jump off the seat to join us.

'Eva.'

Zach runs over to me, picks me up just a couple of inches off the ground and kisses me. His arms feel strong and protective. All I want to do is sink into him.

'I've missed you, babe.' He puts me down and we kiss again.

I've missed this and I can't wait to sleep with him in our bed tonight and have my whole family under one roof.

'You have to see the kitchen.'

'I've missed you so much.' I can't stop kissing him. We haven't seen each other since he came back to Malvern eight weeks ago. It feels like forever. 'And I can't wait to see all that you've done to the house.'

'Seriously, it's better than the photos show.'

Dragging me by the hand he pulls me and I pull Freddie. Caiden is already upstairs checking out which bedroom might be his. We go through to the snug with the inglenook fireplace at the far end. Two huge charcoal-coloured beams strike lines through the ceiling. Then we step into a small dividing room that already contains the ten-seater dining table that I'd kept in storage as we couldn't fit it into the cottage. The old part of the house then opens up to a huge kitchen-cum-family room; the very reason we specifically wanted this house. The uninterrupted, floor-to-ceiling glass view of the pebbly beach and sea below is everything Zach and I dreamed we might be able to afford.

'Mummy, can I have the big bedroom with my own bathroom?'

I laugh and ruffle my son's hair. 'I think that one's ours, Caiden. There are three more bedrooms, go and choose one of the other decorated rooms.' I place Freddie's lead under a chair leg to keep him safe while I look around properly. Brushing my fingers against the deep blue Shaker-style kitchen drawers, I open and close one. The huge island in the middle is topped with the exact worktop I chose and uploaded to our virtual mood board. My eyes well up. 'I can't believe you've done all this.' I head over to the lounge part of the room and press my hand down on the new charcoal-grey sofa, excited about buying soft furnishings to jazz it up.

'I'm glad you approve, Mrs Wright.'

'I do, and I'll show you how much I approve later.' God, I've missed him. I reach up and run my fingers through his full head of dark hair which is slightly mussed-up as always. Linking my hand in his, I feel for the callouses, a reminder of all his hard work, and I stroke them.

'Is that a promise?' He grins and kisses me again.

'Of course, but I think we need to unpack and eat first.' Freddie whines as he drags the chair in an attempt to escape his lead.

'Let's get this done.'

Zach says goodbye to the removal staff and picks up the box marked *Electricals*. 'I should go and set the TV up. I'm guessing Caiden will want to watch something later.'

I nod. 'At the very least, it might give us some peace while we unpack. It's going to be a long evening. I'm heading up to make the beds and then I think we should get a takeaway later. A celebration is called for.' I glance back through the house and see that the front door is now closed, so I release Freddie. He wags his tail and starts to sniff everything.

'That sounds like the best plan.'

However much I want to slump onto one of the sofas and sleep, I know I have too much to do. I run upstairs and hear a voice coming from the room at the very end of the hall. I gently listen at the door to Caiden chatting away to himself. 'This is our new home and this is my room, Doggo.' A bit of clanking around is followed by more chattering. 'Dad, we're at our new home. Mummy said we always came on holiday here but I can't really remember.' He pauses. 'I found this,' he pauses, 'which I'll keep safe forever. I wish you were here and that you didn't die.'

I knock before nudging the door open. 'Caiden.' I don't see the object he says he'll keep safe forever. All I see is Doggo and stacks of boxes.

'I chose this room, Mummy. My bed was already in here.'

He still calls me Mummy sometimes, mostly when he's tired, or he's feeling poorly. I sit on the edge of the mattress, lean over and kiss his cool head. 'Well, I think it's perfect.' There are plenty of built-in cupboards and shelves for all his toys and clothes, and being in the roof of the older part of the house means the room has charm with its uneven angles and vaulted ceiling. 'I know you miss Daddy a lot. Were you talking to him just then, before I came in?'

'No. Daddy's dead. I was talking to Doggo and I know Doggo is only a teddy. I'm ten, not five, but I still like to talk to Doggo sometimes because he doesn't ask me questions.'

I shrug and sit up straight, slightly upset that my son prefers to talk to a stuffed dog over me. 'Okay, but you know you can always talk to me, about anything.'

'I know, Mum.'

Freddie jumps onto the bed and begins licking Caiden's cheeks. 'Freddie, that's yuck.' Caiden giggles and play fights Freddie. As he rolls back onto the bed, he drags his coat with him, revealing something that makes me shiver.

'Caiden, where did you get this?'

'It's mine. I want it.' He snatches it from my hand and storms out of his room with Freddie barking at his legs. I'm open-mouthed with confusion. I want to call him back but instead, I let him go. I spot an opening at the back of one of the built-in cupboards. It's a gap and it's empty.

Why did Caiden have Hugo's toy raven, the one with a

sucker at its base? The one that had been stuck to Hugo's dashboard when he crashed to his death? The one that was never recovered from the wreck of my dead husband's car?

THREE

I lie in Zach's arms and ponder over that raven toy as I snuggle against his hairy chest. I'm still slightly flushed but I think I've come back down to earth now. 'I've missed this.'

'What, the sex?' he asks with a laugh.

I move from his arms and sit up in bed. 'Not just the sex.' I playfully slap his bare arm and then kiss him again as I attempt to put the toy out of my mind. I haven't been this close to my husband in ages and I want to be present.

'Okay, my charm, wit and good looks.'

'Now you're talking.' We have this banter which is why I feel so comfortable with him. He is the complete opposite to Hugo. Hugo was serious and mysteriously romantic. He was my Heathcliff. Zach is funny, more salt-of-the-earth and loves nothing more than rolling around on the floor wrestling with Freddie and Caiden. I imagine our new house filled with more children – once we've settled in, of course. 'I feel so lucky.'

'I can see why. I'm a catch.' He presses his lips together and raises his brows as he waits for me to laugh.

However hard I try to push the toy raven to the back of my

mind, it won't stay there and I don't know if I should bring it up. The last thing I want to do is start a deep conversation about Hugo during our first night together in weeks, just after we've made love.

'Eva, is everything okay?'

I smile as I twist a few strands of hair and accidentally tear a bit out. Damn, I haven't done that since Hugo died. I gently reach for the hair close to my neck, where the bald patch used to be, then I bring my hand back down. 'It's just something earlier...'

'Something?'

'I was listening outside the door to Caiden's bedroom and I heard him talking to himself.'

'Well, he is ten. I'm sure it's nothing to worry about. What was he saying?'

'Nothing really. He was just chattering away to Doggo.' I don't want to mention that he was pretending to speak to Hugo. 'But that isn't why I'm concerned.'

'What's worrying you?' He holds my hand.

'I found something and it...' I felt stupidly overwhelmed after seeing the toy raven but I can't explain why Caiden has it.

'Okay, what did you find?'

'Caiden had this toy. It's a raven with a sucker on the bottom so it can be attached to things.'

'Okay.'

'It wasn't just any toy; it was the one that Hugo used to have on his dashboard. I bought it for Hugo before Caiden was born because he used to watch them nest outside our house, then he lost it when we were on holiday.' I shrug as I have no idea how it could have gone missing. 'I knew he liked it so I helped Caiden buy Hugo the exact same raven the Christmas before he died. As soon as he opened the gift, Hugo put it on his dashboard and it never came off. He literally treasured it.' I pause. 'When Hugo's car...'

Zach shifts away from me and looks up at the ceiling and I know mentioning Hugo has ruined our first night together in our new home. Not once has he tried to erase Hugo from mine and Caiden's past so I'm not sure why he suddenly looks so distant. I continue speaking in the hope he'll mellow again. 'Well, I thought that raven went down with Hugo, and now Caiden has it.'

Zach sighs and speaks in a matter-of-fact tone. 'Could Caiden have found the one that got lost? Or maybe your mum bought it for him.'

'She'd have told me.'

'Is it possible that Hugo never had the raven in his car when he died?'

Thoughts are awhirl in my mind. Could Hugo have given it to Caiden? If so, why, and how come Caiden never mentioned that he had it? 'I don't know. All I know is that Hugo was in that car and he died and I always thought that raven was in the car too.'

That day still haunts me. I'd been away with Mum. I'd missed the calls from the police as we pulled up the next morning to see police tape and officers everywhere. That's when I learned what had happened to Hugo. Hugo hadn't wanted me to go away that Saturday night to watch a show in London with Mum and Caiden, that was one of the reasons we argued. He never wanted me to go anywhere without him. I gasp, feeling momentarily suffocated by how much he cared. When I got back home and the police officer told me what had happened, I couldn't breathe. My mother caught me as I collapsed, and Caiden cried so loud, I was deafened to everything around me. Weeks later, they confirmed that the DNA of the body in the car matched that of my husband.

Zach grips my hand under the quilt and I flinch. 'Sorry, I was in a world of my own. You're right, maybe Mum did buy it for Caiden. That's all I can think of.'

The alternative is unthinkable. Had Hugo left the raven for Caiden, knowing that he was going to die? Had he made our son swear to never tell me he had it?

FOUR

A month has passed and we've settled in nicely. I've filled the house with soft furnishings, completing the look with bright, abstract seascapes. As I chop up some apple and spread it with peanut butter for Caiden, he comes running in like a tornado and begins eating. Zach grabs his tool bag and kisses me. 'See you later and don't stress. You're going to be amazing today. Oh, and I can definitely pick Caiden up from school later so no need to rush away on your first day.' Zach leaves just as a message pops up in the parents' WhatsApp group.

> Nicole: A few of us are meeting for coffee on Saturday. It would be amazing if you could join us.

Caiden loves playing with Nicole's ten-year-old son, Aaron, and I really like Nicole. We chat every day when dropping our boys off at school. She messages me witty parent memes most days, and they make me smile. I never expected to make friends this fast and it feels brilliant. I reply with a yes and a smiley emoji.

I can't even think about Saturday, right now. First, I need to get through today. I feel sick with nerves. Being a wedding planner is a job I love and today I start work at the Sea Horse Hotel.

'Mum, we're going to be late and Aaron will wonder where I am.'

While Caiden washes his hands in the kitchen sink, I check myself one last time in the full-length mirror next to the coat rack. I think the pink suit is perfect, along with the silk frilly blouse dotted with cherries. I ruffle my loose blonde curls a little.

'Mum, you look really pretty and you're really clever too.' Caiden, my thoughtful little boy, is beaming at me in our reflection.

I crouch to his level and straighten his school tie. 'Thank you.' I kiss his forehead. 'And you look smart too, son. Let's go.' We go to fist bump, move our fists and make a pretend explosion with them while wiggling our fingers. He laughs and all of a sudden, I don't feel as nervous.

After catching up with school news from Nicole, I leave Caiden at school and drive to the Sea Horse Hotel – my new work home. It's superbly designed and Instagram perfect. Swings, decorated trees, and a pond half covered with lily pads.

My new colleague, Hallie, walks me around the hotel showing me everything. This is the first time we've met in person. She's showed me the spa, the treatment rooms, the ceremony room and the lavish reception – finally she takes me to my office, and I love it. The high-ceilinged room overlooks the perfect gardens that stretch back into thick, lush woodland. I have a sash window, a ceiling rose and built-in bookshelves. 'Do I share this office with anyone?' This can't be all mine, surely.

'No,' she says with only the slightest West Country accent. Her glossed lips reflect the light from the ornate chandelier above me. 'We're really happy you're here. The last wedding planner left two months ago, so I've been bumbling through the job. I don't know how you deal with the stress of it all.'

'It's challenging, but I do.'

'I have heard those words a few times.' She laughs and points a manicured finger at me. I'm guessing that Hallie is around twenty-five. 'Anyway, I work in admin but I will be available to assist you too, so if you need me at any point, just shout.' She points to the white leather office chair. 'Why don't you check out your seat, see if it's comfortable, and I'll go through some of your upcoming appointments for this week, then we can go to the café and get some coffee. Does that sound like a plan?'

I already like Hallie. 'That sounds perfect.'

'Okay, so you have an online diary. The computer is already turned on, so if you wiggle the mouse you should be able to see your appointments. Have you managed to study our packages and the prices?'

'Yes, I spent last week reading everything that was sent to me.'

Hallie smiles and plays with the end of her honey-streaked blonde ponytail while standing behind me. 'Great, so click into tomorrow.'

I click. 'Ben and Alice at ten a.m. and Theo and Madison at two p.m.'

'They are your first appointments.' She excitedly claps her hands once. 'They're both interested in our bronze package. I don't think you'll budge Ben and Alice, but I know that Madison wasn't happy. She wanted silver but her husband-to-be was trying to keep costs down. We want them to both be happy, but ultimately if we can convert to a silver, that would be amazeballs.'

So, I have my first challenge and I can't wait.

Hallie leaves the room to attend to a customer's billing query, and my phone rings. 'Hi, Mum.'

'Eva, how are things? I was getting worried because you didn't call me back. We haven't had a proper chat since you moved.'

I should have called Mum but I've been constantly sidetracked, and I know how she worries, even though I'm in my thirties. 'I'm fine, Mum, but I can't speak for long. I'm at work and it's my first day. I can't get caught talking on my phone.'

'I should call back later.'

I stand and open my office door. Hallie is nowhere to be seen. 'I'm okay for a couple of minutes but if I cut you off, it means someone is about to come in.'

'Okay, I just wanted to know how you were all settling in.'

'It's amazing here and the house is beautiful. We're really happy and Caiden loves his new school. You've seen the photos of the house, haven't you?'

'I have and I'm worried about you.'

'Why, because of the house?'

'No... yes. All of it. Rushing into your marriage, the house, the new job, the move. You were settled in Malvern; we had a routine and it was good for you and Caiden.'

My stomach clenches. Not this again. 'I was existing in Malvern. I had to pass where Hugo died every single day. It was stifling me and don't get me started on the people and how they stared. Caiden and I needed to get away from all that.'

'You're running away and we know what happens when you run away from things that upset you or stress you out.'

'Mum, I'm not having this conversation again. I love Zach, I wanted to move here with him and I'm happy.'

The day before we left Malvern, Mum had gone on and on about us moving away with Zach and it pains me that she won't accept him when he's been nothing but perfect with me.

She hangs on the other end of the call in silence. 'I'm scared.'

I puff out a breath. 'Why?' I don't know why I'm indulging her. I'm not the same person I was all those years ago. Things have changed for the better.

'I'm scared I'll lose you again.'

'You haven't lost me. You can visit anytime.'

'You know what I mean. Only this time, I won't be close enough to be there when you need me.'

Is she crying? 'Mum. Please stop this nonsense and let me live my life.'

Hallie walks back in and smiles. 'Right, let's get that coffee.'

I hang up on Mum and smile. That's the story of my life. I smile to cover my worries. Ouch, without realising what I was doing, I've pulled another hair from the back of my head and it stings.

Keep smiling, I say to myself but the wider I smile the more my head is itching for me to pull another hair out. A smile can't fix me or the dark feelings that have followed me from Malvern. The anxiety and guilt is eating me up from the inside, but I can never become 'past me' again.

FIVE

As I put the plates in the dishwasher, I keep thinking about whether to call Mum back but I can't face speaking with her now. I post a photo of our lovely view on Instagram, instead.

'Mum, can I have some ice cream now?'

I flinch and drop a plastic cup onto the tiles, where it bounces and hits the kick board. 'You made me jump.' I snatch the cup and pop it in the dishwasher. 'I'll do you some in a minute.' I turn around and notice that Zach has left the table. He was scrolling through his phone last time I saw him. 'Where's Zach?'

'He went up to his office,' Caiden replies.

I didn't notice Zach leave the room which is odd. The doorbell chimes. I peel my orange rubber gloves off and drop them on the draining board. Hurrying, I open the door.

'Nicole.'

She smiles at me, and Aaron stands next to her, holding a Lego car kit.

'I hope you don't mind me popping by. I was passing and Aaron kept asking to show Caiden his new Lego. Kids.' She rolls her walnut brown eyes.

'Of course not. What a lovely surprise. I said pop by at any time, and thank you for taking Caiden to the café after school the other day when I got stuck in traffic.'

'That's what friends are for. If ever you need me to collect him from school, you only have to say. How did the big day at your new job go?'

'I loved it.'

Nicole pulls out a bottle of wine from her bag. 'This is for you, for getting through your first day.'

'That's so kind, thank you. Come in, take your coat off and I'll put the kettle on.' She doesn't know how happy I am that someone has come to visit; and my son has already taken Aaron to his room. 'Zach's doing some admin and I was just cleaning up. Come through. Sorry about the mess, we've just had dinner.'

'It smells lovely in here. Bolognese?'

'Yep.'

I usher her to the couches, where she sits and admires the sea view.

'Wow, this view never ceases to amaze me.'

I frown. 'You've been in this house before?'

'Yes, didn't Zach tell you? I tidied up the front garden, that's what I do. I met Zach in the pub, and he was telling me about the house and all the work he was doing. He mentioned that the garden was a mess, and we got talking. Anyway, I got rid of the jungle, added a few shrubs and pots and presto – all tidied up.'

Zach never mentioned meeting Nicole despite me talking to him about her. I can't help giving her the once-over. She has this long, wavy brown hair that almost reaches her bottom, and her heart-shaped face is cute.

'Do you like what I did?' Nicole asks.

'Er, I love it.' I can't help wondering why this is the first time Nicole has mentioned working on my garden.

'Great. And I love that our sons are such good friends now. Aaron never stops talking about Caiden.'

'You're not from around here originally, are you?' I ask. She has a hint of London in her accent.

'I moved from Kent a few years ago.'

'On your own?'

'No, I was in a relationship at the time. We both had stressful city jobs and packed it all in for the good life. It was that good he left me and went back to Kent not long after Aaron was born. But I love it here.' She stares out at a boat bobbing on the waves.

'Sorry, I said I was making a drink. What would you like?'

'Gin,' she says with a smile. 'Only joking. It's been a long day and gin helps, but I best have tea because I have to drive home. Do you have an Earl Grey or a Chai?'

I bite my bottom lip. I have one solitary Earl Grey tea bag that Zach nicked from a hotel we stayed at, just in case we needed some emergency tea. I smile at how silly that sounds. 'Yes. How long have you lived here?'

'About twelve years. I moved here when I was twenty-five. My husband left two years later.'

'Does Aaron see his father?' Why did I ask that? That was personal and I haven't known Nicole that long.

'Not often. He has me though, and I love him to bits. How are you getting on?'

I smile and pour the drinks. After handing the tea to her, I sit opposite and hug a cushion with my feet up. 'I love it here. It's such a different way of life, a gentler pace. But I am nervous about tomorrow.'

'What's happening tomorrow?'

'I have two new couples booked in at work.'

'Don't be. They'll adore you.'

'I hope so.'

She sips her tea. 'Have you spoken with the other parents at the school much?'

I shake my head. 'I say hellos and we talk about the weather.

I was hoping you'd properly introduce me on Saturday at the café. What are they like?'

'Mostly okay. Christie is a bit of a gossip but nice enough. She is actually cheating on her husband with some mystery man she met on a night out, but keep that one to yourself until she tells you.' Nicole stifles a giggle. 'Sonia is so sweet. She cares for her grandmother full time who has dementia. I try to pop in to see them every week because it's lonely for her. They're both coming on Saturday. You'll love them.'

My heartbeat is ramping up with the excitement of making more new friends. 'I can't wait.'

A rumble of footsteps come down the stairs followed by a barking Freddie. He dives over me and his paws land on the other side of the couch.

'Mum, can we both have ice cream?' Caiden asks.

I nod. 'If that's okay?'

'Of course, that would be lovely,' Nicole replies.

I scoop some chocolate ice cream into a couple of bowls and seat the children on the stools before heading back over to the couch. 'That should keep them happy for five minutes.'

'Thank you. It's really kind of you to give Aaron some.'

'Nonsense. I love that our boys are the best of friends.'

'Which gives mummies more time to enjoy a bit of peace and a cup of tea.'

'Precisely. Here's to tea and sanity.' I hold my cup up and clank it on hers.

'Cheers to that.'

I hear another set of footsteps coming down the stairs, and Zach enters, yawning. 'Hello CaiMan.' He ruffles Caiden's hair. 'Who's your friend?'

'This is Aaron. He's from school and we've been trying to make his Lego car.'

Nicole clutches her cup and remains with her back to my

husband. I wave him over. 'Zach, look who's come to visit.' I don't need to introduce them if he hired her to fix our garden.

My husband's smile instantly drops. He doesn't even say hello to her. 'I err... I think I left the computer on.' He points upwards and makes a hasty retreat.

I glance at Nicole, and her cup shatters on the floor. 'Sorry, I didn't mean to... I really should go, I have so much to do still. Aaron, grab your things.' There's a sense of panic behind her eyes.

'But I'm eating my ice cream, Mum.' Aaron quicky shovels down the last few mouthfuls before Nicole drags him towards the front door.

Before I know it, Nicole has marched Aaron out to her van and they've gone.

I don't know what just happened. For some reason Zach did not want to see Nicole, and she couldn't leave our house fast enough. I need to confront him over this. Now.

SIX

I hurry up two flights of stairs to the small attic room above the new part of the house that Zach instantly bagged as his office. I walk up the narrow staircase and push the door open. Careful not to bump my head on the beam, I crouch and enter before sitting in the chair opposite his desk.

'I've nearly finished. Just got to hit send on this quote and I'm all yours.'

'You didn't mention that you knew Nicole.'

'I didn't know you knew Nicole until twenty minutes ago.'

'I told you that I have a mum friend called Nicole.'

'Yes, but I had no idea it was the same person.'

'And you never mentioned that someone else did our garden. I thought you did it.'

He shrugs. 'I didn't think it mattered. She's a gardener. I paid her to tidy the frontage up and that was it. I didn't think I had to go through every detail with you.'

I exhale slowly. 'We FaceTimed nearly every night. We talked about everything.'

'Are you accusing me of hiding something from you?'

Zach bites the insides of his mouth, and I can tell he's upset with me for quizzing him. 'Look, forget it. She did the gardening and you forgot to mention her.' I don't like arguing. Hugo and I used to have some huge rows and I don't want that for us. I go to leave the room.

'Wait.'

I turn and wait for him to speak.

'I have something to tell you.'

I swallow. Is he about to confess to something that's really going to hurt me? I think back to Mum's warnings: *Eva, you haven't known him long. You're putting nearly all your money into this house. How much is he putting in? Next to nothing. Once you're married and you buy this house together, what's yours is his. Remember how you got this money.* I wanted to shout, *I know, I know, I know. I only have this house because Hugo died.* Have I made the biggest mistake of my life?

Zach throws his pen onto the desk. 'Firstly, I'm sorry I sounded so defensive but you know I would never do anything to hurt you. You know that, don't you?' He comes over to me, his hands on my shoulders as he looks into my eyes. 'It was in early January. I left Nicole here working to go and get some fittings from the DIY place in Ilfracombe. When I got back, her car was still on the drive but I couldn't see her. The front door was open so I walked in, thinking she'd be making herself a drink but I caught her rummaging through my desk drawers in the lounge. She instantly stepped away from the open drawer full of paperwork. When I asked her why she was going through my personal things, she said she was looking for some scissors. The strange thing was, the scissors were already out on the worktop, right next to the kettle she'd been using all day. All my bank login details were in that drawer. As soon as she left, I changed my passwords. She emailed me her invoice. I paid it and I never saw her again until today.'

I can't believe I thought badly of Zach. 'Could she have forgot about the scissors on the worktop? Is there any part of you that could believe what she told you? I've just been speaking to her and I really like her.' In my heart, I don't believe she was planning to defraud him.

He shrugs. 'Maybe. It had been a long day.'

'Shall we give her the benefit of the doubt? I don't want to lose her as a friend, and Caiden has grown close to Aaron. I really like her.'

'I don't know. I mean, she's a stranger. How do we know she isn't dangerous? I'm just looking out for you and Caiden, so it might be best to stay away from her.'

Looking out for us? More like telling me who I can be friends with. As for dangerous, my husband is seriously off the mark here. 'Let's leave this, Zach. I can look after myself.' I didn't move all this way to have him telling me what I can and can't do.

SEVEN

The sun shines down on the Sea Horse Hotel today. I close my office door and do a happy dance, then I quickly compose myself before a guest passes my window. Ben and Alice only went and booked the gold package. It turned out that romance isn't dead. They wanted those special touches like rose petals trailing up the aisle, and the butler assigned to the honeymoon suite because who doesn't want champagne on tap? I head to the canteen to grab some lunch with Hallie.

'My next happy couple will be here soon,' I say as I eat as fast as I can.

'Go nail it again, Eva.'

Hallie reaches across to grab a napkin. As she does, she knocks a ramekin of mayo off my plate and it lands upside down in my lap.

'Damn.'

'I am so sorry.'

We stare at the mayo that has landed right on my thigh, dirtying my mint-green trousers. 'It's okay. It was an accident. Can you let the two o'clock couple into my office while I clean myself up?'

'Anything. Again, I'm really sorry.'

I hurry into the loos and begin dabbing the large oily stain. Nothing is working so I untuck my silk blouse and it falls over the mess. I button my jacket up and check my hair. I'm not looking my best but as my mum always says, it is what it is. I swallow because I still haven't called her back.

As I walk into my office, I see the back of a head of flowing red curls draping halfway down the woman's back. She turns to face me; her nose is covered in light freckles and her green eyes are striking. 'Hi, I'm Madison. The bride-to-be.' She pulls her lemon sundress over her knees.

'Hello, Madison. It's lovely to meet you. I'm Eva, your wedding planner. Are you alone today?'

'No, my husband-to-be has just gone to change the baby. It's typical, as soon as you walk out the door they fill a nappy.'

'They tend to do that. It's been a few years for me but I remember it well. It's like they know,' I reply with a sympathetic smile. 'I'll make a drink. I have espresso, latte, hot chocolate, tea, soft drinks...' I grab a cup in readiness.

'Your assistant already made us drinks.'

I glance at the table and see two cups with steam curling out of them. 'Ah, that's great. How old is your little one?'

'She's three months old.'

'How lovely.'

Just as I'm about to start talking babies there is a tap at the door. 'That'll be Theo.' Then he enters, holding the baby.

He goes to hold his free hand out to shake mine. 'Lovely to meet you,' he says.

I stare like I've never stared before. The cup I'm holding hits the floor and the handle crashes into the side of the cabinet and flies under my desk. The air has been sucked out of my lungs and I can't stop gasping. I look down, thinking that I'm having some unexplainable moment but I'm not. I saw right – the man in front of me is Hugo, my dead husband.

EIGHT

I can barely move. It's as if my shoes have been filled with concrete and the effect is spreading up my ankles and past my knees. All I can do is stare. Where is the shock in his face? I can barely contain mine but the man standing in front of me seems emotionless.

'Eva, are you okay? Are you ill?' Madison hurries over and leads me to my seat.

'I, err...' I don't know what to say. If I blurt out that the man she's about to marry is my dead husband, Hugo, she'll think I'm insane. Does she know? Is all this some sort of set-up? I take a breath and remind myself that I'm new here. Hugo wouldn't have thought for one minute that I could be his wedding planner, so this can't be a set-up. I stare at Hugo again, looking for the slightest hint of recognition, but he isn't giving anything away from behind those fake round glasses he's wearing. All he does is bob from foot to foot, trying to comfort their baby who is starting to whimper. A lump sticks in my throat. He's not only alive, but also he has a baby and he's about to marry someone else. Were Caiden and I so easy to discard? How did he do it?

'Can I get you some water?'

I should be looking after Madison and all her wedding needs and desires; she shouldn't be looking after me. 'No, no. I just felt a little dizzy, that's all. I skipped lunch.' Now I feel guilty for saying that. I don't find lying easy. I despise lies but I can't exactly tell them what I'm thinking – I mean seeing. My head feels as though it's stuffed with cotton wool. From the way he's parted his hair to the black jagged mole on his neck, all I see in the man in front of me is Hugo. His nose is the same as our son's nose. My hands keep jittering away and there's nothing I can do to control that.

The baby starts crying. 'Should we come back another time, when you're feeling better?' The tone of Theo's voice matches Hugo's. Hugo never had an accent and Theo doesn't either. I barely come across an accentless person. That man is my husband. He didn't die.

I frown, not even trying to mask my confusion. There was a DNA test on Hugo's body. DNA doesn't lie. It can't be him. That's what science and logic say, but he's here. How?

'Eva, I think Theo might be right. We should do this another time.' Madison bends over and picks up a part of my broken cup, placing it gently on the desk.

I don't want to jeopardise this job. Since buying the house, we've ploughed every penny into it. If I'm fired, we'll lose our home too. Hallie will be waiting for me to tell her how the meeting went and I don't want to let her or my employer down. Maybe this is all a bizarre coincidence. I've been ill in the past. That's it. It's just an episode of something I have no control over and I need to get a grip. 'I'm feeling better. So sorry about that. I don't know what came over me.' I grab a fudge sweet from my drawer and quickly eat it. 'I just need some sugar and I'll be right as rain.' After chewing on it, I struggle to swallow but I do. 'Right, where were we?'

The baby's cries turn into red-faced bawls. 'I think I'll just take her for a walk, try to get her off to sleep.' Theo pulls a pram from the other side of my room, places the wriggling baby into it and quickly leaves.

'Sorry, I guess it's just us now,' Madison says.

I need to know more because right now, I don't trust my own mind. 'So, how long have you been together?'

She scrunches her brow and returns my smile. 'We met three years ago. Theo does computer repairs and a friend of mine recommended him. I thought I'd lost all my spreadsheets but Theo managed to rescue them. When I dropped it off at his house, I almost wanted to turn back. This little house in the middle of nowhere was overgrown and then a bearded man opened up and looked like some sort of hermit who hadn't seen daylight for weeks.' She let out a laugh. 'I'm not selling him well, am I?'

Hugo had never been unkempt. Although he had graduated in computer science before falling into a job selling agricultural machinery for a living. His fitted suits and tidy hair were such an entrenched part of his identity. He'd always insisted on being cleanshaven even though the general trend for men his age was to have some facial hair. He hated anything fussy, whether it was an awkward watch strap, a stray hair or a jagged fingernail. 'It sounds like a charming meeting,' I force myself to say. I lean in a little, prompting her to continue.

'It wasn't an instant spark. I had to take that dratted laptop back three more times, then he admitted he'd done something to it because he wanted me to come back. That sounds odd, doesn't it? All I can say is, he didn't come across as creepy or controlling. It was his only way of ever seeing me again. It wasn't as if he'd ever bump into me at the pub with him not leaving the cottage. We talked, we dated – by dated, he cooked for me at his place. Over a few months, I fell in love with him. Life has been hard because of his agoraphobia but he's a lot better now since he started therapy. He came here today; he comes to the salon I own and we're getting married. He's come a long way from working in his house and only having food delivered, to planning a wedding. Fingers crossed; we've been discussing a honeymoon.'

'Wow, that's an amazing story.' I'm guessing he didn't want his past identity exposed which is why he never left the house. The word *DNA* flashes through my mind again. Theo can't be Hugo. I'm seriously losing it and I need to do my job. 'How many guests are you looking at inviting?'

'On my side, friends and family – about fifty. As for Theo's side, I'd say about ten. He has no family. There will be sixty guests at the most.'

'No family?' I think of Hugo's mum and sister, who live in Birmingham.

'I know, it's all so sad. He lost his family in a house fire. Ours won't be the biggest of weddings and, because of that, I was talking to Theo and I think we might go for the silver package. I think we'd like a more generous menu and drinks package. Oh, and can we have a garden ceremony? Theo doesn't like to be confined when there's a crowd. But it still needs to be intimate and contained, not too overwhelming for him, if you get what I mean.'

I realise there is a tinge of blood underneath my fingernail. I move my hands from my head and drop a strand of hair on the floor. Pulling hair out in front of a client isn't a good look and when I'm anxious, I don't know I'm doing it. I point out of my window, hoping she'll look at the lovely view instead of my ruffled mane. 'Of course, when we go over the bridge, there is a stunning pergola. I can also arrange for your flowers to be woven through an arch and yes, I totally get what you mean. We have all kinds of moveable trellises to create that intimate setting.'

She smiles, happy that I can accommodate Theo's needs. Hugo was never worried about crowds or open spaces, and he'd never have survived as a loner. He needed people, craved them even. Have I got this wrong? Theo has a mole in the exact same place as Hugo's and I see my son in him. I feel sick so I take a deep breath and exhale to the count of five.

Madison continues. 'This might sound like a strange request, but can you recommend a falconer? He loves birds. We listen to the owls hooting where we live in that once overgrown cottage that is now our home. He's a real nature geek. We have a handful of children attending the wedding and we thought it might be nice to maybe have an owl ringbearer.'

I shiver at the mention of birds. I bought Hugo that raven toy for his car, twice, because he was such a bird geek. He used to stand in our garden with Caiden and they'd listen out for the owls together. My heart is humming and my hands are shaky so I place my pen down.

'That's a beautiful idea. We do have a falconer that I can contact for you.' I'd read in my pack about the birds of prey and their handlers. I know we have a falconer who takes the birds to events to raise money for the sanctuary they work at. 'I think you'd be looking at about four hundred pounds.' I let out a breath slowly, unsure of how I'm keeping myself together right now.

'That's fine. Please book them and invoice me. It'll make Theo's day and anything that puts him at ease will be worth it.' I can tell that Madison adores Theo. She'll do anything for him.

I adored Hugo.

I check the system to see if Hallie took their full address when she made the appointment and she has. 'Have you walked around the grounds yet? Maybe we could do that next and I'll show you exactly where the ceremony will take place?'

'We've already had the full tour when we came here for the wedding fair.' She shakes out her curls, and I catch sight of her beautiful French manicure. I wonder how she can look so perfect so soon after giving birth. She's thin, maybe worryingly thin, and looks delicate in every way.

Throughout the turbulent first year after giving birth to Caiden, I struggled to remember to shower, let alone consider a manicure. I reach up the back of my scalp again, thinking back to how I pulled such a large clump of hair out, how I picked the scabs and kept pulling them up until they joined to form one big scab. Zach has never seen that side of me. Hugo did and during my darkest periods, like when I first had Caiden, Hugo had to do everything for our son because as soon as our son cried, I cried with him. That's when I started to think he was trying to get Caiden taken from me. He called our doctor behind my back and then he called my mother. Mum turned up and I did something I will never forgive myself for. No, I can't ruminate over that night. It's too painful. Is Hugo outside, soothing his new baby while thinking about what I did that day? I thought my secret had died with him. Self-hatred fills me.

'Eva, is that sorted? Can I leave the falconer with you?'

I flinch and come back into the present. 'Yes. So, we're going for the falconer, an outdoor ceremony and the silver package? Is that correct?' I run through all the details with her and we arrange for them to return to enjoy a taste of the food, before making a final decision on the menu. 'We work closely with a baker who specialises in wedding cakes.'

'It's okay. I have that sorted.'

'Great. I'll err... I'll see you in two weeks for the food tasting.'

'I can't wait.' She pulls a card from her bag and passes it to me. It's headed up, *Madison, AveNew Hair and Beauty Salon*. I read the sentence under the salon name. *When you leave, you find the new you in AveNew.*

'I have a salon on the outskirts of Ilfracombe. Can't blame a girl for trying to get more business, especially now I've upgraded our wedding; everyone has to have their hair cut at some point.'

I place the card down on my desk, my hands still trembling.

'Thank you. I haven't been here long and I think I will need a cut soon.' I really like Madison. I feel she is the type of person I could be friends with, if I didn't think she was trying to marry my so-called dead husband. A part of me wants to kick myself. I could have this all wrong. I've got things like this wrong before and I am stressed. Maybe I saw Hugo's face in Theo because I wanted to or because I'm aware that I've left his memory back in Malvern, or is it the guilt I can't let go of? The one person I want to tell all this to is Mum, but I know she'd worry. She'd have every right to.

'Well, I might see you at the salon soon, then.' She stands. I shake her hand. She holds onto me and places her other hand warmly over mine. 'Thank you so much for making this easy. I really feel I can trust you, Eva. Our wedding is in good hands.'

I wonder if she can trust her husband-to-be. After leading her back through reception and out to the car park, we watch as Theo sings, 'Twinkle, Twinkle', to their baby while gently rocking her in his arms. Hugo used to do the exact same thing with Caiden. I want to run over to him, shake him and ask him how he did it? Instead, I wait for Madison to take the sleeping baby from him before placing her in the car seat. As she's leaning into the car, clipping the little one in, Theo glances in my direction before swiftly turning his back to me. Something strikes me: Theo has brown eyes whereas Hugo had blue eyes.

'Hugo?' I say, just loud enough for him to hear.

He doesn't even attempt to turn around, then he gets into the car leaving Madison to say their goodbyes. It strikes me as odd that he didn't even turn around to correct me.

Madison thanks me again, 'And I'm so excited about the owl. I can't thank you enough.'

Maybe I have this all wrong. If Theo is Hugo, how could he stand there and not acknowledge that I'm his wife?

'You're welcome,' is all I can say as I wave them off.

As Theo starts the car, his stare is fixed on mine in the wing mirror. I want to turn away but it's as if I'm hypnotised by him, and he can't break our eye contact either. I'm looking into the eyes of the man I love with all my heart but can't explain the coldness spreading deep within my core. The intensity of his gaze is wild and creepy. I'm scared of him.

NINE

Caiden skips beside me as we head to the café in Combe Martin. I love that my son is happy here even though I'm living in some kind of weird hell. Did I see Hugo the other day? That is a question I've continuously asked myself since the meeting.

Zach has been pushing me to tell him what is wrong, and all I've said is work stress. I mean, I've only been working at the Sea Horse Hotel for a few days and I already look like I'm having a breakdown. Zach doesn't know the real reason, the one where I think one of my new clients is my dead husband. If the last time I mentioned Hugo is anything to go by, I know it's best not to say too much again. How could I even begin to broach the subject? I'll sound crazy and crazy isn't a label I want to wear ever again. The last time that happened, I thought I'd lose everything I cared about. I swallow. After what I did, I deserve to lose everything but I'm lucky I didn't. I grip Caiden's hand, knowing how truly blessed I am. We pass the convenience shop and Caiden points at some toys in the window. 'We'll have a look later.'

I think back to Zach. This awkwardness that has crept between us over the past week didn't exist before. I can't help thinking that Mum might be right. Maybe I shouldn't have made this move but it's too late now. I've ploughed every resource we have into being here.

'Mum, can I have a cookie at the café?' Caiden is reluctantly still holding my hand. He thinks he's too old for public handholding with his mum, but he'll always be my baby. I keep a protective hold of him as we reach a slight bend. A car whizzes by. There's hardly any pavement and some people really do drive like they have a death wish.

A ray of sunshine burns my flustered face. 'Of course you can,' I say as I finally loosen my grip of him.

'Good.' Caiden lets go of my hand. Aaron pulls a face at him through the café window and they both giggle. The last thing I want to do is embarrass Caiden in front of his friend, so I put a bit more distance between us.

I push the door open to the cosy café and I spot Nicole holding a huge cup of something hot, probably an aromatic tea. She waves me over. I follow Caiden through the maze of tables, trying not to bump into the friends who have come out for a chat and the families who eagerly tuck into their brunches. A part of me wonders if I should mention what Zach said about catching her rummaging through his desk drawers but I decide not to. I believe she was looking for scissors.

Nicole stands and points to her bag which is on the other side of the couch she's sitting on. 'Saved you a seat.' She pops it on the floor to make room for me.

'Where are the others?'

She raises her brows. 'Sonia's grandmother's carer was running late but she's there now, so Sonia's on her way. Christie is about five minutes away. Her dog was sick just as she was about to leave. The joy of pets and kids. Do you want a drink? My shout.'

I feel that given the week I've had, I need a good shot of caffeine but I also need something sweet. 'I'd love a mocha, please, and a hot chocolate with marshmallows for Caiden.' I never need to ask Caiden what he wants because he always wants hot chocolate when we come out. Besides, he's already pulling toy cars out of Aaron's bag and they're snickering and talking. He's forgotten about the cookie for now.

The server asks us what we want to drink as she passes, heading back to the counter to relay the orders to the flustered barista.

'I have an apology to make.' Nicole takes a deep breath.

I scrunch my brows, wondering what she could be about to say.

She waves a dismissive hand, sips her drink and lets out a small laugh. The oversized cardigan she's wearing falls forward as she hunches over slightly. I wish I could pull off this woolly, almost hippish style she has. It's almost like she was born of the sea despite not growing up around here. 'I saw the look on your husband's face when he caught sight of me in your house, and know you wondered what the hell was going on. I didn't want you to get the wrong idea and I think I should have called—'

I need to put her out of her misery to end her nervous waffling. 'It's okay. After you left, Zach told me about your misunderstanding.'

'Good, good. Only I'd be mortified if he thought I was trying to steal anything. I saw a desk, needed some scissors and thought he must have some in one of the drawers. I could have waited until he got back, but I was running out of time and had to pick Aaron up from school. I didn't want to miss the bell because I've been late a few times and the staff get annoyed.' She twists her hair up into a clip, leaving a few strands loose.

I smile to put her at ease. 'It's okay. That's exactly what Zach said. It's fine.' I really like her and I don't want her to feel awkward with me and I think Zach is wrong. I wish she'd told me she'd worked on our garden though. It seems strange that she didn't when we were speaking at the school gates, but then again, we always seemed to be rushing to get to work or home.

'Let's forget all that. It was nothing; you don't have to apologise and everything is great.'

That's not true. I've only known Nicole a short while so I can't talk to her about Hugo – Theo – whatever the man's name is. Zach and his silly little issue with Nicole pale into insignificance with all that. I miss Mum, but I can't talk to her about it. She'd arrive at our door by the end of the day, thinking I can't cope. I can cope. I am calmness personified. I rearrange the back of my hair to cover up a sore bit. Why do I try to lie to myself? Seeing Hugo has hit me hard. It is him; I know it is, but I don't know what to do with this newfound information. If it is him, how could he pretend he didn't know me? We were soulmates. He held me when I pushed our boy into the world. He was there throughout my breakdown and gave me nothing but support and love. It didn't feel like that at the time, but hindsight gave me a better perspective. My heart broke when I was told of his death. Even now, I still have nightmares thinking there was something I could have done to prevent his suicide. I am so bloody confused; I don't know what to think. Did I push him to it with the way I was? No, I can't go there. It's too dangerous.

'Eva, are you crying?'

I wipe the tear away. 'No, I was cleaning earlier and I don't think I washed the bleach off my hands properly. I just rubbed my eye.' Gosh, I'm amazed at how easy the lies come when I don't want to discuss something.

She passes me a wet wipe from her bag. 'They've only got water in them.'

I take the wipe and go through the motions, then I realise I've probably rubbed mascara under my eyes. Nicole points under my left eye, so I continue to clean the area but I'm obviously missing the spot because she takes the wipe off me and begins to tenderly clean around my eye.

'There.' She smiles at me then waves as Sonia enters.

Although I've met Sonia, we haven't really spoken much. I wave as she approaches. She hails the server for a mint tea and removes her coat before sitting opposite me.

'No Amelia today?' Nicole asks.

'She's on a playdate. I'd say I'm having a break but I have to get back for Nan in an hour when the carer leaves.'

Christie hurries through the door, looking flustered. She sits next to Sonia and waves at the server. 'The usual, please.' Her daughter, Iris, hurries over to the boys and joins in with their car play. 'Sorry I'm late. Damn dog ate a bag of Skittles that we'd left out last night. It was not a pretty sight. How's everyone?'

I take a photo of us to put on my Instagram, so Mum can see how well everything is going. No one seems to mind me doing that.

Half an hour passes quickly, and Sonia begins to check her watch. 'I'm going to have to get back for Nan.'

I feel in my pocket and my hand happens on the business card that Madison gave me. After Sonia hugs us all in turn, I sit back down and watch her hurry across the road.

'She works so hard looking after her nan. I just want to scoop her up and take her for a big night out,' Christie says. 'She needs to get it on with someone. Maybe I could fix her up.' She laughs. 'I'm sure she'd feel much better after a good night of—'

Nicole laughs loudly to cover up what Christie might be about to say. 'Okay, don't need the details.' Nicole finishes her tea. 'So, how's everything going with you-know-who?'

I guess Nicole is referring to the man Christie is having an affair with.

'A lady never tells.'

'A lady normally tells,' Nicole replies. 'I'm loving living

vicariously through your love life. Maybe it's the absence of not much happening in mine at the moment.'

Christie glances my way. She doesn't know me well enough to let me into her confidence circle. I get that so I smile and wave a dismissive hand. 'I think Christie is entitled to her secrets,' I say. I'm not on board with her affair but it's her business and I don't know her well enough to judge. She might be in a really unhappy marriage. Whatever – it's not my business.

'You're right, Eva. You're a better person than I am.' Nicole winks at Christie.

'Of course she is, hon.' Christie laughs. Christie is the louder one out of all of us. Even her clothes are louder. She wears red jeans and a sparkly black jumper, and how she walks in those heels, I have no idea. Maybe I should ask them about Madison AveNew. One of them might have been there for a treatment or haircut. I show them the card. 'Have either of you ever been here? I need to find a good hairdresser.'

Nicole grabs her glasses from her bag and takes the card from me. After reading it, she passes it to Christie. 'I've never been there. I use a mobile hairdresser.'

Christie sips her drink. 'Madison did my nails until New Year. I can't say I knew her well but she did a great job. She was heavily pregnant if I recall and she couldn't bear the smell of the nail varnish. Poor woman looked green throughout the duration. I haven't been there since then. My sister has started doing nails so she does mine now. Maybe I can give you my sister's card. I know she could do with the business.'

'Okay, thanks,' I say. How do I bring Madison and Theo up in another way without sounding weird? 'Madison and her husband-to-be came to the hotel I work at to talk about their wedding.' I shouldn't really be discussing their personal business but I can't help myself. I need to know more about them. 'He seems like a nice guy.'

'Oh him. He did come by to bring her lunch when I was

there, but he never said much. She talked about him a lot, as you do when you're trying to pass the time. She mentioned their wedding plans. She said they'd been to a wedding fair and there was a silly amount of wedding magazines on the table in the waiting area.'

'That's so sweet. They're such a lovely couple and their baby is gorgeous. When they came to see me, the little one was starting to cry so he left the meeting. Madison and I saw him gently singing to the baby.'

Christie let out a long breath and grimaced.

'That was a look and a half,' Nicole said, a slight nervous quiver to her voice, before smiling. 'Why so serious?' she asked in a comedy voice. 'Do you think there's more? If so, spill.'

Christie playfully tilted her head to one side before continuing. 'Something felt off about them. I tell you what, open her Facebook page. It's her Madison does Madison AveNew – Beauty Specialists, page.'

I type in those words and wait for her page to load. The salon looks amazing, all candy colours like a fifties American diner. If my only interest in them was having beauty treatments, I'd be booking in a shot. There is photo after photo of nails and hair, before and afters, and I realise how amazing Madison is. Then I swallow. If her husband is Hugo, then Hugo is about to commit bigamy, and where does that leave me? Will I be in trouble? I take a couple of breaths. No, I have his death certificate. Then another voice fills my mind. *They will think you're in on it. An insurance scam. The police will come for you and you'll lose Caiden and your house and Zach, then Hugo will tell everyone your awful secret. Everyone will hate you then. You'll lose everything.* All I want to do is hit my head to knock that taunting voice out of me but instead, I reach for the back of my head and tug at a hair. *Stay in control, Eva,* I tell myself.

'Scroll back to December. I was there the day they were arguing about her posting a photo,' Christie says.

I ignore my thrumming heart and do what she says. That's when I see Theo reflected in a mirror. The photo is focussed on a woman's wedding hair, but he dominates the top right-hand corner. Him, with his wrong-coloured eyes wearing the glasses he doesn't need.

'What's off about this?' I tell myself to play it cool. If I come out with my hairbrained thoughts, I'll be committed before the day is out. When a person has a history like mine, they're automatically always under suspicion of a relapse so speaking up without evidence wouldn't end well.

Christie continues, 'The way he spoke to her when he saw that photo got me thinking all sorts. I was having my nails done when he came in and pulled her aside. He was angry that she'd posted it because he was in it. She just kept saying, "No one's looking at you, it's about the hair." Anyway, she shrugged it off and refused to take it down, finishing their conversation by going on at him to get help. He stormed out of the salon, slamming the door so hard the windows shook in their frames and everyone stared. She smiled and all she said was "men" followed by a shrug. She didn't seem too worried but I thought it was off. There's something not right with him but I can't think what.'

I can. I know exactly what was wrong. Pictures of him online would have blown his secret life apart. Now I need to work out what I'm going to do next.

TEN

Caiden and Zach playfight on the floor after watching wrestling. Normally I smile and cheer Caiden on, but this evening all I can think about is Hugo. I scroll through my phone and click back onto Madison AveNew, and I frown at that photo. I've tried to enlarge Theo's face in the corner but when I pinch to zoom, the resolution is poor and it becomes a blur. I tried to search for him on social media. I can't find a *Theo Hudson* on any platform that looks remotely like him, but that was to be expected.

My phone rings. I pick it up and see Mum's name on the screen. Mum has always sensed when something is wrong, which is why I can't speak to her.

Zach holds his hands in the air as Caiden lets him out of a headlock. 'I surrender. You win. Caiden is the wrestling king.'

Caiden runs around the dining table, then he circles the kitchen island twice, arms in the air, shouting 'loser' at Zach.

My flustered husband gets up and falls heavily onto the couch opposite me, where he takes a moment to get his breath back. I check my phone and it lights up. Mum has left a message. I place it face down on the coffee table and stare out into the darkness, and all I see is the light from a bobbing boat on the horizon.

'Who was that?' Zach points to my phone.

'Mum.'

'She's been trying to call all week. Don't you think you should give her a bell? She rang me earlier when you were out with your friends, wondering why you hadn't called. You know what she's like. She worries.'

'She worries too much.'

'So just call her and she'll stop ringing every five minutes.'

I can't tell Zach why I don't want to speak to her, but if I don't call, she'll start messaging and leaving even more voicemails. Even worse, she might just turn up.

'Eva?'

'What?' I look up from my phone.

'You seem a bit distant tonight. You're not having second thoughts about the move, are you?'

Why would he think that? 'No. I love it here.'

'You've seemed distant all week. It got me thinking; you've moved away from your mum, your work friends, your whole support network. Caiden is missing his friends. He told me. It's okay to feel a little bit unsettled.' He pauses. 'You would tell me if you weren't okay, wouldn't you?'

I've only briefly touched on my past. Zach knows that I've suffered with my mental health but he doesn't know how bad it got, how I had a stress-related breakdown after failing year two at uni, then how I had the mother of all relapses when Caiden was born. He's worried about me and I like that. I want to lean over and kiss him, and tell him that everything is okay. Mostly, I want him to not even think about my mental health, especially if Mum is texting him direct. One wrong word to Mum and she'll be over like a shot to take over my life. Actually, I am going to lean over and kiss him gently, show him that I'm fine.

Caiden pretends to put his fingers down his throat and giggles.

'I am so happy. I think I'm just tired, what with starting my new job.' Do not mention thinking you saw Hugo or he'll think you're crazy. A part of me wants to share those nagging inner thoughts, but the little voice in my head is telling me to keep my mouth shut. 'I love you.'

'Love you too. Remember, we're in this together so just kick me if you want me to help with anything.'

I go to kiss him but his lips barely brush mine before he pulls away. Things don't feel right and I don't know why. He's saying the right things but there's a distance between us that I can't explain. Maybe I'm just imagining it. It's been a long day. 'I'll go upstairs and ring Mum.'

'Good idea. That'll be one more job off your plate.'

I'm always anxious when I procrastinate. Maybe that's all it is and I've nothing to get anxious about. 'You're right as usual. Mum is a worry monster and if I don't call her, I'll have three million missed calls before the night is out.' Now I feel mean. I sound like I'm calling my mum to stop her hassling me. It is in part true but I think the world of Mum.

'Great. Me and the CaiMan are going to put some popcorn in the microwave and choose a film to watch on Netflix.'

Zach stands and high fives Caiden as they walk to the kitchen and pull a huge bowl out from the cupboard. It clatters on the worktop until it settles.

I grab my phone and head upstairs to our bedroom.

* * *

A chill in the air sends a shiver through me so I get into bed and prop the pillows up. Phone in hand, I call Mum and she instantly answers.

'Eva, is everything okay? I've been worrying like mad about you.'

'I'm fine, Mum. I've been really busy with the new job, that's all.'

She sighs. 'It feels like you've been avoiding me.'

'Sorry, I didn't mean for it to feel that way.' I allow a silence to replace our conversation. It's as if Mum is waiting for me to speak. I can't help myself so I say something. 'Mum?'

'What is it, sweetheart? Mums know when something's wrong and they know when they're being avoided.'

I know sharing my inner thoughts with Mum is risky but I have no one else to talk to. Mum loves a real-life crime programme as much as the next person which is why I want to open up to her a little. 'Mum, I know we've spoken about things like this before but I've been wondering how accurate DNA really is. Hasn't everyone got unique DNA?' I say that with doubt. I could have searched online for the answer but I didn't. All I have in my head is what the police told me. They concluded that the body at the bottom of the huge hill was Hugo's, and that there was no room for any kind of doubt.

'They do. Is this about Hugo? It's okay to think about him and miss him. I know you're married to Zach now but Hugo was your husband, he was Caiden's father and you had a whole life planned out together. It's okay to still be grieving but you have to accept he's gone.'

'I do. Oh, did you give Caiden a raven toy, the same as the one Hugo used to have in his car?'

'No.' She pauses. 'I let him rummage through a box of things that one of my friends left at the house to add to my charity shop pile. Maybe there was one in there.'

I puff my cheeks out and exhale slowly. 'Maybe.' She's silent. Neither of us wants to talk about the last time I was hospitalised, so I am going to refuse to bring that up.

'Are you looking after yourself?'

'I feel great. I'm eating well, getting my steps in and the sea air really agrees with me.'

'So why are you asking about DNA?'

'I was just curious.'

'Curious? You forget, I know you better than anyone else in the world. From the moment I found out you were growing inside me, I've wanted nothing more than for you to be happy. I know that when you avoid speaking to me like you have this week, something's wrong.'

I swallow hard and I'm sure she heard. 'It's just...' I don't know how to put this without sounding crazy – but I have to try. My thoughts never switch off and I feel this sense of overwhelm; so much so, I want to climb into my wardrobe to shut all the noise out, but I know it will follow me there. 'When I was working the other day, I saw a man who looked just like Hugo,' I say in a hushed voice. I don't want Zach to overhear me. He was worried that I wasn't ready to marry him when I did. It was hurried. Maybe I wasn't ready, but I do love him. Caiden loves him too.

'You do know that it couldn't possibly be Hugo, don't you?'

I need to tell her the rest. 'This man likes birdwatching and has the same mole. He's identical. His eyes are brown though. It threw me. He's an absolute doppelgänger.'

'Sweetheart, a lot of people like birdwatching and have similar features to those we know.'

'It's so specific.'

'Yes, but still. That man isn't Hugo. You know, when I'm in a crowd, I sometimes still catch a glimpse of your nan, then I realise it's not her and I feel this deep sense of loss all over again. Grief hits us when we are least expecting it. Our minds play tricks on us. That's all this is.' She pauses. 'I think you should see your doctor.'

'No. I don't need to. I'm fine.' I can't believe I told her what was going through my mind. Now she's going to be like a dog with a bone. Why didn't I keep my thoughts to myself? I'm such an idiot.

She's silent, which means she totally disagrees with me. 'This is how it started last time, and the time before. First, you see things that aren't real. Second, you believe them and they become real. Please, Eva. I beg of you, go to the doctor. Have you told Zach?'

My silence will probably answer that question for her.

'Thought not.'

'Mum.' Caiden calls me.

'I have to go. We're meant to be watching a film. Please forget I said anything, Mum. I promise you I'm okay. You're right. It's grief and I'm being a silly sausage.' I try to smile so she can hear me lightening the tone of my voice. She used to call me a silly sausage when I was little if I put my shoes on the wrong feet and we always joked about that. I hope she can park what I've said and trust me when I say I'm fine.

'I'll call you tomorrow. Love to you all.'

Caiden bursts into my bedroom and jumps on my bed.

'Love you. Bye.' I put the phone down and pull my son close to me. His warmth feels comforting.

'Are you upset, Mummy?'

'No, lovely. I was just talking to Nanny and she said she loves you.'

'I love Nanny too.' He pauses. 'I miss her.'

Of course he does. Mum spent the last five years bringing him up with me. As I hug Caiden and hold back my tears, I regret mentioning Hugo to my mum. It was stupid, but there is no going back. Could it be that I'm delusional? Or was seeing Hugo in Theo some kind of weird hallucination brought on by grief?

I've seen things before, horrible things. They weren't real.

I'm stressed. I feel alone here. I miss my old colleagues.

These symptoms are a recipe for disaster. But I know what I saw. I saw Hugo.

ELEVEN

I send Mum a selfie of me standing in the hotel grounds. The bridge seemed like the perfect place. My orange suit and white Mary-Jane shoes are cheery enough, and I made sure my make-up was perfect. I share it to Instagram too. It's one of the better photos of me and I add a caption, telling everyone about this amazing place I work at and how the weddings here are the best. Mum has to see that everything is okay, and I hope she's happy with a photo instead of a phone call as I have such a busy day.

I look like Bambi learning to walk as I navigate the boggy grounds, back towards the main building. The rainfall from the early hours is still filtering its way through the earth, and the sea in the distance looks a bit choppy but I love that salty smell in the air. It makes me feel alive. My phone beeps. Nicole has sent me a photo of Caiden and Aaron smiling at the school gates. I really appreciate her dropping my son off at school, and I've promised to look after Aaron for her soon, so that she can have a break. She follows it with a selfie of her wearing a plastic plant pot as a hat, which makes me chuckle.

Hallie waves at me from my office window. She's carrying a

pile of folders containing all the upcoming bride and groom instructions and requests. The management are happy with me. I nailed the wedding on Sunday night. Everything went like clockwork and, for a while, I managed to not think of Hugo.

As I enter the back of the hotel, I check the photo again that I sent Mum and I'm happy with it. She replies.

> Mum: *You look lovely, sweetheart, but you always do. Are you pulling your hair again?*

I look closer. My hair is sticking out slightly. Why did I choose a slightly off-centre shot? My cheeks burn with shame as I rake my hair back into place. My fingernails are slightly russet-brown from where I've scraped the dried blood from my scalp with them. Putting my phone in my pocket, I decide not to reply now, especially as Hallie is beckoning me over. She shakes her head and rolls her eyes. 'We've just had a call and it's not good.'

I frown. 'Who was it?'

'Madison Chalk from Madison and Theo.' She passes me their folder.

'What's the problem?'

'She's cancelled.'

'Is the wedding off?' It's me. Theo *is* Hugo and he knows I recognised him, which is why they've cancelled.

'Yes, she told us to keep the deposit and said they'd secured a cancellation at another venue. They want to get married sooner and we simply can't fit them in before August.'

I know they've changed their mind because of me. A part of me is relieved. I don't think I could watch Theo marrying Madison, knowing that his life is a whole lie. I also hoped they'd be back in so I could see him in person again. I needed to see if I've got it all wrong.

'I booked a falconer for them.'

'It's okay. Miss Chalk said she'd pay the balance and just tell the falconer that they're needed at a different venue. I said you'd contact her about the invoice. They said they'd deal with the change of time and date.'

'Accounts have sent it to me. I was just about to forward it to her. How did she seem on the phone?'

Hallie shrugs. 'I don't know. Matter-of-fact – but she was letting us down, I guess. I don't think she'd have enjoyed making that phone call.'

'No.' I blow out a long breath. 'I'll send the invoice now.'

'Okay. Oh, you've had a couple of enquiries and I've added two appointments to your calendar.'

I thank her and she hurries off. On entering my office, I place the folder on my desk then open it up to Madison's personal details and I call her.

'Hello.' Her voice is low, almost sombre. The baby cries in the background.

'Hi, it's Eva from the Sea Horse Hotel. Just calling about your cancellation.'

'If you're calling to change my mind, you're wasting your time.' It's almost like she's shouting at me. She seemed so pleasant and cheery when I spoke to her last week.

'It's not that, although I am sad you've cancelled. I was looking forward to planning your wedding.' I'm trying here. Planning her wedding was hurting me. Maybe it's for the best that they're not getting married here. 'Hallie, my colleague, told me that you've found another venue?'

The baby shrieks. 'We want to get married as soon as possible because we've decided to move. The Sea Horse was also our second venue choice. We really wanted the Clifton House Hotel. Theo has been calling them regularly, hoping for a cancellation, and one came up on the tenth of May and it's a Saturday, which is perfect.'

I make a mental note of where and when. I also can't stop

thinking that she said they want to move. Madison has a life here with her salon.

'I told your colleague that we'll pay in full for the falconer as soon as you email the invoice, and I want to thank you for sorting that out for us. I'm really sorry that we've let you down.'

'It's okay. These things happen.' As far as the Sea Horse is concerned, we have their deposit and I can take a new booking for that date if we can get one.

I hear Hugo's voice. 'Who's that?'

'It's Eva, from the Sea Horse,' Madison replies over the baby's cries.

'Oh, I see. Come on, Pumpkin.' I hear shuffling over the phone as the baby is probably being handed to him, then I want to cry. Hugo always called Caiden Pumpkin when he was a baby.

As soon as Madison ends the call, after several more apologies, I search through my phone and come across the photo of baby Caiden sitting in a pumpkin. Hugo chopped out the leg holes and we popped an orange hat on our baby's bald head. As he snapped the photo, Hugo said, 'Smile, Pumpkin'. And our little pumpkin beamed the biggest gummy smile, the same smile I'm looking at now.

Everything is telling me to drop this now. It's not good for me. But I can't. It's not possible that Theo is Hugo, but I know he is and I can't drop it. I need to know the truth before this feeling eats me up. There's only one thing I can do. I pull out Madison's card and make a call to the salon, and I book a hair appointment for this Thursday, making sure I specifically ask for Madison.

TWELVE

Thursday is a dreary day and to make it worse, I feel sick to my stomach. The crashing of the sea against the rocks makes me realise how powerful nature is. As I ramble over the rockpools, in the shadow of the cliff and hills above, I take in the tiny pools of molluscs and fish trapped in this temporary refuge from the rough sea. My heart starts to bang as I think of what I'm about to do. It's like the hills are closing in on me. Freddie presses his nose onto the surface of a pool and quickly withdraws it to bark at a seagull.

Why the hell am I going to Madison's salon? A gust carries my hair upwards. I also know she's going to spot the small bald patch at the nape of my neck. I've tried not to pluck any more hair from that part since I booked the appointment, but I haven't succeeded in keeping my nervous fingers away from the ever-growing patch.

Pulling my phone out, I take a moody photo of the sea with Freddie's cute face in the foreground, then upload it to my Instagram. Everyone loves Freddie. He receives a lot of adoration online. I then send Zach a message, telling him I love him and that we're having cottage pie for dinner tonight. Zach and

Caiden love my cottage pie. It used to be Hugo's favourite too. Freddie barks at me and I can tell he wants to play ball, but I don't have time this morning.

My phone rings again. It's Mum. I know she wants to talk to me, but I have more pressing things to do like getting my hair cut and investigating Madison's husband-to-be. I have to hurry back to the car if I'm to make my appointment on time. I've already checked the route and at this time of the day, it'll take me no longer than twenty minutes but I have to drop Freddie home first. Hurrying back over the rocks, I jump onto sand where I burst into a light jog with Freddie, leaving the beach and rockpools behind.

Before I know it, Freddie is settled in his basket and I'm on my way to Madison's salon. As I drive out the other end of Ilfracombe, SatNav tells me to take a right. A row of mostly white terraced houses leads to several large detached bungalows. Then a little further down, I spot the soft pink and white bungalow with its scalloped canopy highlighting the main entrance. The huge sign on the building tells me I've reached Madison AveNew. I have to do something I haven't done in years: parallel park. After driving up the narrow kerb opposite three times, I eventually manage to park. My hands are so shaky, I'm surprised I managed to get my car into the tiny gap.

As I walk across the road, I look through the huge bay window to the left of the entrance. There are three chairs in a row, two are already occupied. The woman wearing the full head of foils glances at me over her Kindle. The other woman is chatting away to the hairdresser. I'm almost taken aback at how beautiful the interior is. The baby blue, lemon and pale pink colours are captivating. All the surfaces are cream and have the fifties vibe I saw in the photo, but the salon looks much grander and prettier in real life. I glance through the other window and see the nail bar and a door leading to a treatment room. On a normal day, I'd be excited about going to a salon like this to be beautified, but right now, my stomach is doing somersaults and my body is itching for me to get back into my car and drive away. I reach for the back of my head and grip a strand of hair, then I let go. *Stop it, stop it.* If I say that in my head enough times, I might just listen to myself.

I can't see Madison. As I push the lemon-coloured door open, I'm greeted by a girl who looks to be about eighteen; she has sleek dark hair that is partly shaved on one side. She gives me a huge smile, and I can see from her badge that she's called *Orla*. I quickly explain who I am, and she takes me to a couch.

'Can I get you a drink?'

There's no way I can stomach anything. 'No, thank you.'

'Madison is out around the back so we'll get you sorted in a minute. You've come for a cut, is that right?'

I nod. 'Yes, a dry cut, thank you.'

I know my hair could do with a fresh colour running through it. It's naturally more of a light brown but I always go blonde. Money is tight with the house purchase and I haven't been paid yet, so I'm going to get a bottle dye to do at home. I try to swallow and I can't. My underarms are prickling and I know I'm beginning to perspire. The wait is making me tetchy so I scroll through Instagram. Nicole has posted a photo of a garden that she's landscaping, so I click *like* and comment, saying how amazing it looks. She instantly drops a heart on my comment and replies with a smiley face. I've been here for two minutes, that's all, and I don't even know what I'm going to say to Madison. I can't tell her I think her husband-to-be is my dead husband; I need to carefully tease something out of her. How? I'm not a detective. It no longer sounds like a good idea to be here. What the hell was I thinking when I booked the appointment? I can't get Theo out of my head. His mole, his nose, his voice, his face; the way he used to touch me and tell me he loved me – why? Because he's Hugo.

'Eva, it's so lovely to see you again.'

My heart feels as though it's about to eject itself from my mouth, I flinch that hard. I place a hand on my chest and smile. 'Sorry, I was in a world of my own. You made me jump.'

'I have that effect on people. Sometimes my lovely staff have to tell me to keep the volume down, but it's noisy here when the hairdryers are on the go so I tend to be loud. Come with me, let's get you seated.'

She leads me to the third chair, the one at the back of the salon next to the sink and a door that says *Staff Only* on it. Madison must have come from the treatment room. I glance back and see a woman about my age, with high-definition brows, paying at the till.

'What can we do for you today? I think we have you down for a trim, is that right?'

I nod. 'Yes, thank you.'

She drapes the pink cape over me then expertly lifts my hair as she ties it behind my neck in one swift move.

'Once again, I'm really sorry about letting you down but we had to take the other venue when the cancellation came up.' Her frown is reflected in the huge lit-up mirror. She looks sincere. Her red curls are clipped up stylishly, like she should be on the cover of a magazine. I normally make an effort with my make-up and hair, but today I feel drab. I can't stop looking at her, drinking her in and wondering if Theo is really my Hugo. Seeing her makes me feel betrayed. I take a deep breath. None of this is her fault because Hugo is meant to be dead. 'Are we okay?' she asks.

'Yes, the Sea Horse are okay with it. It's in your contract that you can cancel when you did, so all is fine.' I let out a nervous laugh and wonder if she can hear the shakiness in my voice. If I could sum up my life in a line, it would be, *I'm fine*. 'I remembered I had your card and I needed a trim so I thought, why not book in with Madison. So just a trim, please, keeping the layers and I think I'd like a fringe, but not too short.' I had a fringe when I was married to Hugo. I suddenly feel a little off with myself for requesting that Madison cuts me one. Am I trying to become the woman Hugo fell in love with back then or is this fringe for me?

She tilts her head and smiles. 'Fabulous, a fringe will really suit you.'

As she starts combing and spraying water in my hair we carry on making small talk. She talks about her baby keeping her up all night, and I talk about Caiden and Freddie. In my mind, I hope she mentions all this to Theo when she gets home. The first thing he'd ask me when I got home back then was, how's your day been? She then mentions the weather. I interject, knowing a chat about the upcoming rain will just eat into my precious time. 'You said you might be moving when we spoke. That's sad considering I've only just found somewhere to have my hair done.'

'It was a huge decision but after the wedding, Theo wants to move to Scotland. He said that was his dream.'

I want to say the Scottish lochs but she beats me to it.

'We're looking at houses near Loch Ness actually. We feel it would be good for the little one. It's big progress for Theo. He's been doing so well getting out and about, and I no longer feel as though we're stuck here.

'I have a buyer lined up for the salon. She's a brilliant hairdresser so I know you'll be in expert hands.' Madison laughs as she snips away but I can tell there is something underneath that laugh, sadness maybe. A wave of nausea passes through me. As she continues speaking, her voice is competing with the sound of my banging heart. 'She's been trying to buy my salon for years so she's more than good for the place.' Her smile has now all but gone.

I'm left in no doubt that she is marrying Hugo. Before he died, we talked long and hard about a move. I hadn't been sure but he'd tried so hard to convince me. My hands are sweaty so I unclench them but now they're shaking. We'd been on holiday up there in the winter after seeing a cute cabin to rent. It had been cold and I felt lonely when he went off walking all day on his own. I remember we argued on that holiday, about how easily he got distracted and sometimes forgot about me and Caiden. The hours spent alone had been long and lonely. The memory is vivid, as if I'm back there and I suppress the urge to cry like I had cried back then.

'Well, what do you think?'

Where did the time go? I got lost in my thoughts and I've barely asked anything. Gazing at my reflection, I see myself as I looked several years ago. 'I love it. Thank you.'

'Anything else?'

'Erm, no. Just congratulations on securing the Clifton House Hotel for your wedding. It's a beautiful venue.'

'It is.'

She disrobes me. Not once did she mention the missing hair at the nape of my neck. She's the soul of discretion. I know she must have wondered why I've been pulling my own hair out and creating scabs on my head.

'I know someone who can help.'

I frown.

'With your trichotillomania. Don't worry. It's common. We see it all the time. We all live such stressful lives, these days. I grind my back teeth.' She pulls a card from a drawer and I see that it's for a local therapist. 'She helped me. I barely grind at all these days and my dentist is grateful for that.'

I want to scream, *I'm only stressed because my husband, the man you're marrying, seems to have come back to life from the dead.*

A part of me assumed she'd mention it so I don't know why I feel this overwhelmed. Maybe it's because someone else can see me falling apart, just like Mum can. 'Damn, I'm running late. I have to go.' I pull a twenty-pound note from my purse, hoping that we don't have to discuss my head any longer. The price on the board for the cut is a tiny bit less. 'Keep the change.'

Madison runs after me and stands at the salon door as I get into my car. 'Eva, please wait. Have I upset you?'

I turn the engine on and edge out of the tiny space as tears fill my eyes. As I drive off up the hill, I see her in my rearview mirror getting smaller as I get further away, then she's gone.

A car horn blares as it's coming at me at speed. I swerve out of the way to avoid the collision and abruptly mount the kerb before hitting a flimsy fence.

The man gets out of his car and runs over. 'Are you okay?' he asks.

Was he driving at me?

'Hugo,' I say. It's him. It's really him.

THIRTEEN

The man stares in the same way Hugo used to stare at me when he was worried. Did I imagine him driving at me or were my eyes blurred by my tears?

'Hugo, why... how?' The only differences are the glasses and those brown eyes.

'Sorry, I don't know who Hugo is. It's me: Theo. Madison and I saw you the other week about our wedding. We had our baby with us. Are you okay? Do you feel concussed? Shall I call an ambulance?' His questions fly at me, then he grabs his phone. 'I should call an ambulance. You nearly hit me head-on, and you've crashed into a fence.' He goes to make the call.

'Stop, I mean I'm okay. I don't need an ambulance.' I wasn't looking at the road. I was looking in my rearview mirror for far too long and not concentrating. My neck is stiff but I manage to glance back. Madison must have gone back into the salon. 'I lost concentration for a second.' Am I in trouble? I keep half expecting a police car to come speeding onto the scene. 'I don't know what to do. Is my car okay?'

Theo circles my car. 'There's no damage at all. Looks like

you've been lucky. All you've done is knocked down a bit of this old rotten fence. If you're sure you don't need an ambulance, I best get on.'

I frown and stare into his eyes, the same eyes that used to look at me with such love, such passion and sometimes frustration and anger. They're brown, Hugo's were blue, but it's him. I'm so confused. I look at his mole again with its slightly ragged edge. I took a photo of it at the same time every year back then, to make sure it hadn't changed because his doctor said to monitor it. 'Hugo, why are you doing this to me?'

Madison's shoes clack on the pavement as she catches us up. 'My goodness. Someone came into the salon and said there had been a crash.'

She runs over to Theo and gives him the once-over. 'Has anyone been hurt?'

'No,' he replies as he lifts their sleeping infant from the car seat.

Madison looks a little red and flustered as she snatches the little one and holds her closely. 'I panicked.' She then looks over at me. 'Eva, are you okay?'

'She's fine. I just stopped to see if she needed an ambulance but I think she's okay. It was just a little accident.' He looks back at me. 'I am worried about you though, Eva. You seem to think I'm someone else. You might have a concussion and not know it.'

'No, no, no. I haven't even hit my head.' No one is taking me anywhere today. A memory floods through my mind. The night the crying wouldn't stop when Caiden was a newborn, and I felt my whole world had collapsed. I sat on the wall next to our house, the very wall Hugo had driven through to his death. As Caiden bawled, all I could do was think of ending it. I'd told myself repeatedly that I was a bad mother, that it was unsafe for Caiden to be around me and my only option was to let myself go; after all, he'd have been better off without a mum like me. My mind kept courting that same thought. If I leaned forward, all those dark worries would have gone away forever, along with the crying and the noise in my head.

'Okay, let's get your car backed out of this fence.' Theo checks the road and nods that it's okay for me to go.

I insert the key into the ignition and start my car up again. Selecting reverse gear, I slowly back out, leaving the small piece of rotten fence behind and I park up properly. The baby starts crying and Madison bobs her up and down while trying to comfort her.

'Theo, I'm going to take her to the salon and feed her. Eva, I'm glad you're okay.'

I watch her walk down the hill, kissing her little one's head and speaking softly. Grabbing a bit of notepaper and a pen from my bag, I quickly write my name, an apology for the fence damage along with my contact details and post it through the letterbox of the house next to the fence. That'll be an expense I could do without. I accidentally drop my keys but snatch them up quickly. As I turn back, Theo is crouching and picking something up off the pavement. I hold my car keys up. The photo keyring of Caiden must have broken away when I dropped them. That's when I see Theo holding it in its little circular plastic casing. He stares at the photo.

'That's Caiden,' I say, hoping for a reaction.

He thrusts the keyring back at me.

'Wait,' I call as he gets into his car. He might not want me to know who he is, and I have no idea why he would go to all this trouble to fake a death and pretend to be someone else, but he is still a father, one who loved his son to bits, and I know that hurt look so well. It's the look of a father who dearly misses his son. 'Why are you doing this to us? How could you do this to Caiden? I know who you are,' I yell.

He leaves me broken and confused.

Several people have stopped to stare. A man shakes his head and a woman rolls her eyes. I get in my car, hands trembling as I drive off. They were all looking at me like I've lost my mind and I know only too well how that feels.

FOURTEEN

I sit on the beach only half an hour later, coat done up as I stare at the sea. All I can think about is how Theo drove off when we both know who he is. He left me there, looking like a crazy woman, in front of all those passers-by. The cliff behind me feels suffocating even though I'm not looking at it. I know it's there, in the same way that I know my past is in reach and it's trying to take my mind. My phone beeps so I pull it from my pocket.

> *Zach: I've finished for the day so I'm heading home. Should be back in half hour if you want to do something. Maybe we could have a pub lunch before Caiden gets home from school?? Xx*

My head is so full it hurts. All I can think about is Madison telling me that she and Theo were moving to Loch Ness and then Theo staring at that photo of Caiden. I don't know what to do with all my suspicions. Everything sounds impossible. And what happens next? I can't keep going to the salon to speak to Madison. What if Theo told her that I kept calling him Hugo? She might not want me near them if she thinks I'm a bit weird. I touch my new fringe, knowing that when Theo saw me, it must have taken him back too.

'It's a bit cold to sit out here, today?' Nicole smiles and sits next to me. Her green gardening wellies are caked in mud, and her wax jacket is done up to her chin.

'I was just taking it all in.' I smile, not wanting her to ask me how I am. The last thing I want to do is go on an unhinged rant about what I'm thinking. I'd like to keep her as a friend. 'I still can't believe I live here.'

'It's charming, even in bad weather. I was heading to the café to warm up a bit before picking Aaron up early for his dental appointment. I think he's going to need braces which he's not looking forward to. Do you want to join me?'

'On any other day I'd love to, but Zach is finishing early and he's promised me a pub lunch.'

'Lucky you. That sounds much better than a coffee. He's a good one, not like Aaron's dad. You can tell.'

I shuffle on the damp sand to face her. 'Are you okay?'

She shrugs. 'He was meant to be having Aaron this weekend but he's let me down, again. You're so lucky having Zach.'

Nicole knows nothing of my past and I don't know if it's too soon to open up to her, but I'm going to give it a go. 'I am beyond lucky to have Zach. He treats Caiden like his own.' I pause, wondering how much to say. 'Caiden's father died five years ago. I didn't know if I'd ever find someone I could love as much, but I did. Zach came into my life and I've never looked back.' I sound sugary sweet and almost make myself feel nauseous.

'Do you still miss Caiden's father?'

'I err, it's odd. I sometimes think I see him still, and I dream about him which feels surreal. We went through so much together and for ages, I thought no one else could ever love me like he did.' I frown. For so long I've kidded myself that the love

Hugo and I had for each other was once in a lifetime, but I know I tested every element of our relationship and I'm scared I'll do the same with Zach, especially if I tell him what's been on my mind lately. With Hugo, the overwhelming emotions and confusion I suffered from the moment I found out I was pregnant with Caiden tested us both.

'What was he like, as a father I mean?'

'He loved Caiden to bits. They were like two peas in a pod.' I want to tell her what I'm thinking, that Hugo did everything for our little boy when I was poorly. How he took time off work to care for us both; and he cared for me when I was in hospital. My heart pounds just thinking about it. I can't imagine Hugo lying to me in the way I think he's lying to me now.

'He sounds like he was a catch.'

I smile and nod. No one's perfect but he was close. Everything we argued about was my fault. I was the imperfect piece of the puzzle.

'I often think about Aaron's dad. We were stupid getting married. I knew it was doomed from the start.'

'How?' I don't know what went wrong in her marriage but I still can't get rid of that niggle my mum has planted about Zach. I rushed into our marriage and if Hugo is still alive, where does my marriage stand? It would break my heart to hurt Zach.

She shrugs. 'We all have a past and he couldn't accept mine.' She pauses and wipes a tear from her face. 'It hurts that he's turned his back on Aaron because he adores his dad. I've tried to make it work but he keeps letting us down. I think I'm about to give up.'

I can tell she's upset and there's nothing I can say that will help. Aaron is a lovely little boy and it angers me that his father isn't giving him the love he deserves. I reach over and place an arm over Nicole's shoulders, and she leans her head on mine. Our friendship feels as though it's at that stage. My friend needs a bit of a hug and I'm here for her.

She continues speaking and lifts up her head. 'I love my boy so much and I can't bear to see him being upset anymore. I give up with Will. It's just me, Aaron and his nanna now.'

'Does your mum live far away?'

'Bristol. She comes to collect Aaron some weekends so they can go to the cinema or out for food. I wish she lived closer but she has a life there.'

'Same, I miss my mum too. When Caiden's dad passed away, she stepped in and helped me with everything.' I think of Mum. When I do see her next, I'm going to give her a huge hug.

Nicole takes a deep breath and dabs her eyes with her sleeve. 'I haven't seen Zach out lately. I thought he might have brought you for a night out at The Ship's Anchor. When he was here alone, he was down there with his friends all the time. He fitted in like a dream. He was even on the pool team but no one has seen him there for a while. You'd love it there.' She pauses. 'That's where we met.'

Zach has never mentioned any of his new friends or going to a pub. I wouldn't have had a problem with him going out, so why would he keep that from me? We spoke most nights and sometimes it was late, so he could have gone out with his pool buddies first. He'd always say he'd been working on the house and that he'd finished the night off with a couple of beers at home. 'I had no idea he even knew anyone from around here.'

'That's strange, he has a fair few friends who he liked to drink and chat with. I got talking to him just after Christmas after he'd had a few too many. He told me about his brother dying, which was sad, and that he missed you.'

Alarm bells are going off for me. Zach barely speaks about what happened to his brother. He only spoke to me about him because we met at a local grief support group. We bonded over our losses and cried together. All I can think of him doing now is being a bit tipsy and talking openly to Nicole in a pub while I was hundreds of miles away. What is more perplexing is how he and Nicole made out they barely knew each other when he came home and saw her in our house. All he mentioned was her rummaging through his desk. I realise now, I don't know Nicole at all because why is she only mentioning this now? We've spoken a handful of times and become quite close because of our boys. Or maybe I don't know Zach as well as I thought I did. Nicole isn't exactly holding back; she's speaking openly to me. Zach, however, has hidden a part of his life here from me, which seems odd. My mum's words ring through my head again. *Why rush things? Shouldn't you get to know Zach better before running up the aisle? I worry about you...*

'Sorry, maybe I shouldn't have mentioned his brother. I didn't mean to upset you.'

I wave a dismissive hand and force a smile. 'It's okay. I'm not upset, just surprised because he doesn't like to talk about what happened to him.'

Nicole blows out a couple of breaths. 'And I'm sorry for going on about my problems with Will.'

'Don't be. Anytime. I hope he wakes up and realises how lucky he is to have such a wonderful son.'

'Me too,' she replies.

My phone beeps.

Zach: I'll be home in five. Xx

'I best get back. Zach's nearly home. Anytime you need to chat, I'm here.'

'We keep calm and carry on for our kids, don't we?' She looks up at me as I stand. 'It's all okay though, isn't it? Caiden will always have you, and Aaron will always have me. No matter what, we are always there for them, for our children. He's my world and I know Caiden is yours.'

'Yes, he certainly is.'

She frowns and goes to speak, but stops before taking a

moment. 'I'm so glad you moved here, Eva. Enjoy your meal and we need to do something fun together soon, maybe a spa day.'

'I'd love that.'

'Oh, your fringe is lovely by the way.' She stands and hurries towards the café. I'll probably see her at the school gates later, but in the meantime, I really need to talk to Zach. He has this whole life here. He's made friends but he hasn't mentioned any of them to me. He confided in Nicole which is out of character and I can't work out why he would.

Caiden is my everything, Nicole was right about that. I hurry back to where I parked my car outside a gift shop and I drive home.

On pulling up, my eyes widen as I see the red Fiesta parked in front of Zach's van, then his text comes through.

Zach: Cancel lunch. Your mum was waiting outside in her car when I pulled up.

FIFTEEN

I exhale slowly and walk through my front door with a fake relaxed and happy expression pasted on my face. She can't see the worry that I'm holding inside. Freddie wags his tail and I pat him on the head. Mum is already there to greet me, her full-length charcoal-grey coat still buttoned up.

'I tried to call you earlier, sweetheart.'

'What is it, has something happened?' If there wasn't an emergency, why else would she be here? I know. She's concerned about me. *I'm* the emergency. Her expression is one of pity and I can't believe she drove all the way here without speaking to me first.

'No, I woke up this morning and was really missing you and Caiden, so I thought, why not visit? I wanted to see your new house. There's a holiday park close by. I've already called and they have a chalet I can rent so I won't get in your way.'

Zach comes up behind her. He raises his brows as if to say, did you know she was coming? I can't answer him, obviously, but if I knew Mum was about to turn up, I wouldn't have agreed to go out for a pub lunch with him.

He clears his throat. 'We were just about to go out for something to eat before Caiden finishes school. I think I'll make something instead, then I'll collect him so you two can catch up. Do you want to join us for lunch, Susan? You must be hungry after the journey.'

'I've disrupted your plans. I'm really sorry.' Mum hugs herself, embracing her bag, like she always does.

'Nonsense, Susan. You're always welcome here. Let me take your coat.' Zach always says the right things.

My mum smiles but that smile doesn't reach her eyes. She passes her coat to Zach. Underneath she is wearing her favourite shapeless orange jumper, the one that needed de-bobbling several years ago.

'That sounds lovely and you're right. I'm famished. We can eat and you can tell me everything. I've already had the house tour,' she says to me.

However nice Zach is to her, she still suspects him of using me which is ludicrous. I may have put most of the money into this house but Zach has been here making it a home. A bit more doubt creeps in. Since talking with Nicole on the beach, I know he, maybe they, are hiding something from me. Now I've had a bit of distance from our conversation, I wonder why she brought up the pub and Zach's brother. Why didn't Zach mention something as silly as joining a pool team, making a few friends and speaking to her at the pub? Why didn't she mention it before now and why did she decide to tell me today? It doesn't help that I feel Nicole and I are becoming close as friends. Maybe that's why she told me. I could do without these worries on top of my suspicions about Theo.

My mum continues speaking, 'This house is gorgeous. I can see why you moved here even though I miss you all to bits.' Her brown wavy hair falls over her shoulders as she fluffs it up.

I lead her to the snug as Zach heads to the kitchen, leaving us to talk. 'Look, I know I've turned up unannounced but—'

'Mum, I'm really busy at the moment with work. It's not a

good time.' A short while ago, I wanted her to be here so I could hug her, but I want to talk to Zach, so I wish she wasn't here. I feel the buzzing in my head again, like I have done in the past. When everything gets too much, the tsunami of thoughts start. My heart thrums hard. If I could, I'd walk away and take some time out. Though, if I dare to do that, my mum will suffocate me with concern.

'I know and I feel bad but I was worried after our last conversation. I've been trying to call you back. You don't answer and you send me that photo, and I can see you've been pulling at your hair.' She walks around me, checking out my appearance to see if I've been looking after myself, then she examines the back of my head like she used to do when I was a child. I hated the mittens she used to make me wear to stop me picking. I told her that my school friends had started bullying me and she still made me wear them.

I flinch and step out of the way. 'I'm okay.' I tease the hair down that she's ruffled. So far Zach hasn't noticed and I want to keep it that way.

'That looks sore. I hate to see you like this again.' She reaches up and strokes my face like she always did when I was a little girl. I've been half a foot taller than her since I reached fourteen. She hugs me. She cares and all she's done is help me with everything. We managed her work shifts and mine so we could both bring Caiden up together after Hugo died. How could I stay angry at her? I enjoy her warmth and the scent of her peach shampoo – the smell of home – she's used the same shampoo since I was twelve. I find that smell grounding when I'm anxious and I'm anxious at the moment. It's in this moment I realise that I need my mum. She knew I needed her and she came.

The words tumble out of me, about crashing into the fence and seeing Hugo again, how his gaze lingered on the photo of

Caiden. 'It's him. I did doubt myself but after seeing him again I'm certain.'

She sits on my plump couch next to the log burner, then she grabs a cushion to hug. Always something to hug, that's Mum. 'Sweetheart, we've talked about this. It can't be him. It's impossible and you know it.'

I check the hallway to see if Zach is close by; he isn't. He's still in the kitchen clattering plates on the worktop as he prepares our lunch. I'm safe to carry on talking. I don't want Zach to worry about me and I don't want him to think I'm not over Hugo because I am... I was. 'It's him,' I snap. 'And I'm worried about Caiden.'

'Is Caiden okay?'

'Yes... no. He talks to himself; well, it's only been twice. Actually, I've heard him talking to his dad like he's in the room. If I hadn't seen Hugo, I'd have put it down to grief; now I wonder if he's seen Hugo too. Something has made him think of Hugo.'

'Darling, that's not possible because Hugo is *dead*. You have to accept it and move on. This is stressing you out and it's all for nothing.'

My thoughts go back to overhearing my son. He claimed to be talking to Doggo and we'd just turned up at the new house. He couldn't have seen Theo before we got here, so I think the raven toy triggered memories of his father. I still wonder if he got it from that cupboard but why, and how did it get there? Or did he have it with him when we left Malvern? 'When did Caiden rummage through that stuff that was destined for the charity shop?'

'Are you talking about the raven and how he might have got it?'

I know I didn't explain myself well but I'm getting confused with everything and my mind is moving at a million miles an hour.

First it's full of Theo, then of me seeing his face close up, then Madison telling me that they're getting married sooner and packing up to live in Loch Ness; and I'm starting to doubt Zach. I drove into a fence. My mind goes quiet as I concentrate on my breathing. I doubt Zach, and that doubt couldn't have come at a worse time because I need him more than ever. If only I'd never had my breakdowns. I'd be able to speak openly to everyone. However, I feel if I show one sniff of me being on my crazy path again, I don't know what will happen; I couldn't bear to be parted from my darling boy if I had to go to hospital. I'd rather die than lose him for a single minute.

'Eva, the raven?'

'Oh, yes. When could he have got hold of it?' I ask.

'It was about two weeks before you moved.'

I blow out a breath and place a hand over my ever-increasing heartbeat. 'That makes sense.'

'I'm glad something does. So is everything okay now?' She tilts her head. 'You're stressed and it isn't good for you.'

'I am not stressed,' I snap. Stress isn't causing all this. It's Hugo, Theo, whatever his name is.

She pats the seat next to her so I sit. 'I'm here for you and we're going to get through this, okay? We're going to book you an appointment at the doctor's and get this sorted.'

No, no, no – not again. I am not having a breakdown and I know what happens when doctors get involved. This is real, not a manifestation of my psychosis. That is all behind me. I want to yell this out loud, but Mum won't believe me and Zach will run in wondering what the hell is going on. 'I'll call them.' I won't but she doesn't need to know that.

She places her cold hand over mine. 'It's for the best, before things get worse. This isn't like that time at uni or when you'd just had Caiden. We know it's coming on now. We know what to look out for and seeing things that aren't real is a biggie.'

'But I saw him and he was there.'

'You think he was there.'

I clench my fists. 'This is not stress-induced psychosis and I am not having another breakdown. It's real.'

Mum's eyes are watering. She's helped me back from rock bottom more than once. She talked me down from that wall, the same one Hugo drove through. She collected me from uni when I thought all my roomies were plotting to poison me because I'd fallen out with one of them. I only ate food out of packets for nearly a month, all because of exam stress. That's why I flunked year two. She knows me better than anyone but she doesn't know me now, because what I'm seeing is real. I pull my phone from my pocket and find Madison AveNew's page. I try to find that photo with Hugo in the background to show her, but it's gone. I scroll and scroll before throwing my phone hard onto the coffee table. 'There was a photo. I could have shown you but it's been deleted.'

'Are you sure it was ever there?'

I bow my head in thought. One of the mums at the café had shown it to me. I remember now, it was Christie. 'Yes. He's made Madison delete it.'

Zach calls out. 'Food's done.'

Mum grips my hand. She doesn't know what to say so she remains silent. We both compose ourselves before leaving the snug and heading to the dining table. The view of the sea is a little brighter than earlier.

'I'd never tire of this view,' Mum says as she sits. I sit next to her and feel Freddie's damp nose on my leg as he waits for me to drop him a treat from my plate.

'I hope you like cheese sandwiches and chicken soup.' Zach places a plate full of sandwiches down and brings the bowls and a bottle of water over.

'This is lovely, Zach. Thank you,' Mum replies as she takes a little triangle sandwich and begins eating.

How can she eat? If I attempt to eat now, I'll throw up, so I sit back and taste the tiniest bit of the soup.

'I have some news,' Zach says as he pours us all a glass of water.

He never mentioned any news to me.

'I was going to take Eva to lunch today to tell her that a job I tendered for has come up. Well, I didn't originally get the job, someone else did but they've let the contractor down, so now they're offering me the work instead. I've accepted.'

I put the conversation that Mum and I were just having to one side and smile. Zach has been working hard to get bigger contracts so that he can earn more and I'm happy for him. 'When do you start?'

'Tomorrow, at seven in the morning. There's this new development and they need a plasterer to work with someone else on twenty houses. We have two weeks to get the job done, and there will be more work from this developer after. They have houses everywhere. They're huge, Eva. It's going to be amazing for us.'

'That's great. Where is it?'

'They mostly have properties around this way, so the next jobs will be closer but for the next two weeks, I'll be based in Worcester.'

That's close to where we lived in Malvern. 'How are you going to travel there every day? It's too far.'

He smiles. 'They're putting me and some of the other subbies up in a rental house. I might be able to come back next weekend to see you and Caiden if I can wangle a couple of days off, but the following week, I'll definitely work right through, then I'll be back home for good.'

I don't want him to leave. We have so much to talk about. How can I mention what Nicole said just as he's about to leave me for two weeks? 'So are you going in the morning?' I know my forehead's creased and my mouth is downturned. He pauses and I can tell he's leaving tonight. 'You're going later, aren't you?'

'I can't turn this down, Eva. It's so much money and we need it at the moment. It's only two weeks.'

I rely on him for so much. 'You look after Caiden when I'm working and pick him up from school when I can't. We're a team. How am I meant to cope?'

'I'm here, sweetheart. I can help.' Mum looks almost happy that he's going.

'That's a great idea and as I said, it's only two weeks then we'll work it out if I do more for them. Why don't you stay here, Susan? I'm sure it'll be more comfortable than staying in a chalet.'

'I'd love that, if you're okay with me staying, Eva.'

'I'll change Caiden's bed for you and he can sleep in the spare room on the sofa bed.' Mum gets a bad back so this seems like the only solution because I'm not sharing a bed with her.

For the first time, Mum seems to be warming to Zach as they exchange smiles. I think mentioning earning money has helped her see him in a better light. As for me, Zach and I still need to talk about Nicole. My shoulders drop. Everything about Mum's sudden arrival feels a bit convenient. Maybe she was due a little later and Zach was going to tell me over lunch, but I almost think they planned this.

SIXTEEN

Zach left a while ago and everything I wanted to speak to him about will have to wait. Caiden goes into the main living space and watches *Despicable Me* for the hundredth time. Mum has gone upstairs to shower, so I sit in the snug with the log burner going and click onto Instagram to check out my posts. I have a smattering of likes, some from my old colleagues and there's a comment telling me I'm missed.

It's at the back of my mind that I have Madison and Theo's home address and both of their phone numbers, though I know using that information would be wrong. I've already typed Theo's number into my contacts. All I want is to hear his voice, for him to slip up and say something so I can prove to Mum that I'm right and that I'm not losing my mind again, and the only reason I'm stressed is because I keep seeing Hugo. I go to call him then I stop. He'll see my number come up and he'll find out it's me because Madison has my number in her phone. To cover my tracks, I open up my phone settings and choose the option to withhold my number, then I call.

He doesn't answer so I call again.

'Hello... hello...' Theo says.

'Is it them telling us the food is going to be late again?' Madison asks in the background.

'Who is this?'

The baby begins to cry. Madison calls out while I listen to this slice of their lives playing out. 'It's probably a pocket dial. Just hang up,' she says. He cuts the call. As before, Theo sounds exactly like Hugo.

The doorbell makes me flinch. Freddie jumps off me and begins to bark. Caiden doesn't even move from his film. I open the door, leaving the chain on, confused as to who is calling at this hour.

'Eva, it's just me.'

'Nicole.' I remove the chain and open the door to her and Aaron.

'Aaron,' Caiden calls out. Aaron runs past me to get to my son and they both run into the main family room.

'Come through. Are you okay?' I lead her to the snug, where she sits in the armchair. I sit and Freddie gets up onto the settee next to me.

Her eyes are red rimmed. 'I had another huge argument with Will – Aaron's dad. I don't know how he can be so...' She bursts into tears and dabs at her eyes with scrunched-up tissue. 'I can't hold it together anymore.'

'Nicole, you can. Whatever it is, Aaron needs you.' I'm shaking with anger now. She mentioned earlier that Aaron's dad has been letting him down.

'I just hate him. I'm so angry, Eva.' She squeezes one of my cushions and roars into it. 'I need to be there and look him in the eyes, tell him how upset our boy is. I try to phone and as soon as the conversation gets tough or heated, he just hangs up.' She stands and throws the cushion at the chair. 'I grew up without a father and I know how much it sucks. He left my mum when I was three to marry someone he'd met at work, and he discarded me like I was rubbish.' She begins to tremble before letting out a burst of huge sobs. 'My dad left me...'

I walk over and hug her. She weakens in my arms so I keep rubbing her back and telling her what an amazing mother she is and how Will doesn't deserve Aaron. I don't know what else to say. Will turning his back on Aaron is unforgivable. Nicole's father leaving her when she was a little girl is heartbreaking. All I can do is allow her to let it all out and comfort her.

'I need to talk to Will face-to-face, which is why I've decided to go to Kent for a few days. I need to do this for Aaron. I need to make Will see sense before he breaks our boy's heart. I'm going to have to pull a sickie with the school and take Aaron with me.'

I think of poor Aaron, caught up in the middle of their arguing and, with that thought, I know a good friend would offer to help. 'He can stay here if you'd rather go alone.' I instantly regret saying that because I know I'd be leaving Aaron on Mum while I'm at work, and I haven't even asked her. 'But I'll have to ask Mum.'

She frowns. 'Your mum?'

'She turned up earlier. Zach is working away for a couple of weeks, so she's helping me with Caiden.'

'You didn't mention your mum was staying. I'm really sorry I barged in like this.'

'I didn't say earlier because I didn't know. It's all been a bit manic this afternoon since I left you.'

Mum walks in with her towel wrapped around her head, wearing fluffy bear slippers and a dressing gown. 'It's no problem at all. It'll make my life easier having a playmate for Caiden.' It's obvious that Mum was listening outside the door.

'Thank you. I owe you both,' Nicole replies before blowing her nose.

I know I might need to ask her for help one day if Zach gets busier with his job, so I feel like I'm doing the right thing, and I like Aaron too. He's good for Caiden. 'It's no problem at all. When are you going?'

'Now. I have some of Aaron's clothes and the hamster cage in the van. I actually came to see if you could look after Aaron's hamster, and now I feel like I'm asking way too much.'

I smile. 'Nonsense, bring the hamster and the clothes in.'

Nicole heads out to the van to get Aaron's bags. Like a whirlwind, she unloads and she's gone and I've said that Aaron can use Caiden's spare school uniform. I place the hamster in the corner on a shelf with some food and water then I leave Freddie watching the rodent run around in circles on its wheel. 'Would you watch the boys while I go upstairs and call Zach? He's been there a couple of hours now.'

'Of course. I'll make them a hot chocolate then they can get ready for bed.'

I leave them in Mum's capable hands. When they're in bed later, I'm going to ask whether she and Zach planned her timely arrival, but first I want to call my husband. He hasn't even messaged me to say he got to Worcester and he normally does. I go up to our bedroom and close the door before pressing his number. It rings out. Maybe he was tired and fell asleep.

* * *

As I come out of the bedroom, I hear a creak upstairs coming from his office. I carefully walk up the attic stairs. When I reach the top, I notice the door is open and the skylight has been left ajar. I grab the stick we use and pull the window down until it clicks shut. A pile of paper has blown onto the floor so I bend down to pick it all up. As I do, I see it's a collection of printed articles and newspaper clippings. They're all related to the murder of Zach's brother, Justin. He told me his brother died in an accident. I read on. Tomorrow it will be twenty-five years since it happened in Bromsgrove, not far from where he's staying in Worcester.

I try to call Zach again. I'm worried and he's not answering. I realise I don't even have an address for him. All I know is he's living in a shared house in Worcester.

I pick up all the sheets of paper and begin to flick through them with tears filling my eyes. No wonder Zach never wanted to talk about it. I read another report. Zach hid under the climbing frame house while he watched his brother get stabbed to death. My heart is breaking for the nine-year-old boy who had to witness that. All I want to do right now is go and hug Caiden.

I didn't think we had secrets but now I know we do. He lied to me about how Justin died, and he never mentioned how well he knows Nicole. These articles might not mention Zach's name but Justin and Zach's mother are mentioned in one of them, and there is a photo of Justin. Why would he lie to me about something like this? And what more don't I know about my husband?

SEVENTEEN

As I head back down, I listen to the boys' giggles echoing throughout the kitchen as Mum pretends to be a bear in her silly slippers, like she used to do all the time with Caiden when we lived in Malvern. I wish things were simple, like they were back then. Yes, I was grieving heavily, but the routine did us good. With all that's going on, it warms my heart to hear Caiden having fun. I burst through the door and roar, making them scream even louder, and Freddie jumps around barking.

'That's enough now, boys,' Mum says as she pants with exhaustion. 'It's time to brush those teeth and go to bed because you've got school in the morning. I'll be up in five to check your teeth, see if you've done enough to keep the cavity monster away.'

They dart past me up the stairs, eager to have a sleepover. 'Sounds like you were having fun.'

She lets out a laugh and sips her tea. 'I've missed this. Did you get hold of Zach?'

I shake my head. 'I think he must have got his head down for the night. He'll probably message later.' It saddens me to think he's all the way over there, thinking about what happened to his brother while alone. Mum goes to make me one of her chamomile teas, so I sit on a stool at the island, thinking back to when Zach and I met.

I'd been attending the same grief counselling support group for over two years in that old community centre and still I wasn't able to make sense of Hugo's death. I couldn't believe he'd take his own life when he had so much to live for. I even wondered if I'd given him the idea when I threatened to jump during my breakdown. There were no clues. Not once had I suspected he was depressed. Then this new man walked in wearing work boots and a paint-splattered coat. He stood beside me to pour some water out of the urn to make himself a coffee. When he said hi, I felt something I hadn't felt in a long time, that telltale tingle of desire. At first I thought that the chemistry we shared might be a fun way to help us both. The last thing I expected was to end up in a serious relationship. When I approached him with the biscuits, I hoped he wasn't a new widower and as soon as he mentioned losing his brother, I sat back and listened. I felt his pain and I shared mine with him. Within a month, neither of us was attending the group anymore. We'd meet up and talk about our loss, but that soon became less frequent and was replaced by bowling nights and going out for cosy meals. Caiden met Zach soon after. They'd wrestle and play games. Zach declared that his all-time favourite film was *Despicable Me* and he won Caiden over. My son loves Zach and Zach loves him. I couldn't bear it if Zach had done something to compromise what we have.

'Eva, tell me about Hugo. It's okay to speak about him. He's such a huge part of your past and I know you loved him a lot,' Zach had said on one of our first dates. That's what I instantly loved about Zach; he allowed me to talk until I was all talked out. I told him about how Hugo grew up in the Cotswolds with his parents, and how they weren't close as a family. They sent Hugo to boarding school. They fulfilled their parental duties by turning up to our tiny wedding but that was it. A part of me always wondered if they thought I wasn't good enough for him. They'd invested so much in Hugo, I think they hoped he'd marry a scientist or a lawyer, not a wedding planner that hadn't even finished her degree.

'Here's your tea, sweetheart.' Mum brings me back to the present with a cup of tea. The mug has a picture of me, Mum and Caiden on it.

I take a sip, almost burning my lips. Mum always forgets to add a bit of cold water to drinks that don't have milk in them. 'Weren't Hugo's parents strange?' I ask.

She nods. 'We said that at the time. They were so... mechanical.'

I frown. 'Mechanical?'

She shrugs. 'Just going through the motions like rusty robots; then again, I only have your wedding day to judge them on. His mother didn't even crack a smile. Me, I was all smiles and happy tears. I always felt sorry for Hugo growing up without any love or warmth. They didn't take up my invite to come over for dinner, and didn't want to do anything with us and Caiden when he was little. I mean, what kind of family doesn't even make sure they visit their grandchildren over Christmas when they live that close? Sending Caiden his presents in the post was awful.'

'Hugo said they were like that all the time.' I pause, not knowing how much to say. Hugo told me things in confidence and even now I feel like I'd be betraying that by speaking. His parents were emotionally neglectful but it was something Hugo never dwelt on. 'Do you know, they never told him once that they loved him?'

'I can believe that.'

'At his funeral, my heart was breaking when they came for the ceremony then left as soon as it was finished, their faces like stone.' I remember them not even coming to the wake at the hotel next door. 'Do you think that's why he's able to be this cold now and lie about who he is?'

Mum stares at me as if I've just said Elvis is in the room, then I remember, I basically have. Hugo is not dead, though, and I need to find a way to make Mum see that too. I need a photo of him or a recording of him speaking. Mum clears her throat and slams her cup on the worktop.

'He's dead. Please stop this, Eva.'

I now know I can't talk to her about this anymore, not without proof.

'Did Zach ask you to come today?'

She shakes her head and goes to reply, but she's cut off by my ringing phone. I answer straight away, hoping that it's Zach but it's a man whose voice I don't recognise.

'Hello, you left a note through my door. I was going to say, don't worry about the fence, Theo came to fix it for me. He explained what happened and it's an old thing anyway.'

'Thank you for letting me know and that was so lovely of Theo. Did he say anything else?'

'Like what?'

'I don't know. About me?'

'He just said you were new around here. These roads are a bit windy. Well, thank you for leaving the note but we're good.'

I breathe a sigh of relief as he ends the call. I could do without any further expense – then I think of Hugo, going back and fixing my mistake, just like he always did in the past. My heart begins to bang in my chest as I think of my big mistake, my big secret. If I get too close to the truth, will Hugo use it against me? My cheeks burn. Caiden can never know. I'd rather die than for him to know what I did.

'I think I got the gist of that phone call,' Mum says, not noticing how flustered I feel. 'I'm going up to have an early night. And no, Zach didn't ask me to come. I came because I want to be here for you. We can talk more tomorrow. Are you okay now?'

I nod, not wanting her to focus too closely on me. 'Yes, Hugo's dead. I'm just stressed and I'm sorry.' Mum doesn't believe me, I can tell. Until I have evidence, I'll pretend everything is okay, and I won't mention Hugo or Theo again. I'll be a good mum and just go to work, and cook food. Everything has to seem normal. 'Mum, would you be able to look after Caiden sometimes in the evenings while you're here? I have weddings coming up and I have to be there, and sometimes my clients can only come after office hours. Zach normally looks after him.'

'Of course. You do what you need to do. Caiden and I are going to have lots of fun.'

'Thanks, Mum.'

'Right, that bed is calling me.'

I hug Mum before she heads upstairs. Freddie comes running down. He must have been up there with the boys. I'll go and check on them in a short while. Opening up my calendar on my phone, I glance at my upcoming appointments.

Theo and Madison are getting married in just over a week, on the Saturday. I have to get my evidence before then otherwise they'll be gone for ever. If I'm right about Theo being Hugo, I don't know what it will do to my relationship; still, I have to know the truth. Mum has to believe that I'm not losing my mind, and I want answers from Hugo.

I try to call Zach again but like before, he doesn't answer. I'm worried about him now so I send him a WhatsApp message, which he replies to instantly.

> Zach: I'm okay, just tired. I didn't know it was you calling. Your number is coming up as withheld. I'm really tired and I have to be up at 5 this morning so I'm in bed. I'll say goodnight now. Love you. Xxx

When I was in Malvern and he was here, we spoke every night. This is the first time we've ended the night on a message when we haven't been together in the same house. I miss his voice and I miss him saying, I love you.

> Eva: I don't know how that happened. Best sort my phone out. Love you too. Xxx

I hit send. A part of me wants to say that I saw the paperwork in the office but it's not right to do that by message when Zach's upset about his brother. I feel as though we're coming apart a little. I know I forgot the upcoming anniversary of his brother's death so I'll need to make it up to him.

I do, however, know why I didn't tell Zach about Theo: I don't want to be wrong. My past will make me look like I'm losing it again and I don't know what will happen to me. Maybe I'm not sure I trust myself. A small part of me wonders if Mum is right. As for Zach, why would he not tell me about his brother being murdered? A lump forms in my throat as I think of Zach watching while Justin was being stabbed to death. Maybe we've both held things back. Zach doesn't know how bad my breakdowns were. Have we based our whole relationship on not being honest with each other and, if so, where does that leave us?

I make sure my number can be seen now and send a quick message to Nicole, to see if she's okay, but she doesn't reply. I had hoped she'd call Aaron to say goodnight but maybe she's midway through an argument with her ex.

Freddie scratches and whines at the front door. That's his way of telling me that there is someone out there. Heart pounding, I follow him. Mum comes out of Caiden's bedroom and shouts down the stairs. 'Is everything all right?'

'I think so. It's probably just a fox. I'm going to lock up and come to bed.'

I hurry to the front door and peer through the spyhole. I can't see anyone around. I remove the chain and open the door slightly, letting Freddie run outside. A breeze fills the hallway and I shiver as I gaze into the darkness. Rain patters down. My attention darts to the rustling coming from the wall of bushes that divide our land from the footpath and coastal road, and I'm sure I hear footsteps behind it. I look down and see the slight outline of a muddy footprint trail.

Freddie barks frantically at the shrubs. I call him back, as I don't want him to run through any of the gaps onto the road and I'm scared the intruder might hurt him. The footprints are already starting to blend into the damp driveway as the rain gets heavier. The sound of an engine roaring tells me that I didn't imagine any of that. I run in my slippers towards the road and all I see are taillights turning a corner.

Someone was here.

Someone was lurking around on my drive, in the dark.

Someone was watching us.

EIGHTEEN

I check every window and every door before heading upstairs. I pass the open spare bedroom door and see Aaron lying on the sofa bed. 'Hi, lovely. Is Caiden in the bathroom?' I try to hide the fear churning inside me, not wanting to startle the children.

He nods. A wet Freddie bounds over and starts curling up at the bottom of the sofa bed. Aaron doesn't seem to mind. He laughs and strokes him.

'Is Mummy going to call me? She said she would.'

I quickly check my phone to see if I missed Nicole's call with all the commotion going on. 'Not yet, lovely. It's late so she probably didn't want to wake you up.'

'Mummy's upset because she was arguing with Daddy.'

'I know. Sometimes grown-ups have fights and get upset. I'm sure everything will be okay when they've spoken.'

'It won't be.' Aaron looks down.

I walk over and sit on the bed. Aaron knows his mum and dad are fighting and I wonder how that's affecting him.

I tilt my head. 'Well, your mum has gone to Kent to see your dad. They both love you and just want what's best for you.'

He folds his arms. Freddie nudges his hand with his damp

snout. Aaron strokes him. 'My daddy doesn't love me.' A stony look spreads across Aaron's face.

He's doing everything in his power to hold back his tears. I don't know what to do and it saddens me to see him upset. Tension starts to pulse through me. I'm livid at Aaron's father for making him feel this way. 'Aaron, your mum thinks the world of you. She tells me how proud she is of you all the time. In fact, she tells everyone that, not just me. I heard her telling the other parents in the playground. I haven't known you for long but Caiden and I love you too. I know Caiden sees you like a brother; he told me. I just want you to know that whatever happens in life, you are surrounded by people who care and people who love you, okay?'

He nods and wipes a stray tear away.

I get up, walk around the bed and give him and Freddie a hug. 'We'll talk to Mummy in the morning, okay?'

He nods and lies down in the bed. 'Okay.'

I pull the quilt up to his chin to keep him warm. 'If you need anything, just let me know.'

As I leave, Mum is standing in the corridor looking slightly emotional. She reaches over and strokes my hair. 'That poor boy.'

'I didn't know what to say, Mum.' The lump in my throat grows bigger.

'You did, and you said the right thing.' We both take a deep breath, and Mum continues, 'Were you outside a few minutes ago?'

I ponder whether to tell my mum about the intruder. There were footprints but I know they won't be there anymore, just like the car that left. If I tell her what I saw, it'll be another nail in the coffin that is my freedom. She won't go home when Zach gets back. She'll march me down to the doctor's and insist on being with me, and she'll check on me all day long because Mum is a worrier. My heart whirls away at speed as everything fills my head, threatening to overwhelm me.

'It was a fox. Damn thing was mooching through the bin. It's gone now.' There is an itch at my nape, a little scab that is begging me to itch it and pull at it, but I hold my hands tightly in front of my body. I will not give into it with Mum watching. I'll do it later when I'm alone.

'So, nothing to worry about. I'll get some sleep then. See you in the morning.'

Mum goes back to Caiden's room and closes the door. I take a huge breath and scratch the back of my head before opening the door to the only room that we haven't done anything with. Old floral wallpaper peels from the walls and the carpet smells like mildew. This is one of the rooms that Zach didn't decorate because this is mine. I'm going to strip it back, fill the cracks with my own hands and make bespoke storage at my leisure. I've always wanted a hobby room to paint and sew in, but right now, I want to look out onto the drive to check that the intruder hasn't come back. I can't see anything out of place, no unexpected shadows or movement. It's bedtime. I have work tomorrow and the boys have school. Friday is a busy day for me so I need to at least try to sleep, though I suspect I'll have nightmares.

I leave my hobby-room-to-be and head to the family bathroom, where I stop and listen to Caiden speaking quietly as he turns the tap off. He's been in there for ages now. I wonder if he's all right. Maybe he's not feeling well. Ear to the door, I try to make out some of the words he's saying to himself.

'I promised I wouldn't say anything and I didn't. What do you think, Emily?'

My blood runs cold at hearing that name. I knock and walk in. Caiden throws something into the bath. I hurry past him and pull the raven toy out of the tub.

'Who were you talking to?' I gently ask.

'No one.'

I bend down to his level and hold both of his hands. 'Who's Emily?'

He pulls away and storms past, almost knocking me over. 'The bird,' he shouts as he runs out of the bathroom, leaving the toy behind.

I lean over the bath and hold it close to my heart while I cry.

The very mention of Emily sends my knees weak. I lock myself in the bathroom and I collapse to the floor, weeping into my hands as I think of her.

How did Caiden know about Emily? This is the one name from my past which I'd never expect him to know about, and I know Mum wouldn't have said anything to him. Zach doesn't even know about Emily because I can't bear to go there. A shiver runs through me. My son is talking to his dead dad and now he's talking to Emily.

I feel haunted but I don't believe in ghosts. Do the ghosts care if I believe them or not? I doubt it. The hairs on the back of my neck prickle. I don't feel alone even though there is no one with me in the room. I feel as though someone is toying with me. Am I paranoid? Did I hear Caiden say Emily or was that my brain playing me up? After all, I was standing at the other side of the door. I swallow, knowing that my brain could be deceiving me like it has done in the past. Was there even an intruder? This confusion that has come back into my life, the same confusion I call the parasite living in my head. Seeing Hugo was the trigger. If I can solve the mystery of Hugo, I know I will get rid of the parasite. I don't need a doctor; I need the truth.

None of this is going away until I work out if Theo is Hugo.

NINETEEN

Saturday comes by quickly and it's wedding day for one of my lovely couples. As expected, Deepak and Millie are nervous. He's flapping around checking that the catering team have all their dietary requirements, and she's nervous because her beauty team is running slightly late, and she has a bridal party of six. I want to tell them to slow down and enjoy their day. You only get this moment once, you pay a lot for it, let me take your stress away. But no, Deepak and Millie are insistent on dealing with certain elements of their wedding directly even though they've paid for my services.

I press the espresso button on my coffee machine twice. Today I need a lot of coffee as I'll be on my feet until eleven this evening.

Hallie pops her head round the door. 'Is everything running to plan?'

I nod. 'Same old. Bride and groom are flapping but everything is absolutely fine. The florists have been and gone. I've finished decorating the room for the wedding breakfast. The photographers and videographers have set up in the function room and the ceremony room. We've done a sound check. The sweet cart is in place and so is the photo booth, along with a collection of silly hats and plastic glasses. The champagne is on ice, and the magician is in the library trying to locate his rabbits.' There are no rabbits, of course; I saw him expertly cutting and shuffling a pack of cards.

She lets out a chuckle and leaves me to it. As I sip my double espresso, I spare another thought for my relationship. Zach has been gone for two whole days and nothing else strange has happened. Caiden has been acting normally. It's as if he never mentioned Emily. I spoke to him about it and he looked at me as if I made it all up. Emily – I heard him say her name. My throat sticks as if I actually spoke her name out loud. I drink some more coffee before grabbing my mint-green jacket. I always make an effort to fit in with my bridal party's colours and today is a green day. Green is popular lately.

I haven't mentioned Hugo to my mum again and she's backing off a little. She's laid off the topic of me going to the doctor's, so I may be in the clear for now. As for Zach, his phone call this morning was brief as he was working, so I couldn't talk to him properly. My biggest worry is Nicole. I haven't spoken to her and she hasn't called to speak to Aaron. He's missing her dearly and I keep having to cover for her by telling Aaron that Mummy is just a little busy but she loves him. I'm really worried about her but I think she needs space to work through her problems with Will.

She's sent one message. All it said was, *Be back on Sunday. Thanks again.*

Time is escaping me again. I need to check on the bride and accompany her team to our salon. Hurrying down the corridor in my white brogues, I take the lift up to her suite. From outside the door, I listen to the women giggling. The bride asks for her drink to be topped up and she moans again about her beauty team. I knock and her younger sister answers.

Millie beckons me in. 'Any news?'

I shake my head as I spot that the group are all wearing *Team Deepak and Millie* dressing gowns. 'Shall I call them for you?'

'No, my sister can do that.' She glares at the teen girl with the braces on her teeth. The girl walks towards the window to make the call, while I shimmy through the party of women to get to Millie.

'I come bearing an update. Everything is ready for you. The celebrant has confirmed that she will be here for two, ready for the ceremony at three. The ceremony room is decorated beautifully and so is the function room. You have nothing to worry about.'

'Only my beauty team. I can't get married looking like this.' She points at her oily t-zone and the spot that has broken out on her chin.

She's trembling so I pull her to one side. We make our way into the ensuite. Not the best place to have a little pep talk, but it's better than a public corridor or a room packed with people. I've been in this position a million times before.

'Millie, you are absolutely beautiful on the inside and out. I promise, you are going to have an amazing wedding. It will be the best day of your life. If for any reason your team doesn't turn up, we have the spa staff who are very experienced in wedding hair and make-up.' I look at her. Her face is only slightly oily but in a youthful kind of way. The spot is tiny but I know in her mind she's seeing something the size of a clown's nose. She's twenty-two with the most perfect heart-shaped face, and her dress is a work of lacy art around the neck area.

She waves a dismissive hand and wipes a tear away. 'I know. I'm just being silly but I can't seem to help myself. Thank you for having my back.'

'Now go out there, smash this wedding and marry the man you love. Remember what this is all about. It's about you and Deepak and your new life together.'

One of the party knocks on the door.

'Come in,' Millie says as she takes a deep breath and fans her eyes with her perfectly manicured hands.

'They've arrived and they're on their way to the salon, sis. We have to go.'

She squeezes my arm. 'Thanks again, Eva.'

I love my job so much. I live for moments like this when brides are happy, when everything is running almost like clockwork. I know I'm forever part of a couple's special day and that to me is the payoff.

I follow the party down, taking the second lift with the bride's mother, who pads from foot to foot in a pair of slippers that look a size too big. We step out. Giggles echo along the corridor that leads to the spa and they all turn left into the salon. As I reach the door, I'm almost taken aback. Two women wheeling make-up storage units stop at one end of the room, and three hairdressers set up along the other side. I've been a part of so many weddings now, I know exactly what to expect, but I didn't expect this.

'Eva, hi.' Madison smiles, and my heart begins to bang. Given how certain I am that Theo is Hugo, I don't know what to say to her so I stare with my mouth open.

Talk, Eva, talk. 'Hi,' that is all I can say. What I have here is the opportunity to find out more. I can't exactly say, *can I be frank? Is there any chance that Theo could be my dead husband, Hugo?*

She glances up at me, and her forehead creases with a look on her face that says, *I don't want to be here.*

She knows who I am and what I'm up to.

TWENTY

It's nearly ten thirty at night. The wedding reception is in full swing. The cake has been cut, the first dance was superb and the family is now in a merry state on the dance floor doing the Macarena. I hoped to have a few moments with Madison this morning but I struggled to find her. I didn't even see her leave. It had been a shock seeing her. I had to go outside and get some air and when I returned, she was gone.

When she was cutting my hair on Thursday, we chatted and she was friendly. Today, it was as if I didn't know her. I wonder if she suspects it was me who called Theo's number the other night. I breathe out and catch the sight of the bar manager. He gives me the nod which means I can finally leave. My feet are throbbing after being on them all day.

I give Millie a wave. She lifts up her wedding gown and staggers towards me. Her face has reddened and her make-up has long gone but she's happy. 'Eva, I just want to say thank you. I've had an amazing day and also thank you for keeping me sane.' She throws her arms around me, and I hug her back.

'It's been an absolute pleasure.'

Millie nods to Deepak, who walks over to the cake and

places a huge chunk in a bag before coming over. Millie takes it from him. 'Have some cake,' she slurs.

I thank her and take the cake. After saying goodbye, I'm in my car and ready to leave the Sea Horse Hotel, and I'm going to have the mother of all lie-ins in the morning. I check my phone. Mum messaged to say that she'd ordered a pizza for her and the boys, and that they were now asleep. I know Mum will be in bed now, so I won't message back.

It's dark and dreary tonight. Reaching around the back of my head, I grab a few strands of hair and gently tug, relishing the moment before the follicles pop out of my scalp. I wince, realising I pulled too many in one go. I can feel a thin trickle of blood which I rub vigorously in the hope that it'll scab.

Instead of turning right to go home, I turn left. The truth is within reach and I have to go and find it.

TWENTY-ONE

I need to check out Madison and Theo's house under the cloak of a dark, starless sky. Twenty-five minutes later, I'm driving along this single-track mud path which I've been on for about a quarter of a mile. The satnav's instructions ended at the entrance to this road. I haven't passed a house for ages, and I can't see one further ahead. I need to turn around but I don't think I can manage a three-point turn as there's not enough room. It's too narrow. I'll end up bonnet first into a row of trees and I already scratched the car bumper the other day.

My heart thrums. I need to get back on the main road. I can't see anything and there is no one around. Maybe I can reverse back out... The idea of that fills me with dread. I hate reversing, especially over a long distance. It'll be like the other day when I crashed my car – and then, I was going forward. I gasp. I can't breathe. I'm stuck. Letting the window down a bit, I turn the engine off and try to fight my breathlessness. I'm safe. It's just a panic attack. *You are not dying. You will get out of this situation.* I repeat those words in my head until I can breathe without feeling like I might pass out.

I put the car back into first gear and start the engine up

again. The earth below me is churned up so the car hops as I drive forward. There's the orange glow of a light in the distance that I catch when the breeze momentarily parts the trees. Another thought unsettles me. If that is Theo and Madison's house and one of them drives out, I'll be blocking them. They'll see me and questions will be asked. Just as I'm about to panic again, I spot a clearing next to a huge gate that leads to a dense thicket of trees. I gently pull forward and park my car as far away from the narrow dirt road as possible. I get out.

In the distance, I hear the shrieking of foxes and an owl hooting. Rustling sounds come from the shrubs, setting my nerves on edge. Shivering, I grab my green jacket from the back seat and put it on before leaving my car behind and heading towards the house on foot. The ground below is so rocky, it's hurting to walk. It doesn't help that my feet are swollen from standing all day.

On approaching the house, I spot Madison's car. Theo's is parked in front of it. Then there's a gate that has a tree arch over it. The whole house is surrounded by dense evergreens. It's like the owner is telling any prospective visitor that they're not welcome. Light is cast from that one window upstairs. Madison walks over to it and stares out. I stay behind the tree, peering through a gap where she can't see me. Theo walks in and it looks like they're arguing. She has her hands in the air and he's trying to move closer to hug her but she pushes him away.

Theo grabs her arms and forces the hug, just like he used to do with me when I was upset. I didn't like it when he did that to me. It was as if he was trying to suffocate me rather than allowing me to get my emotions out. I wonder if Madison feels the same. I watch as his mouth meets hers. At first she resists him and I almost think she might release a hand and slap him, but their kiss gets more passionate. This shouldn't hurt me because I have Zach, but it does. I close my eyes, remembering how Hugo's touch felt on my body, how expertly he would caress my skin until it tingled. As I open my eyes, I see the room is now in darkness. The sounds of an infant crying and a dog yapping come from the back of the house. I guess they're attending to their baby.

I gently open the squeaky gate and take in the ivy-clad house. It feels oppressive and suffocating, not like the huge open-plan house in Malvern that we once owned. Hugo came here to hide away from me, and this dark corner of Devon was perfect. I try to ignore the niggling voice at the back of my head, telling me that none of this is possible. DNA proved that Hugo was dead. But he isn't: I keep seeing him. He is in this house. I dart across the overgrown lawn, sure that my trouser hems are now damp. With my back to the side of the house, I eventually shimmy towards the long garden that is embedded in the base of a hill. At the far end is a wide summer house or maybe it's an annexe. A light in one of the rooms glows from behind the closed blinds.

Glancing back, I see that the lights are on around the rear of the main house. I can hear the baby's cries are louder. Madison bobs up and down behind the almost closed curtain. I can't see Theo.

Back in Malvern, I remember Hugo working at all hours. He loved it when Caiden was asleep and I was in bed. I'd hear him tapping away in his office at the end of the landing as I put my earplugs in. It looks like his working habits have remained the same.

I dart along the pathway that cuts through the lawn until I reach the annexe. The door is unlocked and I'm sure they're both in the house. I should go in, have a look around. I imagine Theo keeping his deepest secrets here, not in the main house where Madison could easily find them.

After listening at the door, I nudge it open and I'm in a tiny hallway, facing a small room with a toilet and wash basin in it. I'm almost holding my breath, trying to creep around in silence just in case he's close by. There is a closed door to my right and one to my left. What if I'm wrong thinking Theo is in the house? He could be here. What the hell am I doing? I should be at home with Mum, Caiden and Aaron – not playing detective, alone in the dark. But then again, I am alone. Not even Mum believes me so I have to do this. *Be brave, Eva.*

I press the handle down on the door to my left and peer around the corner. It's a room full of old dismantled PCs on work benches. Boxes in all sizes are piled up everywhere and leads spill out of drawers and cabinets. It reminds me of the chaos that Hugo used to surround himself in. The rooms in our house that were his reminded me of a hoarder's space. It was always me who made sure that chaos didn't spill out into the rest of our house. After a quick poke around using the torch on my phone, I know there's nothing for me to investigate here.

I leave that room and place my ear against the door of the other room, the one with the light on. There isn't a single sound coming from that room, and yet I can't bring myself to press the handle with my trembling hands. What if he's in there? I don't know what he'll do if he catches me here. Will he try to keep up the pretence that he's Theo or will he call the police to take me away or... My chest tightens. I'm the intruder here. No one knows I'm here and if I confront Theo and Madison, they could kill me and bury me in their woodland to keep Hugo's secret. I could vanish forever. A thought flashes through my mind as I imagine Caiden missing me when I am not at home in the morning, making his peanut butter apple slices. I imagine Mum's face as she wonders where I am. How would they be in a week, a month or even a year after I vanished?

Then I hear the back door slam at the main house, and I have no choice but to go into that room. Someone is coming, so I press the handle and breathe a temporary sigh of relief when I see it's empty. It's a spacious room with sofas, a fireplace, a desk at one end topped with two huge screens that are on. It looks like Theo is editing a nature video of two foxes at night. Bookcases full of IT and editing manuals cover the walls of the room.

'My phone must be in here,' Theo calls back as Madison asks what he's doing.

It's him. His phone on the sofa starts buzzing because Madison is obviously calling it.

I run over to the desk, pull the swivel chair out and crouch underneath before pulling the chair back in. My phone starts to ring so I grab it from my pocket. Just as Theo walks through the door, I end the call and the only ringing left is his phone. As I hold my phone to my heart, I know I've had a lucky escape.

Glancing between the chair and the desk, I watch as Theo stands in front of the patch of dirt and dead grass that I must've left behind when I stepped into the room. I check the floor and see that there isn't a trail that leads to me, so I hold my breath and hope that Nicole doesn't try to call me back. His phone stops ringing and the silence is now my enemy. He walks over to the couch and once again stands there. I slowly exhale and place my hand over my mouth in the hope he can't hear me breathe.

My right leg is crunched under me and I can feel the onset of a cramping spasm.

'Hello. It's you,' Theo says.

What do I do? Do I stand and beg him not to call the police? Do I hope they won't bury me in the woods? He knows I'm in here. Just as I go to release my leg, he continues to talk, then he shouts. 'Don't you ever call me again, do you hear? Call me again and you'll wish you were never born.'

Phew, he's not talking to me. He's on the phone. I grit my teeth as the cramping in my leg worsens.

'You come near me or my family, I will fucking kill you.' He ends the call and I let out a slight squeak as he kicks the door so hard, the window frame seems to shake. Again, hand over my mouth, I pray he didn't hear that. *I will fucking kill you.* Those words ring through my ears and as I'm about to let out a sob, he turns off the light and leaves. I cry like I've never cried before. I'm shaking, and the muscle in my cramped leg spasms really hard and I want to yell, but I don't. It's just me and my silent tears. I need to get away from this room. After a stretch, I creep out of my hiding place and poke my finger through a slat in the blind, and I see there's no one in the back garden. I run out of the door into the hallway and go to open the front door but it's locked.

I'm trapped.

TWENTY-TWO

I run into the storeroom panicking. The windows are nailed shut. Who nails windows down? I run to the small bathroom and there is a window above the toilet, but that too is nailed down. Back in the main room, I check the back and front windows again. There is no way out unless I smash the glass, and then someone might hear me.

He's not here. You are alone and safe. I keep repeating those words in my head. I don't know how reassured I feel because Theo threatened to kill the person who called him. While glancing through the slats of the blind, I can see their house is now in darkness.

Using the torch on my phone, I scan the room and see a large filing cabinet in the corner. I should be getting out of here but I need to find evidence to show my mum. If I can get her onside, I can deal with this and any repercussions.

I jump as my phone rings. It's Nicole again. 'Hello,' I say in a stage whisper.

'He's not who you think he is,' she says in a slurred voice.

'Nicole, are you okay?'

'Did you not just hear what I said?' she shouts.

I take in her drunken words and I think back to what she told me about knowing Zach from the pub. 'What are you talking about?' Though I'm not sure I want the answer, I have to ask. I quickly peer through the slat again. The house is still in darkness.

'He's a liar. You can't trust him. You can't trust me. Don't trust anyone.'

'What's going on?' She goes silent. I'm biting my nails here and all she can do is say nothing when I say, 'Nicole, tell me.' Her sobs come through my phone. 'It can't be that bad.'

'I don't know how to tell you. I can't. I just can't. I will lose you and I don't want to. We're friends.'

'Nicole, you won't lose me and we are friends.' I know we haven't known each other for long but if she's done the unthinkable and slept with Zach while I was in Malvern, I will damn well blame him.

'I've got to go.'

'No, don't.'

'I'm going to be sick.' She hangs up.

I don't know about Nicole, but I feel sick. She could only be calling to tell me she'd slept with Zach, and she obviously backed him up when it came to the little story about her rummaging for some scissors, the only stupid thing he could come up with on the spot. They shared a look. Zach wasn't expecting her to be in our house. I invited her in. She knew how he'd react. Why the hostility on Zach's part? Had he hoped he could sleep with her and she'd just fade away as soon as I moved down here? I turn my phone onto airplane mode and place it in my pocket. It's just gone midnight and I have to get home. Nicole and Zach can wait.

Before I work out how to escape this mess, I gently open one of the drawers. All I see are suspended files with company and business names on the tabs. I peer through a few and there's just the usual kinds of things like invoices and quotes and a breakdown of works completed or problems diagnosed. I open the next drawer and it's full of similar paperwork. Then the third drawer – nothing. As I push it closed, it doesn't make the same noise as the other two. I pull it out again and reach around the back. There is an envelope caught inside the filing drawers, so I tug at it until it comes out.

I open it and tip the contents out onto the rug beneath me, and I sit. There is a ragged old photo of two tiny babies in a plastic cot, wearing white romper suits that are much too big for them. Both are sleeping, their little fists balled inside scratch mitts, and one thing strikes me: their slightly long noses. I place the photo in my pocket and hurry to the bathroom. It's time to leave. I found what I came for. Why would *he* have a photo of *our* babies if he wasn't Hugo? I run to the water closet, grab the metal toilet brush and slam it as hard as I can through the window, knocking the flimsy frame out in one piece. It must have already been loose. Squeezing through the gap, I put my hands out, breaking my fall as I land on a bed of mulched leaves.

Before getting my bearings, I hear the dog yapping from behind the back door. I run around the front of the building, and the upstairs light flashes on. Knowing I need to get away, I dart across the lawn, half limping until I reach the side of the main house. Flapping my arms in a panic, I catch my jacket on one of the spiny evergreens. I yank it as hard as I can to free myself from its clutches and it tears. Someone must have opened the back door because their chunky Lhasa Apso is tailing me. Without looking back, I dart through the gate, ignoring my throbbing feet. The dog is nearly upon me. The lights to the front of the house flash on. I need to get to my car – now. The dog barks at my calves, wagging its tail like we're playing a game. After pressing the central locking button, I open the driver's door and grab the cake that Millie gave me earlier and I fling it in the verge. It's a sponge, not a fruitcake so

I know the dog will be fine. It runs towards the cake, leaving me to make my escape. I catch sight of something through the trees as the moon appears from behind a cloud. There's a small wooden structure in the distance. Shivering, I know I need to get away.

I hear the front door opening. Theo calls out for Buster who I presume is the dog. I select reverse gear, pull out and hop the car all the way to the main road with the lights off. As soon as I'm far enough away, I pull over in a layby and jump out of the car, feeling that I'm either about to pass out or vomit.

Neither happens. Without warning, tears fill my eyes as the photo of the babies burns an image in my brain. While Caiden was crying night after night when I brought him home from hospital, I kept hearing two babies, not one. The baby we lost at birth and Caiden. I lost sight of reality as I imagined that my twins were fine. Denial, delusional – yes. The moon's light casts a milky white glow onto me as I weep for my other baby. I can't believe he created such an elaborate way of abandoning me.

And he kept a photo of the baby we lost: Emily. Why is he doing this to me?

TWENTY-THREE

It's lunchtime and despite trying to call Nicole all morning, she hasn't answered. She's meant to pick Aaron up today but I don't know when. I want to speak to her about that phone call.

'Sweetheart, stop picking your head.' Mum gently takes my hand and applies a bit of pressure until I move it away from the clump of scabs that have crusted at the nape of my neck. Embarrassed, I pull some hair across the back to disguise the patch, realising it's thinning out a bit too much. I'll need to attach the emergency hairpiece I own next time I leave the house.

'What's happening? Please talk to me, Eva.'

'Nothing,' I snap, and instantly feel guilty. Mum is the one who has been there for me throughout everything. 'It was just a busy one last night.'

'I saw.'

I frown.

'Your clothes in the utility, next to the wash. Looked like you'd been wrestling in a pigsty. You've ruined your jacket, sweetheart. I did take a look, see if I could sew it up but there's a big chunk missing.' She pauses. 'I woke up at one in the morning when I heard you pulling up. I thought you were going to be home about eleven.'

I blow out a breath, wondering if now is the right time to show Mum that photo. No, I can't do that now. If I do, I will start crying again. It's too raw. I'll talk about it when I've had chance to process it. It's not like it's going anywhere. I swallow, wondering if Madison or Theo suspect I was there, and I also wonder if he's found the pushed-out window and called the police. My fingerprints will be all over his office. 'It got a bit rowdy which is why I had to stay later.'

'I see. They don't pay you to break up drunken fights.'

I hate lying to Mum so I look away. If my gaze meets hers, she'll see through me. 'I know, and I'm all right.' I let out a nervous laugh. 'You should see the other guy.' A cliché, I know, but Mum laughs too.

'Have you heard from Nicole?' she asks.

'Yes, she called me while I was working.'

'I didn't want to worry you but she came here last night to pick Aaron up. She was drunk and he was asleep, so I managed to convince her to come back today. She came in a taxi and could barely walk. She was in no fit state to take Aaron home like that. Anyway, she saw sense and said she'd come back today. I think she'd been crying. I asked her if she was okay and she said yes. She wasn't though.'

'She's been having a hard time with her ex-husband.' The boys run around upstairs and laughter rains down from above, followed by Freddie's yapping. 'I'll call her when I've had a quick shower.'

I feel as groggy as hell this morning. I check my phone. Zach hasn't tried to call or message. I'm going to ring him, too, when I've freshened up. I need to get to the bottom of what's going on between him and Nicole, and I'm going to tell him that I know his brother was murdered. It's the anniversary of that horrible incident and he didn't even mention it. I don't know how to tackle both of these issues in the same call. Maybe a shower will clear my head. As I leave the room, Mum starts prepping some pancake mix.

Ten minutes later I'm lathering up and massaging all the bruises on my arms and legs from that fall out of the window. I flinch while rubbing shampoo into my hair as it stings the open wounds on my scalp. Once finished, I turn the shower off and step out, grabbing my fluffy bathrobe before heading back downstairs.

Caiden sits at the table with a pancake and a dollop of strawberry jam.

'Where's Aaron?'

Mum sits next to him. 'Nicole collected him five minutes ago. I didn't want to disturb your shower, and she was in a hurry. She said she'd call you later. She took the hamster too.'

Damn, I wanted to speak to her.

'I asked her if she wanted to join us for pancakes, but she said she was in a rush. To be fair, she looked hungover. Poor Aaron didn't even get chance to put his coat on properly before she bundled him into her van.'

I call Nicole but her phone goes to voicemail. I run upstairs and throw some joggers and a sweater on, my hair still soaking. Running back down, I call out 'Won't be long' to Mum and head to Nicole's. I have her address but I've never been to her house. This can't wait.

Several minutes later, I pull up outside her home. All the curtains are closed and her van isn't parked on the road. A neighbour comes out after I've knocked for ages.

'There's no one in. Mr Burton is still in hospital.'

I have no idea who he's referring to. 'I was actually looking for Nicole. Have you seen her today?' I inhale the stench of stale sweat coming from the bald, stocky man who stands there in a grimy white vest and overshirt.

He furrows his brows. 'Nicole, my daughter Nicole?'

I pull out a photo I took of Aaron, Caiden and Nicole when we were at the café. 'This Nicole?'

'That's her.'

'I thought she lived in that house.' I know I had the right house number but then again, she has never invited me to her house. She collected Caiden from school a couple of times, took him to hers and dropped him home to me. Caiden never mentioned her dad being there and from what Nicole told me, I assumed she wasn't close to her dad.

'She did but she lost it. Story of my life, picking Nicole up. I persuaded my landlord to let her rent it, but she blew that too and now she's living with me – again!' He shakes his head and tuts. 'I'm sick of it all now. I'm sick of being used to babysit while she galivants all over the place, which is why I had to put my foot down the other day. If you're her friend, when you see her, can you try to talk some sense into her?'

I feel sorry for her. Her father shouldn't moan about her on their doorstep with a stranger. I think of her bringing up Aaron alone and his dad constantly letting him down. Given my past, I should have seen what was going on. Maybe Nicole is having some sort of breakdown.

'But she's been through so much with Aaron's dad. Maybe cut her some slack?'

He huffs. 'You really don't know Nicole. That poor man deserves a medal.' With that, he turns and slams the door before I can ask him another question.

TWENTY-FOUR

With my thoughts all over the place, I head to the beach and watch the waves lapping against a huge rock in the hope that they'll deliver the clarity I truly need right now. Sea spray bursts over the wall, spilling into the rockpools. As I inhale the salty air, a flock of ravenous seagulls fight over a dead mackerel.

What I can't do is sit on this beach all day and ignore my problems. I call Zach.

Several rings later, he answers. 'Eva, I'm working.' He sounds out of breath.

'It's three on a Sunday afternoon.'

His moment of silence does nothing to put my mind at rest; and then it sounds like he's put me on hold while he finishes what he was doing. I wonder if Nicole was with him while Mum and I were looking after Aaron. After all, if I'm to believe her dad, she's lied to me – big time, so why do I keep feeling sorry for her? I can't stop thinking about everything else she said. Nicole told me I couldn't trust her and I'm assuming the *him* I couldn't trust is Zach. There's no way she could know about Theo and my suspicions.

Zach is back on the call. 'Sorry, I just poured a coffee. I

know I shouldn't be working now but I couldn't sleep last night, so I had a lie-in. There's no one managing the site today so I'm on my own, which is why I started late.'

'You sounded out of breath.'

'I ran downstairs to grab my phone when you called.'

'Zach, I know.' This is where I hope he'll confess to whatever he's hiding. I want him to talk about his brother and Nicole.

'What?'

'I know.'

'I don't know what you're on about, Eva. Should I be worried?'

My mouth waters and I feel nauseous. I'm not a confrontational person, not normally, but I'm feeling far removed from my usual normal self. When I go down this dark path, I become more confrontational but this time I hope I haven't put two and two together and come up with five. 'I know about your brother.'

'I-I can't do this right now, not over the phone.'

I'm going to make him. He can't leave me hanging like this, full of uncertainty and anxiety. I won't let him. 'I went up to the study. You left the skylight open and I saw all the articles scattered on the floor. You never told me the truth about what happened to Justin.'

The sound of something hitting a wall makes me flinch. I think Zach is hyperventilating or is he breathing deeply? I can't tell. I wish I'd FaceTimed him. 'I don't want to think about it, I can't.'

'It's okay, Zach. Is that why you took this job, to be close to him on the anniversary?'

He pauses before answering. 'I needed to be here. It's twenty-five years since I lost him. I had to be with Dad.'

'Why didn't you tell me what happened to him?'

'Why do you think?'

I'm at a loss. I told him all about Hugo. I think of what I omitted from my story. I left out how bad my breakdowns were. Mum warned me about withholding that from Zach, but I told her not to worry because I'd never end up like that again. 'I think it's painful and sometimes we don't want to confront things that hurt so much to talk about.' I wish I didn't sound like our ex-grief counsellor but I don't know how to handle this.

'Exactly. I hid in that wreck of a wooden house in the park because my brother said they were coming, that they were going to hurt him. I didn't even know who they were. I...' I hear the pain in his voice. 'The kids came for him and one stabbed him. They were never found. I miss Justin.' He paused. 'The other day, Dad and I visited his grave. We said a few words, had a drink and I went back to work the next day.'

'I could have come with you.' I know what it is like to feel alone in grief.

'I needed to do this with Dad, just the two of us.'

It feels wrong to ask about Nicole now but I have to. 'I was speaking to Nicole and she told me you met at the pub, that you were on the pool team and you told her about Justin.' The silence is deafening. 'Zach?'

'What are you trying to say, Eva?'

'You never told me that you talked to her about Justin and how he had died. I had to find out from some old newspaper articles in your office. You've never taken me to that pub or mentioned your friends, or mentioned chatting away to Nicole about things you haven't even opened up to me about. I'm your *wife*. I feel like there's another side to you, one I don't know.'

'If you believe what you're insinuating, you don't know me at all. Are you asking me if I was sleeping with Nicole?'

I can't deny it but I don't want to say yes, so I remain silent and hope he'll continue talking.

'Why would I risk everything for a fling? I spoke to her like I spoke to the rest of the regulars. I didn't single her out and yes, I think I drank too much one night and I mentioned Justin to a few people. Mostly, I was drunk and missing you. That was all. I hadn't seen her or the others for a while until I booked her to do the gardening work for us. While she was doing the work, I saw her rummaging through my desk drawer and then you invited her over for a drink. I will say one thing: I don't trust her one bit. I thought I did, she seemed nice enough, but there's something... I don't know... Maybe you should try to distance yourself from her for a while.'

'I agree.' What Zach is saying makes sense. I think Nicole saying not to trust him when she drunk-called me was to make trouble, but then again, I don't like being told who I can meet up with by my husband. I'm not happy with either of them at the moment. I've readily let Nicole into my life. I've trusted her with my son and I've looked after Aaron. I've been a good friend to her. Now I have to consider that she's trying to drive a wedge between me and Zach, and I don't know why. 'Mum and I had Aaron staying over for a few days, while she went to sort out some problems with her ex. She didn't live at the address I had for her. After speaking with her father, I realise I know nothing about her.' I go to tell Zach about Theo and about me sneaking into his annexe but I stop. I've already piled too much on him and I think I trust what he's told me.

'You can't trust Nicole. She says some weird things.'

'What like?'

'Look, it doesn't matter. She's trying to come between us, end of. I think it's best to keep out of her way. She's trouble.' He pauses. 'You sound stressed. I don't want you to be stressed. I'll be home a little after Saturday lunchtime. We can do something. You, me, Caiden and your mum; we can go out for a late lunch, maybe?'

I feel as though Zach is trying to keep me away from Nicole by telling me she's trouble. Really, I need to figure this all out for myself before he returns. 'I have a wedding to orchestrate on

Saturday so I'll be at work.' I don't have a wedding but I've decided that I have to be there to stop Theo and Madison's wedding because that photo of our babies confirms that Theo is Hugo. When everything is out in the open, I'll tell Mum and Zach, when no one can accuse me of losing my mind. After that, I'll deal with the Nicole issue.

'I thought you were off that day. We were going to have a bit of family time when I got back.'

'I was but there was a last-minute wedding booked.' Just not at the Sea Horse Hotel. Madison deserves better. I have to convince her she's making a big mistake. I can't go to their house again. It's too risky. The only way I feel safe doing this is in a very public place.

'Cool. We'll do something Sunday. Love you loads.'

'Love you.' I hang up.

On Saturday, the truth will come out and I don't know what the repercussions will be. I fear blowing apart everything I love, but I fear not knowing the truth and this spiralling feeling of losing my mind more. I only hope that Zach can forgive me for what I'm planning to do.

TWENTY-FIVE

After three uneventful workdays and a day off, I'm back in work today, then I'm off until next week. Over the past few days, I've struggled to sleep, spending hours staring at the ceiling and pacing around Zach's office, reading those horrible articles. I can't get Justin's murder out of my mind, and I can't stop thinking about Madison and Theo's wedding.

The playground fills up with parents. Sonia pushes a frail lady in a wheelchair, who looks to be in her nineties. She stops next to me on the playground. Amelia runs over to Caiden to play with the children. 'This is Nan. I thought we'd get some fresh air because the weather is glorious today. It's lovely, isn't it, Nan?'

The woman ignores her and stares at the children with a smile on her face.

Christie runs towards us, looking flustered as she chases behind Iris. 'See you later,' she calls to her daughter. The bell rings and we wave our children off. I had hoped to see Nicole but she isn't here. I still haven't managed to contact her and she's ignoring my calls.

'I hate being late,' Christie says. 'That'll teach me for pressing the snooze button one too many times.'

'Have either of you seen Nicole? I'm worried about her.' Maybe she's met up with one of them or even better confided in them.

Christie steps closer to me. 'I spoke to her dad. He seemed to think she went to see her ex-husband.'

Sonia piped up. 'I looked after Aaron last week for a few hours and she didn't seem herself.'

I nodded. 'Mum and I looked after Aaron over the weekend. She came to collect him while I was in the shower and I haven't heard from her since. I went to her house on Sunday looking for her and I had no idea she lived with her dad. She's not speaking to me and I don't know why.' I know it sounds like I'm gossiping and they've known Nicole for longer than me, but I'm hoping they can tell me something I don't know.

'I wouldn't take it personally,' Sonia says as she pulls the fallen blanket back over her nan's knees. 'Nicole has a lot going on – most of it is her own doing.'

'Her dad said a few things. Are you talking about her ex?'

Sonia continues. 'Yes, my mother is friends with her father. Nicole treated Will quite badly from what Mum told me. She left him and he was devastated at the time.'

'I thought he left her and Aaron.' This is all news to me.

Sonia shrugs. 'It was definitely the other way around. Then she was in a new relationship with a lovely guy but that ended too. Nicole told me she'd been sending Facebook messages to a man and her new partner thought she was having an affair and, in return, she accused him of being possessive. She told me she had been speaking to someone online and she wouldn't tell me much about it. Only that she had to do what was right. Of course, I was really curious. When we went out for drinks, I tried to get her to talk but she wouldn't open up about the mystery man.' Sonia looked down and shook her head. 'She needs to end the lie.'

'The lie?' I have no idea where this is going.

'When Nicole and her ex were having a heated argument about who was going to have Aaron last Christmas, she told him he wasn't Aaron's father. The man was distraught after taking a DNA test; he still is.'

'Did he abandon Aaron?'

'No, he was just trying to come to terms with the news. Reading between the lines, he's been really depressed and still needs time to wrap his head around it all. He had a bit of a breakdown. He loves Aaron and I know Aaron loves him, but Nicole often turns up at his in a state, and I don't know what that's doing to him.'

I'm silently seething. Nicole was right, I can't trust her. She is a liar and all I wanted to do was be a good friend to her. I cared for her son; I looked after her hamster and my son adores Aaron, and now she's totally ditched me as a friend at a time when I could do with someone.

'Are you okay, Eva? I know all this is a lot to take in.'

I shrug. 'She's just not who I thought she was. She called me up the other night, drunk, saying that I can't trust her and that I can't trust him.'

'Him, who?' Sonia scrunches her brows.

'I don't know but because of all this I all but accused my husband of having a thing with her.' I reach for the back of my head and dig my nails under my hairpiece and begin pulling and picking. 'I can't help thinking that he's the man from her past.'

'I didn't want to be the one to tell you this but I like you and I hate to see a friend of mine lied to in this way.' Sonia steps back from her nan and speaks in a hushed voice. 'Before you moved here, I remember seeing her looking all cosy at the pub with Zach.'

TWENTY-SIX

So Zach had been seeing Nicole before I moved in. It's not my imagination running wild. Sonia could see that. My lack of sleep is written all over my face and the nightmares aren't helping. I keep waking up in a sweat after dreaming that Theo is in the house, doing all he can to play with my mind. One moment I see him, the next he isn't there, like some elusive shadow that refuses to be defined. Mum has started to go on at me again to see the doctor. She thinks I'm going downhill fast. Maybe I am. I don't know what's real and what isn't anymore. Maybe I didn't even see footprints in the rain the other week. The dog could have been barking at a fox. I'm scared that I'm seeing things that aren't there, and the words 'stress-related psychosis' gnaw at me. Am I looking at Theo while wanting to see Hugo? I want to scream or hit something until my hands bleed, at least blood is real.

As soon as I got home from the playground, I told Mum I felt sick and went straight up to bed. Before school, Caiden kept asking when he could see Aaron again, and he keeps walking around talking to that damn toy raven. Sometimes he's whittering on to Emily and other times he's whispering to his dad. I ask him to talk to me and he keeps saying he can only talk about it to Aaron because only Aaron understands. In all this, I'm losing my son too.

I pull the photo of the two babies from under my pillow and take in their poorly looking premature faces and closed eyes. Something isn't quite right but I can't put my finger on it. The baby on the left looks just like Caiden, especially the nose. Tears fill my eyes. How could I forget what my beautiful little Emily looked like? For so long I've buried the pain of losing her. Emily was stillborn but Caiden made it. I can still feel the pain of having to eventually let her go. I don't remember this photo being taken but then again, I don't remember much from that night. All I remember is the dark cloak of depression that I hid under for months followed by my inability to cope with day-to-day life. Unable to nourish my body to feed my baby boy – my first failure. I couldn't tend to him, leaving Hugo and Mum at the helm.

My heart bangs like I'm the lamb behind the door that the wolf is jumping at. It will stop at nothing to get in and I will stop at nothing to get to the bottom of this confusing chaos that is taking over my life again. I can't be ill. My experiences feel so real.

I stand up and pace, banging my palm on the side of my head. I want my brain to work but it's like it's not mine. I don't feel like me anymore. I could call Hugo's mum or his sister. I think of how cold they were, how they thought I wasn't good enough for their well-educated son with prospects, how disappointed they were when we got married and I got pregnant. I have to tell them about my concerns. It's not like they can come here and force me to go to hospital. They don't even know where I live.

I grab my phone and call Hugo's mum, and she answers.
'Hello, Eva.'
'Cynthia.'

'What can I help you with?'

She didn't even ask how Caiden was. I imagine her wearing her cream wide-leg trousers with a white blouse, done up to the neck, stylishly fitted – the only clothes I've ever seen her wearing. 'I err...' How the hell do I word this? 'I saw Hugo.'

'Hugo's dead. Are you all right, Eva?'

'Yes,' I snap. 'He lives in Devon and he's getting remarried. It's him. I think I'd know my own husband. He's got the same mole.' I don't mention his different eye colour. He could easily disguise that with contact lenses.

She sighs. 'Are you ill again?'

'No, I'm not ill. I saw him. He is alive and well.'

After a short spell of silence, she continues, 'Just like he was dead when he was alive?'

She's mocking me now, taking me to a place I don't care to revisit. 'That was different.'

'Was it, really?'

'Yes, because I was mistaken. I was ill.'

'And it sounds like you're ill again now.' Her voice is patronising and it's winding me up. 'Please see a doctor, Eva, for Caiden's sake.'

Only now she cares about Caiden. Hugo's family have never made an effort to have any kind of relationship with him. 'Look, I saw Hugo. He's alive. I don't know how he did it but he did. He did not die in that accident.' I can't bear to call it a suicide. She hasn't said anything for at least a minute so I continue. 'I can prove it.'

'Eva, just leave it. Please.'

'Leave what?'

'Leave it all.' She hiccups a sob. 'Go back to your life, look after your son and stop this nonsense.'

'There's something you're not telling me, isn't there? You never cared about Hugo. You never got the baby photos out like a normal parent would. How could you be so cold towards your own son?'

'I did my best for him. I knew Hugo better than you ever could.'

I'm floored by that comment. Now I know she's keeping something important from me. 'What's going on, Cynthia?' I flinch at the bang. I'm guessing that she's lashed out at something.

She sniffles. 'I tried. I gave him everything.'

'Everything but love.' Is that why he left me and somehow faked his own death? Did he not know how to love because he'd never been loved by his family? 'Now tell me, what should I leave alone? What am I getting so close to discovering, Cynthia?'

'Please let this drop. I'm begging you.'

'I can't and I won't.'

'In that case, you're going to have to live with the truth when you find it, but I will not have anything to do with it, or you. Let it drop for Caiden's sake. Is this like that time you said he was dead, when he was clearly alive? Don't call me again.' She's gaslighting me and I don't know why. She knows he's alive too but she's hiding it.

He was dead, when he was clearly alive...

Those words she spoke were like a dagger to my heart.

TWENTY-SEVEN

It's Theo and Madison's wedding day and I've never felt so alone.

Amongst other things, Nicole won't answer my calls. Zach didn't say much to me when I called him earlier. It's as if he's avoiding talking to me. If I could, I'd get into my car right now and drive to Worcester, but Caiden needs me and Mum would ask too many questions. The more Nicole and Zach stay away from me, the more I suspect them of having an affair. A sick feeling whirls inside me. I have to get ready for the wedding.

I glance out of the bedroom window at the sea and I wonder if I'm about to lose my dream home and half of everything I own, and I've never felt more stupid. I almost want to cry for Caiden. My boy adores Zach and if he's been playing me all this time to get his hands on my money, it's a sick game. I'd have to sell the house. Boats bob in the water and I wish that Caiden and I could leave on a boat and escape all this stress.

The conversation with Cynthia has been going through my mind. She knows Hugo is alive. What isn't she telling me? Everything she said has only made me more determined to speak to

Madison and stop this farce of a wedding. I try to call Cynthia. She doesn't want to talk to me but I can't let this drop. Maybe she has spent half the night replaying our conversation, just like I did.

Cynthia answers.

'Hello,' I say after checking that Mum isn't listening close by.

'Eva, I'm sorry about the way I spoke to you yesterday. I owe you this much. The truth is dangerous and you need to stop digging for the sake of yourself and Caiden...'

After she finishes explaining everything, I stand there, speechless. I can now see why Cynthia wanted nothing more to do with the boy they adopted after what he did to their daughter. I know why they sent Hugo away to school, why they didn't want to come to the wedding and why they've kept their distance. It wasn't them; it was Hugo all along. They were scared of him and they still are.

A knock at my bedroom door makes me jump.

'Eva, I thought you might want a cuppa before work.' Mum sits on my bed and places the drink on my bedside table. 'You're shaking.'

'Too much coffee. It's going to be a long day.' As I turn away from the window, I flash my best smile at Mum.

'Have you been crying?'

I shake my head. 'No, the sun caught my eyes, that's all. Are you sure you'll be okay today? I bet you can't wait to get home.' My hairpiece has become dislodged. I feel around the back of my head and feed it back into place. I can't let Mum see how bad my head is now. It took ages to stop the bleeding and wash my hair through. I'm not ruining the plan now, not before I've done the deed.

She looks at me sympathetically, knowing that I won't respond well if she mentions my head. 'I've loved being here and quite the opposite, I'm going to miss you both. I think I'll take Caiden out for an afternoon tea somewhere. He seems keen to go out for cake.'

'I'll try not to be too late. Zach should be home this afternoon but I think he'll be tired.' I wonder if he's even coming back but this pretence is all I have. The truth will be in whether he comes home to me or runs off with Nicole. I'm not going to keep calling him.

'We should be back before then.' She looks me up and down. 'You look lovely today.'

I'm not wearing my usual pastel trouser suit and Mum has noticed. I'm wearing a blue dress and a jacket that's far from showy. I don't want to stand out when I'm sneaking around the Clifton House Hotel. Blending in is my aim.

'I thought it might make a change to wear a dress.' My stylish pumps are reassuring, just in case I need to make a fast getaway. Once I've said my piece, I'll leave. Cynthia's words keep whirling through my mind and I feel sick.

'Right, I guess I'll leave you to finish getting ready. Maybe we can have a chat later.'

By then I hope to have the evidence I need and plenty to tell her. 'Bye, Mum, and thanks for the tea.' There's no way I can stomach it and my bladder already keeps telling me I need to pee when I don't.

She looks at me for a bit too long, like she doesn't believe anything I'm saying, so I open my wardrobe and begin rummaging so she'll go. Several minutes later the front door slams. They've gone out.

It's time for me to go. I head downstairs and take the hugest breath while I check my appearance in the mirror by the door. A flash of aquamarine catches my attention in the reflection. I turn around and see nothing but myself reflected in the mirror above the fireplace in the snug, then another reflected me in the reflection – never-ending exact replicas of me – none of them bearing any aquamarine. Running into the snug, I glance out of the window and I can't see anyone on the drive or in the front garden. I'm shaking. Was there someone there or did I imagine it? I'm jumpy, that's all it is.

I head towards the kitchen-cum-family room and go to grab my keys off the island, then my blood feels as though it's running cold. Someone was here. That toy raven is on the worktop and its beady eyes are staring at me.

I don't care if someone is trying to scare or intimidate me. I'm going to the Clifton House Hotel to stop Madison making the biggest mistake of her life. Her husband-to-be is nothing like the person he's pretending to be. If I'm right, she's in danger and only I can help her.

TWENTY-EIGHT

The Clifton House Hotel is at least twice as big as the Sea Horse. It's easier to get lost in here with all the staff rushing back and forth. I check out the main ceremony room and duck behind a pillar as I see Theo speaking to the celebrant. He's wearing a grey suit with a waistcoat and a single pink carnation in his buttonhole. We chose pink carnations on our big day. The celebrant leaves so it's just Theo and me in this vacuous room full of decorated chairs and flower arrangements. Blood pounds through my head and my heart booms like there's a jackhammer in my chest.

As I peer around the pillar, I'm glad his back is turned to me. He sits on a chair in the front row. He places his head in his hands for a few seconds, then inhales loudly before standing again. He walks up to the lectern and takes several huge breaths. His hand reaches his chest and he does a few breathing exercises. Hugo was a confident man, not like the man in front of me. I can see that he's struggling. Madison told me he had agoraphobia, but I chose to believe that he was avoiding going out because of his deception. Then again, I've shown my hand by breaking into his office. Maybe that's why he's anxious.

He slowly lets out a breath in a vocal way. I step back behind the pillar and knock the leg of a trestle table.

'Hello?' he says.

The table is set up for later, when the room becomes the venue for the evening and the cake is placed there.

He clears his throat and I hold my breath, knowing that I'm about to be busted. His footsteps fall heavily on the wooden floor as he makes his way towards me.

'I know you came to my house. I'm sick of the phone calls and the stalking.'

His footsteps get closer and closer until he's almost upon me. I exhale and my shaking hands and the tears running down my face make me unsteady as I scramble for somewhere to hide but he's fast.

'You couldn't just leave it alone and get out of my life. I gave you every chance but you asked for this. I will not let you ruin my life. I'm going to kill you.'

TWENTY-NINE

I see his brown leather shoes from under the white cloth that covers the table, and my heart booms. Any second now, he's going to lift it and do who knows what to me. He said he's going to kill me. I hold my breath and to my relief, his phone rings.

'I'm on my way,' he says.

Spent, I lean back against the wall and gasp with relief, my face red from holding my breath for so long.

I have to warn Madison before it's too late.

Hurrying out of the room, I take the first corridor, then another. This place is like a maze. I end up in a library that leads to a room full of people who are sipping a welcome glass of champagne while eating arancini balls. They frown at me as I stand there looking flustered. Madison is nowhere to be seen, but why would she be here? She'll be getting ready for the biggest day of her life, the one I'm about to ruin. I step backwards into a videographer, sending his tripod crashing to the floor. 'I'm so sorry,' I mutter, before running off.

I follow the signs to the spa and hope that the layout is similar to the Sea Horse, and I carefully open one of the beauty room doors – it's empty. After opening a row of doors, I burst into the final room, where someone is midway through having a body wrap. Again, I apologise and dash.

'Can I help you, are you lost?' A woman wearing a pale blue suit smiles.

'Are you the wedding planner?'

She nods.

'I'm looking for Madison. I have her "something blue",' I say with a beaming smile, hoping she can't see my trembling legs or hear the quiver in my voice.

'She's in the bridal suite. Shall I take it to her?'

'Can I give it to her myself? She's expecting me. We're sisters,' I add.

The wedding planner's brows furrow. Madison and I look nothing like each other, there's not even a smidgen of a resemblance.

'Half-sisters, I mean.'

'I think I'll get the groom.'

'No, I don't want to put him out. I'll get the garter from my car and you can give it to her. I'll come and find you here.' Before she can answer me, I run and I can only hope she stays right there so I can reach Madison before she does.

I quickly search for the hotel website on my phone and click on the details for the bridal suite. It's the penthouse. Getting into the lift, I select floor four and take several deep breaths as I press my back into the corner of the ascending lift. *You can do this, Eva.*

As the lift door opens, I hurry towards the door marked *Bridal Suite* and knock. All I can hear is a group of women singing along to the Black Eyed Peas' 'I Gotta Feeling'. Thuds come from behind the door which is why no one heard my knock. I hammer on the door until a woman who looks like a slightly older and curvier version of Madison answers, a glass of bubbly sloshing in her hand.

'I need to speak to Madison.' I glance behind her and see

four other women, a couple of kids and the baby. Then I catch sight of Madison.

Madison places her glass down and frowns at me. 'Er, Eva from the Sea Horse?'

I nod. 'I need to talk to you. It's important,' I yell above the music.

She stands, her hair half up, wearing a white slip with lace trim along the bottom. Her party start asking what's going on, and who I am, but I'm grateful she joins me at the door. 'Carry on,' she calls out to the others. 'I'll just be a moment.'

'Theo isn't who you think he is.' That's it, I've said it. She isn't responding. In fact, she's looking at me like I'm mad. 'He's my husband, I mean my dead husband Hugo. Look.' I pull out my phone and show her a photo of Hugo and Caiden. Then I show her the photo of the babies. 'See this, this is our son, Caiden, and our daughter, Emily, a short while after they were born.'

'Where did you get that photo?' She stares at me, her red tresses beginning to fall from the pile on her head.

I snatch my phone back.

She continues. 'You broke into our house. It was you the other night.'

'He's not Theo. You have to believe me. I can prove it. I'm not going mad. I've just been speaking to his mum, Cynthia.'

'His mum is not called Cynthia. Seriously, Eva, get out now or I'm calling the police. In fact, I'm going to call them anyway, just not today because you're already ruining my big day. It's as if that bump into the fence the other week has fried your brain. You want to know why we cancelled the Sea Horse? Theo had a bad feeling about you and now I can see why.'

'He's going to kill me.'

A worried look spreads across her face then she slams the door. I wonder if she feels that something has always been off about Theo. I knock again and a bridesmaid opens it and swears at me. The lift pings and the door opens. The wedding planner steps out so I hurry to the stairwell. I'm going to find somewhere to sit while I gather my thoughts. I'm confused. Madison said she knows Theo's mum and she's not called Cynthia. I thought Theo had no family. That's what Madison told me. After running down the stairs, I step out into a corridor and hear a voice booming. It's Nicole. She's slurring and not making any sense. There's a loud crash. As I turn the corner to see what's going on, Nicole has left and there's a smashed vase on the floor. There are flowers everywhere and water seeps into the carpet. She's wearing an aquamarine-coloured T-shirt. 'Where did the woman you were just talking to go?'

The receptionist shakes her head. 'Out the main door. Tell your friend to never come here again.'

After darting out of the hotel into the sunshine, I check all the vehicles to see if I can see Nicole's. I spot her van but I can't see her. I dash between the vehicles, heading to the spaces along the back that are almost hidden by weeping willow branches. All I can hear is blood pumping in my ears. There's a chill at the back of my head. I reach around and realise that my hairpiece is missing. I turn around to check the ground but I can't see it so I carry on looking for Nicole.

White hot pain flashes through my head. I fall and my face hits a rock that's embedded into the earth. All I can think of is Caiden as my attacker lifts my head only to smack it into the rock again. I drift into unconsciousness and this strange fever dream takes me back to the dark parts of my past that I've avoided all these years, and I can't stop them playing out. I try to fight and wake up properly but I feel this is my punishment. Cynthia knows of Hugo's faults and how dangerous he is, but I am a bad person too because I don't know what's real and what's not.

I think of the days surrounding Hugo's death where my mind really did a number on me.

I'd heard noises coming from the living room at our house in Malvern. Terrified, I crept downstairs thinking that we were being burgled and that Hugo might need me. Then I saw him lying on the floor amidst a smattering of glass from the coffee table. I checked his pulse but he was dead. My phone, I couldn't find my phone. It had to be upstairs. It had been by my bedside but it wasn't there any longer. Someone had moved it, or had I left it in the kitchen?

I want this dream to stop but I can't seem to bring myself out of it. My head is throbbing and confused. What Cynthia told me is fighting to be heard, but I'm not hearing her in my inner voice anymore. It's just Hugo and that night in question and it's taking me back there, whether I want to go or not...

On creeping back downstairs, I noticed that the door to the living room had been closed. If Hugo was dead, who had closed it? Caiden was asleep upstairs. I couldn't run and leave him. Hurrying to the kitchen, I grabbed a knife while I searched for my phone, then Hugo walked in from the living room, bottle of wine in one hand, glass in the other. 'Eva! You made me jump. I thought you were asleep.'

'You were dead.' The knife fell from my hands.

He put his wine down. 'I fell, that's all. The coffee table is ruined but I'm not dead.'

'Were you unconscious?'

He shook his head. 'Nope, just dazed. Don't you think I'd be worried if I'd knocked myself out?'

My mind takes me to what happened on the night Hugo took his life. I try to fight it, but I can't. The conversation I had with Cynthia has opened the floodgates.

I went away with Mum overnight to watch a show with her and Caiden. When I arrived home, Hugo had driven over the hill's edge in his car. Seeing him lying there by that coffee table only two nights before had felt like some crazy premonition, a foretelling that he was going to die.

That's what I'd thought, back then, but now I know better, thanks to Cynthia opening up to me. I know who I'm dealing with now and that scares me more than anything. Now Hugo has me right where he wants me. I also know what I did and it's hideous and I'm so ashamed it hurts to even think about it. I try to open my eyes but they're so heavy. All I can do is murmur.

Hugo knows. If my secret comes out it will kill me. He can hurt me all he likes but nothing can hurt as much as what I did to my Caiden. I sob with my face buried in the stone on the ground, unable to muster up the strength to move.

I feel another blow to my head and I don't even fight. Right now, I feel as though I deserve it.

I hear a voice but it's robotic. Trying as hard as I can, I manage to turn my face away from the stone and I catch a reflection in the side panel of a silver car just before my world goes dark once more – aquamarine.

I don't know how much time has passed before I slowly come round. Every part of my body screams in pain and I can't see. I don't know if I've been out of it for ten minutes, or several hours. Actually, I can see but there's nothing to see except the four sides of the pitch-black box that I'm contained in.

I panic. I've been buried alive. I touch the side of my head and it's sticky with what has to be blood. Heart banging, I yell, scream, and pound on the hardwood then I remember seeing aquamarine. I know who put me in this box. 'Help me. Let me out, Nicole,' I yell as I burst into tears. Why has she done this to me? My head hurts and I can't think straight. It's like my brain has been substituted for cotton wool. I'm going to die and although I feel like I deserve it, I want to go home to Caiden and hug him hard, tell him how much I love him and how sorry I am for what I did all those years ago.

I'm never getting out of here. It hits me that I'm never going to see my son again. My mind is telling me Hugo brought me here because I know he is capable of murder – but he didn't. For whatever reason, Nicole smashed my head into a rock several times and she's put me in this box and left me here to die, and I deserve it because I left Caiden to die all those years ago. This is my punishment. There is one thing I can't fathom: why is Nicole doling out the punishment?

THIRTY
MADISON

Madison glances at the clock on the wall behind her client. Being pregnant was a miracle, that's for sure. Or was it simply biology? She was going with biology with miraculous undertones. 'I adore this mistletoe-berry red,' she said to Christie, one of her regular customers, while trying not to think about the nauseous churning in her gut. It's typical; she's a beautician, a hairdresser and a nail technician. Why couldn't she have an aversion to sausages instead of nail polish or nail polish remover? And why were her assistants, Orla and Tammy, both at lunch at the same time?

'Are you okay? Your green complexion isn't exactly complementing your red hair. You look more Christmassy than my nails,' Christie replies, her head tilting in sympathy.

Chuckling, Madison waits for Christie's nails to cure under the lamp. 'It's the nail varnish. I thought the sickness went after a few weeks; I've been sick all the way through.'

'That sucks. It happened to me too. I bet that little bun in the oven will be out soon.'

Madison places a loving hand on her bump. 'And Mummy can't wait because Mummy would like to not have to pee every five minutes; she'd like to be able to cut her own toenails and she'd definitely love a glass of wine.' She grimaces. She intends to breast feed so wine might be out of the question for a long time.

'Weather's a bit yuck at the moment.'

'It is,' Madison says for the fourth time that day. It's still grey and there is still a frost on the road outside, but then again, it's early December. What did anyone expect?

'Have you been on holiday this year?' Christie asks.

Another question that always gets asked. 'Yes, we stayed in Loch Ness.'

'Did you see the monster?' Christie chuckles.

Madison forces a smile. It's pretty obvious she didn't see a monster because the monster is a myth as far as she's concerned, but she's learned never to express an opinion, because that would result in losing customers. 'I saw a monster.'

Christie scrunches her brows. 'Tell me more.'

Madison shakes her head. 'Only joking.' But she's not joking. She knew it had been a tall order getting Theo to go on holiday, what with his agoraphobia. If he had it his way, he'd never leave the house; but she had needed to leave the house before she went insane; anyway, if he couldn't leave the house, what had all the therapy been for? What she hadn't banked on was him leaving her alone in Loch Ness with no phone signal, in the middle of nowhere, for a whole night, in a creaky cottage. He'd left a note that said, 'I need some space'. On his return, he apologised profusely, saying he had some sort of anxiety meltdown and didn't want to upset her. What kind of monster leaves someone alone with no way out, no provisions, and no phone and car, with no word on when they'd be back? So much for his agoraphobia. She remembered having her hiking bag packed the next day, just before his return. It was only seven miles to civilisation, but still, it was far enough.

'Right, you can remove your hands now.' She grabs the cuticle oil, ready to massage it in.

Speak of the devil. The door rings as Theo walks in, carrying a box of something she knows she'll find yummy. He's frowning and that bothers her. 'Excuse me a moment, Christie.'

She leaves her client and leads Theo to the other side of the salon, knowing that Christie can still see them through all the mirrors. He thrusts the box at her. 'Pasta salad,' is all he says.

Madison takes the lunchbox and places it on one of the empty salon chairs. 'Thank you. Is everything okay?'

His brow is a little damp with perspiration. He removes his glasses and begins massaging his tired looking eyes. 'It's the photo.'

With furrowed brows, she waits for him to elaborate. 'What photo?'

He pulls out his phone and starts scrolling through her Facebook page. 'This.'

He holds it up in front of her face.

'Faye's wedding hair?' Madison is proud of her work. It's one of the best she's ever done, which is why she chose to show it off on her page, and it's the only photo she took. She had planned to put that photo onto her website too.

He jabs at the phone with his index finger. 'That's me, in the corner.'

So that's what his mood was about. He'd popped into frame just as she snapped the photo. 'No one's looking at you. It's about the hair. You're barely in it and does it matter really?'

He starts speaking in a hushed voice but she knows that Christie can probably hear them. 'It matters to me. You know I don't really like social media. We've discussed this.' No, *he* discussed it. She knows he has issues, but him being an arsehole right now has nothing to do with his agoraphobia, and she's also aware that he has an Instagram account.

'And I have a business to run and this is stupid.'

'Take it down.'

He's shaking. For my own sanity, I'm going to make him face this part of his irrational self. 'No, so please don't ask me again because you're wasting your time and mine.' This isn't how a loving couple should speak to each other, Madison knows, but she also knows she has to speak her mind, otherwise she'll bottle things up and explode later. She places her hands over her huge belly and feels baby Emily kicking hard. 'Look, I don't need any stress right now, okay? I don't know whether you've forgotten. But I'm carrying your baby. We can talk about this at home later.'

'Take it down.'

'Get some help. You need it.' She hated saying that but it was true.

He looks like he wants to say more but instead he takes a few breaths before turning away from her and storming out. She stares at her reflection in the mirror. Gone is the bubbly, glowing pregnant woman. In her place is someone with glassy eyes and a slight tremor. She hates confrontation but it's become too regular with Theo. She loves him, though, so she'll keep pushing him out of his comfort zone until he gets better. As she opens the lunchbox, her stomach churns at the smell of tuna and pasta and she knows it will have to go in the bin. There's nothing like a bit of bickering to ruin an appetite.

She walks back to the other side where Christie remains in her seat. 'I'm sorry you had to hear that. I'll give you a discount because that can't have been nice.' She pauses, not knowing if Christie is happy with her offering. She doesn't want to lose her as a customer or end up with a bad online review. 'Men.' Madison shakes her head and smiles.

'Bloody men,' Christie says. 'No need for the discount. Good on you for saying what you thought.'

The rest of the day is a blur. Madison still can't believe that

Theo came in and spoke to her like that with a client in the salon, all because of a stupid photo.

She parks up outside the cottage and has a little flashback to the first few times she came to this cottage with her broken laptop. He'd admitted not fixing it properly so she'd come back, which in itself was a bit devious. He could have just asked her out on a date and explained that he had agoraphobia. She was smitten with him on first sight. He was gorgeous and she'd been single for over a year. But the house looked unloved, dark and brooding, just like he was. He was her man of mystery, a man who didn't like to discuss his past or what trauma led to him being such a recluse. Then he told her about the terrible accident, the one where his twin sister, Emily, had died, along with his parents, all because his mother had fallen asleep in their house with a lit cigarette in her mouth – and it melted her heart. Madison knew from then that he needed care and love if he was to ever come out of his shell.

Now, as she gets out of the car, she pats her belly, knowing that their Emily is going to be the most loved little girl in the whole world.

He waves from the window with Buster, their Lhasa Apso, under one arm, yapping away. She'd rescued Buster four years ago and when she moved in with Theo, he'd lovingly accepted her gorgeous little furball into his home.

She pushes the creaky gate open and stares at the ivy that is taking over the front of the house. It won't be today, but she'll mention it to Theo. She wants the place made perfect before Emily's arrival. Swallowing, she thinks of their little argument at the salon and she hopes he's lightened up because although she said they should talk later, she doesn't want to talk. As she goes to unlock the door, Theo is already there, a smile on his face. He wraps his arms around her tightly as Buster yaps for attention at her feet.

'I'm sorry about earlier. I shouldn't have come in like that, moaning and demanding you take the photo down.'

She inhales a deep mushroom aroma as she hugs him tightly. Their tiff hadn't sat well with her. 'I'm sorry too. I should have been a bit less angry.'

He pulls back. 'No apologies from you. It was all me. If the internet was asking who is the arsehole, or should I say the asshole, in this situation, it would be me. I wanted to make it up to you so I've made mushroom risotto.'

She'd craved that dish all through her pregnancy and the thought of eating it made her salivate. 'Forgiven, asshole,' she says as she hurries to the kitchen ready to tuck in.

Earlier she'd pondered whether their relationship was over. She wondered if she'd made the biggest mistake of her life agreeing to marry him, but now she knows it was nothing more than a blip and a part of his condition. They could work through it because that's what couples did. They have to work hard at a relationship; she is learning that lesson fast and hard.

THIRTY-ONE

It's New Year's Eve, and though she hates leaving her staff alone with such a busy schedule, this baby is coming early, whether she wants it to or not. An agonising contraction ripples through her, causing her to clench her teeth. Phone in hand, she calls the salon and Orla answers.

'Maddie, everything's fine. Don't worry about anything. You have a baby to bring into the world and Tammy and I can't wait to meet her.'

Orla's sweet voice is reassuring, considering Madison's waters had broken midway through cutting the hair of a new client. Relinquishing control to Orla and Tammy was proving to be challenging; however, she didn't call for an update: she needed to know where the hell her husband was. Theo wasn't answering his mobile despite knowing she might need him at any given moment. Their baby wasn't due for another two weeks but that's no excuse, babies can come at any time when the due date is close. 'Have you seen Theo?' Another contraction sends Madison screaming. 'The baby's coming, I need him here,' she yells.

'I'll keep calling him.'

'Thanks.' Madison ends the call and places the phone down while taking another gulp of gas and air.

'I'm sure he's on his way,' the midwife says.

She doubts that. Since she became pregnant, he'd changed, become a bit more reclusive and angrier at having to leave the house. The tiff they'd had at the salon, about the photo, had been the tip of the iceberg which had forced her to insist that he booked a couple of emergency sessions with his therapist.

Maybe it was the baby. At first he'd been dead against bringing a baby into the world, but Madison wanted their little peanut more than anything, including him. After two miscarriages during a previous marriage, she'd longed for this baby. In the end, he proposed. She'd always wondered if he proposed because she was pregnant or because they'd been together over two years, and it seemed like the natural thing to do.

Her sister, Camille, barges in and throws her coat onto a plastic chair in the corner of the room. 'I came as soon as I could. Neil has left work early to look after the kids.' She runs over and hugs Madison before grabbing a cloth and wiping the sweat from her brow. That should be Theo's job. 'How often are the contractions?'

'I don't know, all the time.' Madison begins to breathe like she was shown in antenatal class, to ease the contractions. It does little to help. In fact, nothing helps. The midwife is annoying her and the so-called antenatal expert was a liar. Every position is painful. She's been on all fours, standing at the side of the bed, hunched over, on her back, walking – nothing helps. 'I feel like I need to push but I can't. Theo needs to be here. I can't do this without him.'

'Look at me, Madison.' Camille leans over and strokes her hair. 'That baby will not wait for anyone. That baby doesn't care that you had a busy day of doing hair so that everyone would look great for their New Year's Eve parties. That baby doesn't care where Theo is. She just wants to come out and meet her amazing mother, and Aunt Camille, of course.'

Madison grips Camille's hand. 'We can do it, can't we?' She needs her sister's reassurance. Her sister has been through this twice already when giving birth to Madison's gorgeous niece and nephew.

'We can. Sisters rule!'

They always said that growing up and their parents used to laugh. She is also annoyed that their mum and dad are on holiday in Lanzarote; but they'd get to meet Emily soon. The midwife finishes examining her. 'Your sister's right and this baby is ready to come out.'

She pushes, over and over again. Screaming, panting, sucking on gas and air – it is happening without Theo. He has let her down. Tears stream down her face as she hears the word *crowning* come from either her sister or the midwife. Everything is a blur. The pushing and pain feels like it will never end. All she wants to do is sleep with her beautiful baby next to her.

'Oh, my goodness, Maddie. I can see her gorgeous little head.'

It doesn't feel little, she wants to yell but she can't because it's happening again, so she keeps pushing with what little energy she has left. It has taken approximately four hours from waters breaking to almost having her baby, and Theo hasn't even looked at his messages or responded to her calls. Anger fuels her as she pushes one more time and within a few seconds, she hears the first cry of her baby before the placenta follows after more pushing.

'You have a beautiful baby girl,' the midwife says as she passes the wriggling baby to Madison.

Camille starts crying. 'She's so precious. She's amazing, Madison. She's bloody perfect and you, you're amazing too.'

'Can you cut the cord?' Madison asks Camille. That was meant to be Theo's job but still, she is aware he's let her down.

'It would be my honour, sis.'

Theo or no Theo, she finally has her baby and she's so high right now, she laughs and cries at the same time, while her little one is being weighed, cleaned and wrapped in a blanket.

'My baby.' She can't stop saying those words repeatedly. She never thought she'd say them and she feels this instant rush of love that people speak about.

'Your baby,' Camille repeats. 'Look at those scrumptious little fingers and her blue eyes. They're just like yours, like ours.'

'I love her so much. How is it possible to feel so much love?' Madison bursts into tears. She's a mother and this is her baby daughter, the little peanut that grew inside her for eight and a half months. She holds her baby to her chest, offering the little one a breast, and the baby struggles to latch on. 'She needs to feed. Why won't she feed?'

'It's okay.' The midwife hurries over and helps Madison to adjust her position then the little one takes Madison's breast in her mouth and begins to suckle.

Madison weeps tears of joy but the beaming smile on her face is tainted by the fact that Theo isn't here.

'What are you going to call her?' Camille asks as the midwife works around them to tidy up the delivery room and make notes.

Theo barges in. 'I'm so sorry, Maddie. I was filming in the woods with my phone on silent. I'm such an idiot.' He stares. 'I missed it. I'm so upset I missed her being born.'

How can she stay angry at him? She takes in his windswept hair and rain-dashed glasses. That's how he always looks when he's been outside filming the wildlife. He often goes out for hours and his phone barely gets a signal out there.

He throws his coat on top of Camille's and kisses Madison's head before leaning down to kiss their feeding newborn. 'She's perfect, Madison.' His phone beeps twice. He frowns as he reads the messages before shoving the phone in his pocket.

'Don't keep me in suspense, guys. What are you going to call her?' Camille asks again.

They had decided to name her after Theo's sister who died when she was a baby. 'Emily,' Theo and Madison say at the same time. 'Emily,' Madison repeats because it felt so good to keep saying her name.

THIRTY-TWO

Theo collapses the pram and wedges it into the boot. Spring has emerged from nowhere and Madison loves the cottage when the daffodils begin to grow. They cheer up its creepy exterior, almost making it look pretty. As always, the birds squawk in the woodland that surrounds them but that doesn't wake Emily. Madison strokes her soft baby hair as she places her in the car seat and straps her in. Emily has a round face and a dimple in her chin, like her. Her heart hums when she sees their baby changing every day. She grieves for yesterday's Emily but is excited to see future Emily. Why do babies have to grow so fast?

'Right, let's do this,' Theo says as he gets into the car. She appreciates the effort he's making lately. He's going out more and is even speaking about them going on holiday again, which excites Madison as she keeps dreaming of having a honeymoon in Loch Ness or should she say, a familymoon. His setback in December was nothing more than that. They are back on track and she couldn't be happier. His phone beeps.

'Are you going to see who that is?'

'Nope,' he replies as it beeps again.

He ignores his phone a lot, which is worrying. Madison

fears he might be missing out on work and, with a new baby, they need all the money they can get, which is why Madison is already back at the salon a couple of days a week. She also wonders if the messages are work related. He looks anxious every time his phone beeps.

She glances back at the cottage, watching Buster standing on the top of the lounge chair, barking at them from the other side of the window. 'Be back in a bit,' she shouts to him, knowing full well that he can't hear or understand. She checks her watch. 'We have time to pop to the salon first.'

'Really?' Theo begins to reverse the car to get out of their tight drive.

It's then she notices how overgrown the ivy and shrubs have become around the house. All the daffodils in the world won't make the exterior look better given the mess it's in. They were never tackled in the winter and with Emily coming early, it had slipped both of their minds. Theo spent far too much time in the cabin and out in the woods filming the wildlife to sell to his network of wildlife YouTubers. What he really needs to do is make the cottage look nicer. She'd do it herself but managing the salon and most of Emily's needs has been all-consuming. 'I just want to see how Orla and Tammy are coping today. I know we're overbooked.'

'I thought you sorted that yesterday?'

She shrugs. It's her salon and it's down to her to keep it going. Times have been tough and if she didn't keep a close eye on spending, it could easily get out of hand. Orla is terrible with figures and Tammy is worse. Besides, she's had an offer on the salon, again, and she's considering selling in the near future, but there's no need to mention that to Theo yet because she's still not sure about whether to go ahead. He will only get excited and she has to be sure before properly considering a move to Scotland with him. She doesn't even know if she'll ever take the offer, but it is a good one and she knows that Theo would be overjoyed at it. Besides, she hopes the familymoon will help her make a firm decision.

'I ended up cutting hair and doing nails yesterday. I just want to check the purchase orders today. I'll literally be five minutes.'

'You should be enjoying some maternity leave.'

She presses her lips together and smiles at him sarcastically. 'I work for myself. It's not as easy as that and you know it. If it was that easy, why are you in the cabin most of the day working? You could take more paternity leave instead.'

'Point taken.'

'See, we both value our businesses, and Camille has been great at looking after Emily for us.' She's become reliant on Camille when it comes to being able to get back to work. As a childminder and mother of two under-fives, Camille welcomed her baby niece into the fold and Madison knew the extra money helped her lovely sister out. She'd find it hard to tell Camille if they decided to move.

Within minutes they arrive at the salon. Madison runs in, checks the purchases and runs back out. Everything was okay and she was worrying over nothing. 'Let's get to the Sea Horse.' She rubs her hands together with excitement.

Theo takes a few breaths and undoes the top buttons on his polo shirt.

'Are you okay?'

'I don't know. It's coming out to a hotel. It's a big venue and there will be lots of people and the sea.'

She should have known how hard this would be for him. The therapy had been going well and he was able to come to the salon and go out for the day with her – at a push; but is this a push too far? 'I'm proud of you, Theo. We have to get used to the Sea Horse because we're getting married there. It's going to be the happiest day of our lives' – she glances back at baby Emily – 'except for when that little one was born, of course.'

'You're right, as usual.' He steers with one hand and places the other on her knee.

She gives it a reassuring squeeze. 'Just keep breathing like you were shown. You can do this. We can do this. Okay?'

As he pulls up outside the hotel, he stares at the sea beyond the main building. 'It's vast, isn't it? The sea?'

'It is, and it's also exciting and beautiful.'

'I'm ready.' He steps out of the car and gets the pram from the boot. 'Let's get you in your pram, Pumpkin,' he says to Emily.

Madison leans in and gently lifts Emily from her car seat. She inhales the lingering scent of milk caught in the creases of her baby's neck. Emily's lips pucker into a pink rosebud before she yawns and goes back to sleep. Madison places the little one into the pram and then Theo pushes her towards the entrance. He uses the pram like a crutch as he grips it tightly.

A young woman called Hallie leads them to a pretty room where she makes drinks while Madison casts reassuring looks Theo's way. If she could place a hand on his heart, she knows it would be thrumming. 'Eva will be with you in just a minute. Take a seat. If you need me, I'll be at reception.'

'It's stunning here.' Madison glances at the very gardens she'd dreamed of getting married in as soon as they saw them at the wedding fair. With the sea view in the background, they are perfect.

Emily fidgets in her pram. Theo leans in to check on her. 'She needs changing.'

Madison goes to grab the changing bag that hangs over the pram handles.

'It's okay, I'll do it. Make a start without me.' He picks up Emily and leaves the room.

She knows he'd rather not be here, and she also knows that

he has to keep facing his fear. He's been doing well but she has no idea why today of all days seems so challenging for him. It's like he's regressed. In her mind's eye, she pictures him behind a locked door doing breathing exercises as he changes Emily, dreading coming back out.

Madison's sundress is crumpled already. She sits and waits for Eva, the wedding planner, to arrive; it feels like forever. Maybe her own anxiety is acting up because all she wants to do now is run to the toilets and see if Theo is all right.

Eva makes her flinch as she breezes in from behind. She offers them another drink and asks about their wedding plans. Madison isn't listening properly; she's half listening out for Theo and Emily. Eva seems nice, like a perfect wedding planner. Her suit is charming, if not slightly tight around the bust, and her smile is welcoming. Her blonde hair frames her face though her ends are a little split. Being a hair stylist and beautician, Madison can't help but notice these things.

There's a tap at the door and Theo walks in holding Emily. He manages to half push a hand out from underneath our baby to hold out to shake Eva's. 'Lovely to meet you.' He frowns and clears his throat. Madison is sure she catches him doing his breathing exercises discreetly. In her head, she can almost hear him counting. He withdraws his hand. Emily is asleep in his arms until the clumsy wedding planner drops her cup, waking her. Eva stares directly at Theo, and she's shaking. Emily is whimpering, and all Madison wants to do is take her from Theo and cuddle her. Theo bobs their baby up and down, and the wedding planner looks like she might keel over as she backs away from them.

'Eva, are you okay? Are you ill?' Madison helps Eva to her seat despite Eva looking like she wants them to leave. There's no way Madison would leave her looking like this. Eva could pass out and then she'd be on her own. 'Can I get you some water?'

'No, no. I just felt a little dizzy, that's all. I skipped lunch.'

Eva stares at Theo and Emily, which seems odd. Madison feels her own heartbeat start to ramp up. It's like the atmosphere changed as soon as Theo entered. Eva seems woozy, like she's about to pass out. Madison glances at Theo but all he does is shrug.

'I'm feeling better. So sorry about that. I don't know what came over me.'

Eva eats a sweet, and Madison can see that Theo wants to leave. The rise and fall of his chest shows her that his breathing isn't under control. He places Emily in her pram and decides to take her outside, which Madison is grateful for. Maybe she should have come alone.

Eva seems to be back on track after her strange little episode, so Madison answers a few questions about Theo and herself.

'How many guests are you looking at inviting?' Eva asks.

A part of her now wonders if Theo will be able to get through a wedding. He couldn't even stay in the room for this discussion. 'On my side, friends and family – about fifty. As for Theo's side, I'd say about ten, if that. He has no family. There will be sixty guests at the most.' She doesn't want to explain the tragedy of Theo's past, and she wonders if any of Theo's friends will come. He has his friends around now and again, the local wildlife filming club, but they're more like acquaintances. He gets some work from a company and is mildly pally with a couple of men there, but again, she wonders if they will turn up. Theo truly is a loner.

'No family?'

Eva's face is intense. Madison carries on speaking in the hope that the meeting will be over quicker. 'I know, it's all so sad. He lost his family in a house fire.' Madison waffles on about the wedding package, but Eva looks distracted. She wonders if it has anything to do with the blood smear across the top of Eva's fingers. Madison tries not to stare because that would be rude, so she keeps the conversation going by talking about having the ceremony and celebrations in the garden, and asking about the falconer. She knows how much Theo likes birds of prey and that his dream would be to have an owl at the ceremony. It might put him more at ease on the big day. Madison taps her manicured nails on the desk, hoping to wrap their meeting up, but she's not sure if Eva has got the hint that the meeting needs to end. 'Eva, is that sorted? Can I leave the falconer with you?' Phew, it seems like the meeting is a wrap.

Madison passes one of her business cards to Eva. She's always trying to promote the salon everywhere she goes, and Eva's hair looks like it could do with a bit of love. It's dull and a bit frizzed up at the back. Her roots need touching up too. 'I have a salon on the outskirts of Ilfracombe. Can't blame a girl for trying to get more business, especially now I've upgraded our wedding package. Everyone has to have their hair cut at some point.' Madison forces a nervous laugh. Self-promotion isn't natural for her, no matter how many years she has been in business. She notices how shaky Eva's hands are as she holds the card. Something isn't right but Madison can't put her finger on it. Maybe Theo's nervous behaviour started Eva off, or maybe it was the other way around. Madison can't tell.

Eva leads Madison out to the car park. She hoped that Eva would leave her to it so that she could see if Theo was all right but Eva seemed insistent on coming all the way to the car – awkward. Theo sings 'Twinkle, Twinkle' while rocking Emily, which makes Madison instantly forgive him for leaving her alone with the wedding planner. Again, she has had to handle all the arrangements; it's basically what she signed up for when she chose to spend the rest of her life with Theo. Madison gently takes Emily from him and clips her into her baby seat while Theo closes the boot.

'Hugo?' Eva calls as Theo gets into the car, but he ignores her.

Madison thinks that was strange, but Eva sees so many people a day, she must have mixed him up with someone else.

As he drives, he has one eye on the mirrors as they get further away from Eva. Madison glances in the wing mirror her side, to see Eva staring like a weirdo. It sends a shiver through her.

'That woman is strange. She called you Hugo. Did you hear that?'

He nods. 'I don't like her. She kept staring at me which is why I had to leave.'

'Me neither.' Madison can't deny his account of what just happened. Eva is weird and the last thing she ever wants is to go back to the Sea Horse Hotel, let alone get married there.

THIRTY-THREE

It's been hours since they got back from the Sea Horse. Madison places Emily in her cot for her afternoon nap, before heading towards the cabin with the phone in her pocket just in case the baby monitor app alerts her to Emily stirring. There's a chill in the air and she can't decide whether it's because the day is coming to an end, or if it's because as soon as they got back from the Sea Horse, Theo basically abandoned her and Emily in the kitchen, barely saying anything before rushing off to the cabin. As she goes to nudge the door open, she can't help but overhear the shouting coming from his office, or man cave as she likes to call it. The couches, TV and coffee table make it more homely than office-like. He even has a more expensive coffee machine in there than they have in the house.

Deciding to nudge the main door, she steps in and listens outside his office. The door to the WC creaks as the breeze from the open main door flows through. She closes the main door quietly.

'Stop calling. I am not the person you think I am... I said stop it or I'll...'

There is a loud bang and Theo roars. Madison flinches and

inhales sharply. If she enters now, Theo will know she's been standing outside, listening.

Buster whimpers at the door and begins to scratch to be let in. He hates being excluded from anything which is why all of their doors are scratched to death at Buster-height. Madison goes to exit the building quietly, but it's no good. Theo walks from the other side of his office, catching her as she's just about to step outside.

'Madison.' His hair is ruffled and his glasses are slightly smudged.

'I was just about to make a drink and thought you might want one. I, err, I thought we could talk about something but...' She knows she'll have to mention overhearing him shouting on the phone. He knows she heard. Her red face is giving her away. 'Theo, is everything all right? I heard you shouting.'

He huffs out a breath. 'It was just a wrong number but they've called several times already so I got annoyed. I didn't handle it well but I'm stressed, so there we go.'

'How long has it been going on?'

He shrugs. 'Only a couple of days. It's nothing. I'm sure they'll get bored.'

'What do they say?'

'Nothing, nothing. They err...' He takes a few breaths. 'They think I'm someone else. Wrong number. It's just annoying, and I overreacted, but it's nothing, really.' He smiles at her and pulls her into him.

She feels the firmness of his body against hers and places her arms around his neck. It feels nice to be close to him because this has barely happened since they had Emily. He kisses her gently and then again more deeply and slowly. 'I love you,' she says as they part.

'I love you too.'

'You know you mentioned maybe moving to Scotland one day?' It was more than mention. Theo has become obsessed in recent days. It's okay for him, he can work remotely from anywhere, but she would need to start up again. However, the firm offer she received for her salon had been upped by twenty thousand pounds recently. The more she thinks on it, the more she knows she is ready for the new start that Theo is keen for.

'Yes.'

'I think I'm ready to make the move.'

He picks her up and spins her around. 'I think it will be amazing for us and Emily. What brought this on?'

She shrugs. 'An offer on the salon, the thought of a new adventure in life and I got thinking. Emily is a baby; it won't disrupt her if we do it now.'

He kisses her. 'What were you going to tell me before?'

'Something felt off at the Sea Horse earlier.' In her head, she mulls over Eva calling her husband Hugo. 'It's odd that the wedding planner called you the wrong name and now you're getting phone calls from someone who thinks you're someone else.'

'It's a coincidence, that's all. The phone calls started before today. I must have one of those faces, but I agree with you, I got a bad vibe from that meeting and the whole place. I don't want to get married at the Sea Horse, and I didn't want to say anything because I thought you'd be angry, but if you're not sure either…'

'I want to get married,' she tells him. If he thinks he's going to put their wedding on the backburner, he's mistaken. She has a baby and getting married is important to her. She knows other people don't think much of marriage these days but she always wanted the full package. Marriage and kids, just like what her sister Camille has, and what her mother and father have.

'And I do too. I want to marry you more than anything, Madison. You and Emily are my world, which is why I've been looking into the Clifton House Hotel. It's a bit grander. I also think we can stretch to pay for a better package there and they have a day in May, Madison.' He looks into her eyes. 'Will you marry me even sooner? Because I can't wait for us to become husband and wife, and I want us to marry at a place that doesn't give off bad vibes.'

Excitement fills her tummy. What she anticipated might be an awkward conversation about her not being comfortable at the Sea Horse, has turned out to be one of the easiest conversations ever. 'Yes, yes and yes, again.'

He reaches out, grabs her hand and pulls her close again. Buster begins to yap at their feet, jumping up against them excitedly. Madison lifts Buster up before kissing his furry head.

'I'll call them and book the day. We can let everyone know later and if they can't make it, I don't care if it's just us. All I want to be is your husband,' Theo says.

Her phone shakes in her pocket. She snatches it out. 'It's the baby monitor.' Pressing the app, she waits for the footage to load. Emily is screaming her little heart out, her fists balled and her blankets nowhere to be seen. 'Something's wrong.'

'It's okay, Madison. She's just been thrashing around a little.'

Madison runs, Theo following as he tries to calm her down. Maybe she's panicking over nothing, like she does a lot, but if anything ever happened to Emily, she'd never forgive herself. Emily is her life and she knows what it's like to lose her babies and she couldn't bear to lose Emily. Up the stairs and through Emily's bedroom door, she sees that their precious little girl is fine, just a bit gripey.

Theo sidesteps past her and lifts Emily up. 'She feels a bit warm. Maybe she's sickening for something. I'll take her down and feed her if you want a rest. There's some expressed milk in the fridge, isn't there? You look tired.'

She catches a glimpse of herself in the mirror. All her make-up has worn off and she agrees: the bags under her usually youthful green eyes are a purplish red. They've been like that a lot since she became a parent; nonetheless, she wants to feed Emily herself. She shakes her head. 'It's okay. I want to feed her.'

Theo passes her over. 'I'm sure she'd love that, won't you, Pumpkin? I'll head back to the cabin and book the Clifton, if you're okay calling to cancel the Sea Horse.'

She nods. She'll do it when someone will be there to deal with the cancellation.

Theo has already gone. It's just her, Emily and Buster, who is sniffing around at the corner of the room. He barks at the dresser. She glances around, feeling like someone is there, watching, but there is no one. With Emily in her arms, she quickly checks the other three bedrooms and the bathroom, but they're empty; then again, what was she expecting? A homicidal maniac lurking in the wardrobe? Buster is still barking at the same corner in Emily's room. She calls him out and pulls the door closed. 'Let's get you fed too. Come on, boy.'

After putting food down for Buster, she heads to the living room and undoes her nursing top and bra, and then proceeds to feed Emily. Her thriving baby gulps and gulps like she can't get enough. After a few minutes, she swaps breasts and Emily continues to suckle. A full up Buster curls up in his basket.

Just as she's about to close her eyes with Emily resting in her arms, she catches a glimpse of something black beyond the gate at the bottom of their garden. The foliage is too dense to see through now. She wonders if it was a raven or a crow. They get a lot of them in the woodland. It was something far bigger than a bird though. She places a sleeping Emily in the baby basket next to her and does her bra and top back up. She goes to open the front door but it's on the latch. Maybe Theo left it like that when he went back and forth to the car carrying Emily's baby luggage in.

She stands in the garden, her sundress billowing in the breeze. Buster dashes past her, barking into the bushes and dashing around all over the place, wagging his tail. He senses that someone has been here.

Daytime has all but gone and darkness is falling. If someone was out there, they'd have to have driven up their long, bumpy drive, but she doesn't hear any vehicles leaving. She hurries down the path, nudging the gate open and continuing a little way down the turning space. There's no car there. Maybe she imagined seeing someone, and Buster is probably trying to get her to walk him through the woods but that isn't going to happen tonight. She's tired. While rubbing her eyes, she begins to walk back. It's dark now. A flurry of bats fly above. On entering the house, she removes the latch and closes the door behind her.

Emily is still asleep so she heads to the kitchen to put the kettle on. A cup of decaffeinated tea is in order before she works out how she's going to tell the Sea Horse about their cancellation. Her thoughts go back to Eva earlier and the way she kept looking at Theo. No wonder her poor nervous husband had wanted to leave with Emily. It was creepy. She was creepy. As she pulls the tea bags out of the cupboard, a glint of light catches her eye.

She reaches for the shiny object in the fruit bowl. It's a wedding ring. Not only is it a ring, but it's half covered in mud.

THIRTY-FOUR

Madison gently lifts Emily up even though she knows it might wake her but she has to get out of the house. After popping the ring in her pocket, she hurries out through the back door, and heads to the cabin.

'It's booked. We're now getting married on the tenth of May.' He gets up out of his office chair and comes over.

He fails to see the frown lines on her forehead as he brushes one of her red curls from the corner of her mouth.

'Theo, I think someone has been in our house.'

He furrows his brows. 'When?' He runs to the door and she follows.

'I don't know. I was feeding Emily in the lounge and I saw someone outside.' She doesn't tell him that it was only a fleeting something out of the corner of her eye, that in the absence of a car it may have even been a bird. She's so sure that it was a person and that they left the ring in their kitchen. 'The door was on the latch.'

'Damn, I must have left it like that earlier when I went to the car.'

As they trudge through the house, she goes to tell him about the ring but he's already outside, using the torch on his phone to check out the bushes with Buster excitedly following. Several minutes later, they're back and he locks the door. He runs upstairs and she hears him going through each room before he runs back down. Then he heads into the other two rooms, the one that contains his gym equipment and the large room that has become a dumping station for all Emily's things. 'Nothing. Are you sure you saw someone?'

She pulls the ring out of her pocket. 'They must have left this.'

He takes it from her and holds it up to the light. 'Love you forever,' he mutters as he reads the inscription. 'Where did you find that?'

'In the fruit bowl.'

He runs his fingers through his hair again, the ring still in one hand. He's been doing that a lot lately. 'No one has been here. I found it in the garden the other day. It must have been there for years.'

He never mentioned finding a ring. And when did he put it in the fruit bowl? She'd been in the kitchen earlier and it wasn't there. She rubs her eyes and yawns. 'But you've been here years.'

'Well longer than me.'

'It wasn't here earlier.'

'It was. Maybe you didn't notice it.' His Adam's apple bobs up and down as he swallows.

'Theo, what aren't you telling me?'

He's going blotchy, the way he does when he gets anxious. She has a feeling he's lying but she doesn't know why. If she hazarded a guess, it would be that he had no idea that ring was in the fruit bowl until the moment she showed it to him.

THIRTY-FIVE

Time ticks by quickly today at the salon. Madison checks her messages. It's probably because Eva is booked in for a trim. Madison contemplates whether to go home and leave Orla and Tammy on their own but there are too many customers coming in today. It wouldn't be fair on them. She checks her emails again and almost lets out a happy shriek as she peruses the offer on the salon again. The new owner will also keep the staff. She's been honest with Orla and Tammy, and they're happy for her, even though they'll miss her. Madison has already checked out small commercial premises around the area they're looking at moving to, and there are some great opportunities. This time, she wants to invest in a wellness centre, get something bigger and grander than the salon. She wants a pool, a sauna and a yoga room, and she'll have a worthy deposit and a winning business plan to present to the bank for the loan she needs.

Damn, Eva will probably be waiting. She finishes Kellis's brows and shows them to her in the mirror. 'I love them. Thanks, Madison, and I'll see you again soon.'

Kellis has left and it's just her in the treatment room on her own. The panpipes play as she lies on the treatment table enjoying the calming vibes of the music and the scent of rose petals floating in a bowl of water. After taking a few minutes to build up enough momentum to continue, she stands and leaves the room.

'Eva, it's so lovely to see you again.' Eva is nervous too because she flinches as soon as Madison mentions her name. After a bit of chit chat, she leads Eva to the third chair along. The woman with the foils in her hair is still happily reading her Kindle as she waits for the colour to take. 'I think we have you down for a dry trim, is that right?'

'Yes, thank you,' Eva replies.

Madison pulls a cape over Eva's head and begins to comb and spray her tangled blonde curls. The situation feels awkward since the cancellation. 'Once again, I'm really sorry about letting you down, but we had to take the other venue when the cancellation there came up.' She asks Eva if she's okay about it, and Eva reassures her that it's all fine. After a few minutes, she's cut the fringe that Eva also asked her to do and she's dried it straight. She talks about her life and Madison mentions that her baby keeps her awake at night, all the usual banal conversations she has a million times a day. Same conversations, different people. Madison wonders if she prejudged Eva a bit harshly. She seems quite friendly and pleasant, not all confused and weird like when they had their meeting. Theo's reaction to her had maybe been due to his anxiety. Madison finds herself opening up to Eva and wondering why she also felt uncomfortable around her. 'After the wedding, Theo wants to move to Scotland. He said that was his dream. We're looking at houses near Loch Ness actually. We feel it would be good for the little one.' She pauses, wondering if what she's saying to Eva is remotely interesting, but Eva looks keen to hear more. 'It's big progress for Theo. He's been doing so well getting out and about, and I no longer feel as though we're stuck here forever. I have a buyer lined up for the salon. She's a brilliant hairdresser so I know you'll be in expert hands when you come again.' Madison knows she's wittering on now.

Eva's smile has turned into a frown. She's staring in the same way she did during the meeting and, all of a sudden, Madison feels a nervous flutter in her stomach. Why did she say so much and let her guard down? Eva is still a little strange; she should have stuck to talking about something safe, like the weather but it was easy to get carried away. It's time to end this appointment and get Eva out of her salon.

'Well, what do you think?'

'I love it. Thank you,' Eva replies, a more relaxed expression spreading across her face.

Maybe she imagined that Eva had been frowning, as she seems normal now. She has a lot of scabs on the back of her head and a lot of missing hair. Madison doesn't see this a lot but sometimes a person comes in and it's almost a cry for help, which is why she keeps the card of a good therapist at hand. It's actually Theo's therapist; she's been wonderful and patient with him so she recommends her to everyone. She did after all recommend her to Theo after getting help herself years ago. Maybe Eva's frown was because of the state of her head and, for a second, Madison wonders what Eva could have gone through that would make her pick her scalp until it was raw.

'I know someone who can help.' There, Madison has said it. She chats away about how good the therapist is, and she is sure that Eva's eyes are glassing over. Is she about to cry? Has Madison said too much or not enough?

'Damn, I'm running late. I have to go.' Eva drops some money on the counter and darts away from her.

Madison feels bad now. She runs to the door and calls out, but Eva ignores her and gets into the car and drives away. She heads back into the treatment room and lies back on the couch, turning the panpipe music up. It was like Eva wanted to say more, but what? She decides to forget it. Eva is not her problem.

As her thoughts drift, they go back to the wedding ring that Theo claims to have found in their garden. *Love you forever.* She also knows there was someone outside watching them, and then there are the calls and messages that Theo keeps receiving. She should be looking forward to her wedding, but something is telling her to halt the plans. Everything is moving too fast. She's going to sell the salon. They're going to move. They have a baby. Her heart begins to bang. All the calming music in the world can't take away the worries that are brewing inside her. Is it pre-wedding jitters? What if she's making the biggest mistake of her life?

Orla barges into the treatment room, yanking her out of her thoughts. 'That customer who just left was in an accident and it looks like Theo's involved.'

THIRTY-SIX

Madison darts out of the salon, heart racing like she's about to go into cardiac arrest. Theo had called earlier to say he was going to bring Emily to see her during his lunch break. What if Emily has been injured? All she can think about is her baby. She clacks up the hill in her low heels, struggling to put one foot in front of the other as her legs grow more jelly-like with each step. She sees Theo's car ahead and it's in the middle of the road. Then she spots Eva standing on the pavement, her car crashed into a fence. 'Theo,' she calls but he can't hear her. He's too busy talking to Eva.

Where's Emily? He's not holding her. She must be hurt. As she reaches them, she runs over to Theo. 'Emily,' she says under her breath. 'Has anyone been hurt?' she calls out.

'No.' He steps towards the car and lifts Emily out of her seat. Emily's still asleep. Relief floods through Madison's veins, and she almost wants to slump with relief but instead she snatches Emily and holds her closely, rocking her tiny baby in her arms.

Madison looks over at Eva. 'Are you okay?'

'She's fine. I just stopped to see if she needed an ambulance but I think she's okay. It was just a little accident.' Theo looks at Eva coldly, and in that moment, Madison feels like she's interrupted them. She feels like a spare part who has just turned up and isn't welcome given the looks between her husband-to-be and Eva.

'I am worried about you, though, Eva. You seem to think I'm someone else. You might have a concussion and not know it.'

'No, no, no. I haven't even hit my head.' Eva looks at him with furrowed brows.

Emily starts to cry as Theo helps Eva back her car out of the fence. Madison knows Emily needs a feed and she needs to get her daughter away from the chaos. 'Theo, I'm going to take her to the salon and feed her. Eva, I'm glad you're okay.'

* * *

Madison kisses Emily's soft head as she enters the salon and heads towards the treatment room to feed her. Her breasts are starting to leak, responding to Emily's cries.

'Is she okay?' Orla asks as Madison stands in the treatment room doorway.

She nods. 'Yes, nothing to worry about. Our last customer hit a fence and Theo was just seeing if she was okay.' With that, Madison closes the door on everyone and sits on the treatment table. She pulls down her top and unclips her nursing bra, ready for Emily to latch on. Her baby suckles away eagerly in huge gulps until her tired eyes start to close again.

There is a slight tap on the door and Theo opens it. 'Hi.' He walks in and pulls up the chair from the corner of the room, the one she normally throws used towels onto. 'She's gone now. At least she crashed into a fence and not us,' he says with a smile.

All Madison keeps thinking about is what she heard Theo saying to Eva: that she mistook him for someone else and that she might have a concussion. That's the second time Eva has mistaken Theo for another person. She called him Hugo when they had their meeting at the Sea Horse Hotel. What seemed more disturbing was the way Theo spoke to her, like he was insinuating she was crazy. She's also a bit confused about Theo and how quick he'd been to diagnose Eva with concussion when she claimed not to have hurt her head. And why did he say those things so loudly in front of Madison? Did he think she'd heard more than she had? She wished she'd appeared on the scene a minute or two earlier because she feels as though she'd interrupted something.

Madison has a feeling that Eva didn't come to the salon just for a haircut; she'd come to see her. Could Theo be lying? Doubt creeps in and she doesn't know what to do with that doubt. Was it pre-wedding nerves or a genuine worry? Or maybe it was the stress of being a new parent.

'Eva seems to think she knows you. The way she looks at you...' She doesn't know where the sentence is going so she leaves it hanging.

'How could I know her? That's ridiculous. The woman is mad. She seems to think I'm someone else.'

The woman is mad. Madison doesn't like the way he said that but she's going to let it lie for now. It's in that moment she realises she doesn't know Theo as well as she thought. Their whole relationship has mostly been played out in his cottage. She feels claustrophobic, which is ironic as he claims to be agoraphobic. She wants to laugh but that would look mad. Would he then accuse her of being a mad woman?

Their wedding is just around the corner and she has this overwhelming urge to postpone everything, but she can't put her finger on the exact reason why.

THIRTY-SEVEN

Madison can't wait to get back home after the odd day she's had. She'd waved Orla and Tammy off early, as their last customer had cancelled, and now she's pulling up outside the cottage, just as Theo is about to leave for the therapy session she insisted he booked. After a quick kiss on the drive, Theo hands Emily to her and Buster runs circles around their feet.

'I'll see you about seven,' he says before he gets into his car and reverses down the long driveway, leaving only the sound of the crows squawking above.

'Hello, my gorgeous girl.' Emily grabs her red locks and gently tugs them.

On entering the cottage, she notices that Theo has packed a couple of boxes. There's a pile of printouts on the coffee table. With Emily in one arm, she bends down and takes a look. It's the specifications of a house to rent near Loch Ness. Theo has written a note on it, saying that they can view it a week after their wedding. Her lip quivers as, once again, she tries to digest how fast everything is moving. She calls Camille, but her sister doesn't answer.

In the kitchen, she notices that the wedding ring is gone

from the fruit bowl. After placing Emily in the baby seat by the kitchen table, she begins searching for it. She rummages through the drawers, in the cupboards and even checks the floor. Maybe it fell under the table. On her hands and knees, she feels around and looks for it, but all she comes face-to-face with is Buster's wet nose. The bin – she runs to the bin and begins sifting through the empty wrappers and potato peelings from the night before, until she reaches the bottom of the bag and touches the smooth round piece of metal. She pulls the ring out and washes it under a cold tap until it shines again. Why would Theo throw something so precious away?

'Shall we go for a little walk, Emily?'

She picks her little one up in the carrier and heads to the cabin, where she opens the door and places Emily down by Theo's desk. Buster jumps onto the couch and begins to dig up the cushions. She nudges the mouse, hoping that the computer is on but it isn't. Theo's tablet sits next to the keyboard. She knows how to get into that. He doesn't do anything confidential on that device and Madison knows his password is his birthday. With slightly trembling fingers, she types in the six numbers and unlocks the device. Her heart skips a beat and her stomach rolls. Spying on Theo doesn't feel right. She's always trusted him, but she has this niggle she can't let go of. She opens up his Instagram and it lands on Eva's profile. There are so many photos of Eva's old house in Malvern, and her new house in Combe Martin. It's a stunning house, everything Madison would love for her family. Madison also knows that house; she remembers it coming up for sale. It's not creepy at all and it has an amazing view of the sea. Everything is in good taste; Eva has a designer's eye, from her wedding to the way her little boy is dressed. Her dog is unbelievably sweet too. After going back three years, Madison stops scrolling on a photo of Eva looking solemn next to a candle that she's lit in memory of her dead husband, Hugo. Madison's gaze turns to the photo of Hugo next to the candle, and a shiver runs through her.

Madison gasps. Theo looks almost identical to Hugo. That's why Eva was taken aback. That's why she behaved strangely during the meeting. She zooms in and looks closer at Hugo. His eyes are a different colour and his hairstyle isn't like Theo's. Hugo is slimmer than Theo and he doesn't wear glasses. They are not the same person, but she can see why Eva might think they are. It's like Theo has a doppelgänger.

As for the phone calls and messages – has Eva been making them? Maybe Theo was being stalked by a woman who is hell-bent on seeing her dead husband in him. She sits on the couch next to Buster and spots something else out of place – a thin pile of photos she's never seen. She picks them up and scrunches her brow while looking at several photos of two babies. They're such tiny dots. Theo has never shown her any photos of his family. He never had any, he'd said, because everything, including his family, had been destroyed in the fire. She feels a lump in her throat as she thinks about how terrifying that would have been for his parents and his baby sister, and then she spares a thought for Theo growing up in the care system.

'Madison.' Theo hurries in.

'What are you doing here?'

His eyes are wide. 'I could ask you the same. This is my office. I have confidential client records in here, you know that.'

It's not like she's going through his work files. He's overreacting. If she did look through his work, she'd have no idea what any of it was. She's taken aback by his abruptness, and she's extra disappointed in Buster for not alerting her to his presence. At least the light on his tablet has gone off, so he won't know she'd been looking at his Instagram.

'I need some envelopes.' *Really, was that the best she could come up with?*

He stares like he doesn't believe her, but she'll say that until she's blue in the face so he's going to have to let it go. Reaching over his desk, he opens a drawer and pulls out some envelopes before dropping them next to her.

'Why are you back so soon?'

'She cancelled. Family emergency.' He glances at the photos in her hand. 'What are you doing with those?' He snatches them from her and pops them on the filing cabinet.

'I err... I found them on the table. I was just looking.' She pauses to give him a moment. 'Theo, what is it? You know you can talk to me.'

He sits next to her and his eyes begin to water. 'That's me and Emily when we were born. She died in the fire, and that tiny pile of photos is all I have.'

'I'm so sorry.' She places a hand over his. He never mentioned having photos of his sister before.

'I feel like a piece of me is missing.'

'Losing your parents and sister would do that to a person.' She can't begin to imagine how much that would hurt. For a moment, she tries to picture what her life would be like without her family, especially Camille, and she can't.

'There's something I haven't told you.'

Her heart begins to bang again. This is happening a lot lately. Was it something to do with Eva? 'What?' She strokes his hand.

'My mum didn't die in the fire. We've been in touch recently.'

'I thought you said she died.' How could he keep something so big from her, when they had a baby and were about to marry? She thinks back to her last marriage. It ended because of his lies. Not being able to have a baby together didn't help, but the lies surrounding his affair had been the final straw for their relationship as they knew it. Theo's secrecy is bringing all those insecure feelings back.

'I think I was burying the trauma. I've been talking to my

therapist about it and it led me to wanting to find her, which I've done.'

'Why didn't you tell me, Theo?'

'It's something I had to do on my own. I'm sorry I shut you out.' He pauses. 'My mother had a breakdown after the accident, and I was told that she'd been hospitalised. She didn't want to lose me but she also knew she had no chance of getting me back after what happened. She fell asleep with a cigarette in her mouth and the settee went up in flames... My sister used to cry a lot and I was the quiet one, which is why we were in separate rooms at such a young age.' He wipes the corner of his eye. 'Dad was asleep in his chair. They'd drank a lot. Anyway, Mum woke up when the fire was already spreading downstairs. She managed to call the fire brigade before running upstairs for us. The fire followed her quickly.' He swallows. 'The flames split the landing in half, which meant she couldn't get to Emily. My mum and me were rescued...' He puts his head in his hands and begins to sob.

She's never seen Theo sob like this, and it's the first time she's heard his story properly. Survivor's guilt is what she suspects he's suffering from but she isn't a therapist. Without hesitation, she throws her arms around him and vows to support him through this. 'I love you and everything's going to be okay.'

'I keep thinking, what if? I went to all those homes and had so many different foster families. All the abuse, and Mum just let it happen. She could have come back for me. She could have fought to keep me.'

'You have us now. Emily and I love you more than anything.' She knows she owes him this fresh start in Loch Ness, away from the prison he's cocooned himself in. It'll be different there, though she can't help thinking about the time he abandoned her that night when they were on holiday. Things are different now. He's opened up. The therapy is helping and she hopes his mum turns out to be good for him. 'Maybe your mum would like to come to the wedding?'

He pulls away and stares. 'That was unfair of me to judge her like that. My mum left me because she had to. She wasn't in the right place. People deserve forgiveness, don't they?'

She nods. 'Of course they do.'

'Even when they abandon their children?'

'She didn't do it on purpose. She wasn't well. What matters is she's a good person.'

Madison has no idea how she'd feel if her Emily died. She could understand how Theo's mum fell apart. Madison breaks the silence. 'She's a good person. A good person who got dealt a shitty blow and couldn't cope.'

'You might be right, but I think I don't want her to come. I need to take things slowly with her and maybe see her on my own a few times first.'

His phone rings and he cuts the call. It beeps with a message and then another. He angrily jabs at it until it's silenced.

'Who is it?'

He ignores her question, picks Emily up in her seat and calls Buster. 'Come on, let's go and order a takeaway.'

Madison follows. She isn't comfortable by the way he walks away without explaining the calls. She feels sick that he's already found them a house to view, and then there's the packing, and the wedding ring in the bin. She takes one last glance at the photos of the babies and closes the door to the cabin.

THIRTY-EIGHT

Madison stares through the window at the back garden, right into the rock face that Theo's cabin is almost embedded into. What secrets is he keeping in that cabin? She wants to go into the lounge and ask him straight up, but she can't. He needs time to process the fact that he's back in touch with his mother. It's obviously causing him some distress.

She picks up the wedding ring and tries it on her wedding finger. It's loose on her. After slipping it off, she throws it in the junk drawer. It's not right to bin it, like it's nothing.

'The food will be here in fifteen minutes,' Theo calls. Emily coos as he plays with her in the other room.

She finishes emptying the dishwasher and leaves two plates out, ready to put their curries on, then she heads to the living room. She normally loves this room but not tonight, not with the pile of boxes stacked up at the far end.

'I see you started packing.'

He nods as he sings 'Twinkle, Twinkle' to Emily.

'And I see you've been looking at houses.'

He blows a raspberry on Emily's cute pudgy belly as he finishes his song. Theo is such a good dad and that's making her feel unreasonable for bringing all this up when they're tired, especially as Theo has had such an emotional evening.

'Yes, I found one. The appointment's in our joint diary.'

'You should have spoken to me first.'

He lifts his head up from Emily, leaving their little one wriggling on the baby blanket that Camille knitted. 'There's no time. We need to get on with it, so that's what I was doing.'

'I have a business to deal with.'

He shrugs. 'You've got a buyer. Sadie has wanted to buy it for years and she's made a good offer. It's as good as sold.'

'But I want a say on where we live.'

'And you will have a say. I haven't put a deposit down or anything. It's just a viewing. If you want to view other places, start looking and book some appointments for that week.'

'I thought we could have a little holiday, a familymoon first.'

He rolls his eyes. 'We can combine the two. It'll be fine, won't it, Pumpkin?' He kisses Emily's feet and she reaches for his finger, which he gives to her to play with. 'Think of our new life up there. Clean air and lots of scenery.'

'We have all that here.'

'But you've never liked living here.'

'Here,' she says, pointing at the floor. 'I don't like living in this cottage. I like Devon. This place has never felt like mine. I can't do anything to it. It's dark and I feel like it's eating me up some days. That drive is a nightmare and the ivy, it brings all the spiders into the house, and I never see you because you're always in that cabin, and the woodland is slowly suffocating me. I want neighbours... civilisation... space to invite friends over.' She didn't realise she was raising her voice.

Theo takes his glasses off. 'I didn't know you felt like this. Why haven't you said anything before?'

'I have. I've asked repeatedly if we can knock that wall through to make a family room, or if I can paint the walls. I've said more than once, let's lay a patio, or can you sort out your junk so we can have some entertaining space? You never want to do anything or change anything.'

He leaves Emily, puts his glasses back on and throws the printout at her. 'I know. I don't want to do anything to this house. I don't want to spend a penny on it. I want to leave. My therapist has made me realise that I've made myself a prisoner here. This is the prison I've built for myself but I'm getting better now. I need to leave just like you do, but I think better things wait for us in Scotland. We've spoken about this.'

He's right. She'd been keen after getting caught up in the idea of it. 'Maybe we can move out and rent around here for a while until we've sold. Take some time to properly think about Scotland.' A part of her still thinks she might be able to afford her spa here, but she doubts it.

He huffs out a breath. 'But I'm excited to move. You were excited too.'

'But I'm going to miss Camille. Francesca and Eden won't grow up with Emily.'

'They can come and visit anytime. Look.' He points to the printout. 'Did you see that there's an annexe above the garage?'

She takes it off him and looks in more detail. It's a beautiful house with more room than they could ever afford down here, and everything about it is modern. New kitchen, new bathrooms. She knows it's a rental but she's daring to dream of bigger and better things than this damp, poky cottage. She imagines her new spa and that house with its sprawling garden and bifold doors to the most amazing views she's ever seen.

'Imagine it. Francesca, Eden and Emily all playing out together when your sister visits. It'll be like a holiday that they can keep repeating at their leisure. This house is in a cul-de-sac. There will be neighbours, other people with children. It'll be much better for Emily. Your friends can come and stay anytime, and I will do everything I can to get you up and running with a new business.' He clears his throat. 'I was saving this good news, but I've already managed to find work. I've been jobbing for this company remotely from here but they say there will be more onsite work when I get there, and it pays double what I'm on here. Also, it's what I need. I feel ready to start working outside the house. It'll help me get better faster and that'll be good for both of us.'

He's putting up a convincing argument for the move, and she guesses it wouldn't be a problem for Camille to visit. It might be exciting for her and her family to stay with them. She's already picturing Christmas dinner at a huge dining table in the open-plan family room. Her mum and dad could come and stay too.

Theo's phone rings, bringing her back to the present.

'Hello... hello...' Theo says.

'Is it them telling us the food is going to be late again?' Madison says.

'Who is this?'

Emily starts crying. It's past her feeding time so Madison picks her up and begins to open her nursing top and unclip her bra in readiness. 'It's probably a pocket dial. Just hang up,' she says.

He ends the call and begins to bite the inside of his cheek as he stares at his phone. 'It was a withheld number.'

Normally she wouldn't think twice about a strange withheld number but the uneasiness within is now amplified by it. She holds Emily to her breast and her baby feeds. As she strokes the back of Emily's head, Theo leaves the room and barges out of the front door.

Buster yelps and snuffles, wondering why Theo didn't take him out too, so Madison walks over to the window and watches Theo staring at his phone. He paces as if pondering what to do. The security light doesn't come on. The bulb must be out, but he's lit up by the moon and stars. He starts to prod his phone and it illuminates his face in a ghostly fashion. He walks away and she can't see him anymore, all she can see is the glow of his screen occasionally peeking through the trees as the breeze parts them. She heads to the junk room, wading through all Theo's clutter. Emily is still latched on and seems content. Madison resists the urge to scream as she catches her side on the handles of Theo's exercise bike. Once at the other front window, she gently unlatches it and nudges it open, just in case she can hear what he's saying.

His voice carries slightly in the breeze. He's on the phone speaking quietly but she can hear snippets of the conversation. 'I told you to never call again. You're a fantasist, nothing but a fucking fantasist.'

The call ends as quickly as it started. She needs to get out of this room. She pulls the window closed and hurries past the piles of junk and the exercise bike. He's already coming through the front door.

'Madison,' he calls.

She escapes the room of doom, as she calls it, with Emily still suckling away. 'I was thinking, I wouldn't mind getting some exercise. I wondered if you could get the bike out for me when you get chance.' She has no intention of peddling for hours to get nowhere. That was Theo's thing when he struggled to leave the house. For the second time that day, he looks at her like he doesn't trust what she has said. First envelopes, now the exercise bike. She wants to rub her sore waist but resists the urge. 'Were you on your phone? I thought I heard talking.'

'It was work.'

Liar, liar, liar. Just like her ex-husband. Enough of the lies. 'I heard you on the phone. I can tell something is wrong, Theo. I'm not stupid and I resent that you're treating me like I am.'

'I'm sorry. I'm such an idiot.'

Sorry – he's always sorry. Her ex-husband was always sorry too.

'It was my mum. You know I said she had a breakdown.

When she's sober, she's really nice but when she's had a drink, she blames me for everything. Like how I could be responsible for the fire that killed my family when I was a baby.'

Her mouth downturns and she feels a tear welling in her eye. Again she'd jumped to conclusions. Theo is going through far worse things than she could possibly ever imagine. If she'd have thought with her brain, she might have realised sooner that he wanted to move to escape here, the very place he'd spent living alone in his head for years. She walks over to him and squeezes his hand.

'I know I've been a bit weird but I will sort it. I'll sort her and she won't be a problem anymore.'

The knock at the door makes her jump and let go of his hand. Emily stops suckling and begins to wail. It's as if she can sense that the air is thick with tension. Theo answers the door and takes the bag of food from the delivery driver, offering him a tip before closing it again. She feels this deep anger rising, anger because Emily is distressed and anger towards a woman she didn't know existed until earlier. Theo seems stressed, which is rubbing off on her. She also wonders what he was thinking of doing so that his mother won't be a problem anymore, then Madison thinks of the wedding ring again. If it was found in their garden, whose was it and how did it get there and again, why did he bin it?

'Madison, are you okay?' He holds the bag of food up.

'Err, yes. I think so. What happened to the ring? I couldn't find it when I got home.'

'I don't know. I didn't do anything with it. Maybe you misplaced it. You haven't seemed yourself since Emily was born, but that's to be expected.'

She scrunches her brows, confused as to why he would bring this up now and not earlier if he'd been worried. 'In what way am I not myself?'

'You forget things. The other day, you asked me where your

car keys were. They were in your bag and I told you they were probably in your bag. I'm worried that the stress of everything is getting to you. You're a new mum. Your hormones are everywhere and you keep working yourself to death at the salon. Maybe when we move to Loch Ness you should take a bit of time out, just a few months.'

She *had* lost her keys but that's not how she remembers it, and she didn't want to take time out from her work. She begins to doubt herself. Had she accidentally thrown the ring in the bin? She was tired all the time.

'Look, let's have dinner. I'll run you a nice hot bath and keep Emily happy while you relax.' He kisses her head and goes through to the kitchen.

She can't make sense of the evening or their conversations. Maybe a hot bath will fix things for now.

THIRTY-NINE

Madison lies in the bath while Theo is putting Emily in her cot. To help her relax, he'd added one of her jasmine bath bombs to the water and left a huge glass of alcohol-free wine. The flickering candles make the mildewy old bathroom look quite charming.

'Emily's fast asleep,' he says. 'I'm going to head to the cabin for a bit so I can do some work.'

She yawns as she finishes the pretend wine and lies back in the steaming hot water. 'Okay.'

'I'm also going to head into the woods to see the badgers and record some sound of the owls if I can.'

Before she gets the chance to answer, he's already gone. She's glad to be alone with her thoughts after such an intense evening. She has her upcoming appointment with the wedding dress sewers soon, to make final adjustments. Everything is moving at breakneck speed. At the back of her mind, she's mentally preparing for Millie and Deepak's upcoming wedding and the fact that it's at the Sea Horse Hotel, where Eva works. A sense of dread washes through her. Maybe moving is the only option.

Her phone rings. 'Camille.'

'Hey, sis. You called earlier. Sorry, Francesca hasn't been well. Nothing to worry about, just a twenty-four-hour thing so we've mostly been in the bathroom. Things calmed down and I fell asleep. I think you and Emily should stay away for a couple of days.'

'Thanks for the warning. What a shame. Poor Francesca. I just wanted to talk but if it's not a good time, I can call tomorrow.'

'No, now is perfect. I'm lying in bed with a hot chocolate so I'm chill now.' Camille laughs.

Madison loves how Camille takes everything in her stride. She's sure she'll be a panicking mess when Emily gets poorly for the first time. 'You know I mentioned Scotland, and possibly moving in the future?'

She hears Camille inhale before speaking. 'Yes.'

'We're going to look at a place soon.'

'Really? Have you thought this through?'

'Yes, we both want this.'

Camille goes silent. It's like she can read Madison's mind and sense her doubts. 'You know you don't have to go. You could stay here for a bit longer, think about it.'

'We've thought about it and we've found a lovely house. You and the family can stay anytime. There's an annexe.' She can't let Theo down, not after they spoke about his mother.

'I don't want an annexe; I want my sister.' She pauses again. 'I'm sorry. I shouldn't have said that. I know you have your own life to lead but I can't imagine not having you here, especially as Mum and Dad aren't close.'

Their parents moved to Penzance in Cornwall several years ago, leaving her and Camille living alone in Ilfracombe.

Camille continues. 'You were here for me when I had Eden and Francesca, and I wanted to be there for you with Emily. I want to see her grow up... why so soon?'

She clears her throat. Maybe she should confide in Camille. She always has done before. 'Theo has been in touch with his mum. She's not dead, like he said.'

'If that's not a huge red flag, I don't know what is. How could he lie about something so huge?'

'It's more complicated than you think.'

'Really,' she replies. 'You spent years being lied to by that prick you married and you kept going back to him, and now this. You've put me through a lot of heartache, sis.'

'It's not the same.'

'Isn't it?'

The problem with Camille is she always thinks she knows better and that annoys Madison. She hasn't even told her about the conversation she had with Theo earlier. She wanted to say so much more, like about seeing those photos and how Theo had been looking at Eva's social media. As she begins to speak, she hears Francesca talking to Camille.

'Mummy, my tummy's bad again.'

'Look, I have to go. Just promise me you'll think things through properly, Madison. We love you loads.'

'I promise,' but it's too late; Camille has already ended the call.

Madison sinks into the bath, her ears submerged while she tries to calm her racing thoughts but it's not working. Instead, she grabs her phone from the window ledge and searches for Eva on Instagram. Her profile isn't even private. She scrolls through the photos of Eva's dog and house until she stops at Eva's wedding photos again. After pressing the photo, she pinches it to zoom in. Eva looks so pretty in her ivory dress, and he looks quite brooding and handsome. She refers to the man she loves as Zach in the description but she hasn't tagged him.

Madison stares at him for longer this time; she's seen him before but she can't work out where and when. He wasn't at the

Sea Horse Hotel when they went for the meeting, and he didn't pick Eva up from the salon; she drove herself.

Maybe she has got baby brain? How could she have ever met Eva's husband?

That's it. She remembers. She saw him with another woman around Christmas. They came to speak to Theo about setting up a computer system for their new business.

Madison scrolls on and sees a photo of Zach with Eva, and underneath Eva calls him *The best plasterer in the world*. There is no mention of the other woman, the one with the little boy. Maybe he'd been helping her out. No, she remembers Theo describing them as a couple who had a business selling something. They'd been holding hands when they arrived. As soon as she'd made them a coffee, she'd left them talking with Theo in the cabin. She scrolls down further, seeing if she can see the woman on Eva's posts, but she can't. There is the back of a woman at a café and it could be the same woman, but she can't be sure. All she can see are her long, wild brown curls caught under her coat.

FORTY

Madison jolts up in the bath to the sound of a car engine pulling up outside the front of the house. It's one in the morning and rain patters against the rattling windowpane. Shivering, she steps out of the freezing cold water and grabs a towel to wrap around herself. She'd been asleep for over an hour. Buster interrupts the silence by barking at the front door. She stands on the landing, dripping water on the carpet while listening out for a knock at the door, but a few seconds later, Theo calls out as he comes through the back door.

After checking on Emily and putting her bathrobe on, she creeps downstairs to find Theo sitting at the kitchen table with a cup of tea.

'I heard the car pulling up. Did you go out?'

He furrows his brows. 'No, I've just finished up in the cabin. I didn't hear a car.'

Maybe she'd been half asleep. She'd been having this disturbing dream about Emily crawling across a flame-filled landing, then a crazy drunken woman who failed to save her when she could have. The woman in her dream couldn't have been Theo's mother; she was too young. It was the woman who came with Zach to see Theo, the free spirit with the brown curls and the pink wellies. 'How did tonight go? Did you film the badgers?'

He shakes his head. 'I gave up in the end and left the wildlife cams running from the den. I went back to the cabin instead and worked on the McKinley job and built a PC for another client. Have you just got out of the bath? I thought you'd have been in bed.'

'I fell asleep and woke up freezing cold.' She pauses, wondering how to ask about Zach. 'I was thinking, do you remember a couple that came here before Christmas? They wanted to talk to you about their new business and their computer system?'

'Er, can you be more specific?'

'Woman with really long brown, curly hair with a little boy. She was with a man who had dark hair. We don't get many people bringing their kids along. The little boy asked for the Wi-Fi code so he could play a game on his mum's phone.'

He closes his eyes for a few seconds then clicks his fingers. 'Yes, they didn't go for my quote so I didn't do their job. What's this about?'

'Can you remember anything about them?'

'I don't know them, so why would I?'

She waves a dismissive hand and pours a glass of water. 'I think I'm just having weird dreams. It's nothing. I thought I saw him the other day.' She didn't see him the other day, but she needed an excuse to bring him up.

'Where?'

Now she has his attention but she doesn't know why. 'At the grocers by the salon. I said hello but he ignored me. He obviously couldn't remember me so it's nothing really. Are you ready for bed?'

'I think I'll just wind down a bit. You go up. I'll be there soon.' He stands and kisses her. 'I'll check on Emily when I come up. I saw that you left some milk in the fridge, so I can feed her again if she's hungry.'

As she goes to leave, she spots Theo's trainers at the back door and they look saturated and mucky. He was wearing his walking boots when he left for the cabin, so why were his trainers there? It *was* him pulling up in the car. She hadn't imagined it. But where had he been at this time of the night, and worse, why was he lying – again?

FORTY-ONE

Yawning, Madison feels the weight of her tiredness creeping through her bones. It's Millie and Deepak's big day and Theo wasn't happy that she wanted to go to work but it's not fair to leave all the organising to Orla and Tammy. Besides, she needs to get out of the cottage for a while.

She doesn't trust Theo and things have gone from weird to weirder. This morning, she left him with Emily and he didn't even say goodbye. Here she was, trundling along the corridors of the Sea Horse Hotel, hoping to not bump into Eva.

She thought back to Eva's social media and wondered if she should speak to her. Her dead husband Hugo did look a lot like Theo, but it was obvious that her husband didn't come back to life, change his eye colour and morph into Theo.

'Hey, boss.' Orla drags a make-up trolley along and carries a huge bag of hair-styling gadgets and tools over her shoulders.

'Sorry I'm running late. I had a flat and I had to change it.' Tammy hurries down the corridor while brushing dust from her trousers with one hand and wheeling another trolley with the other.

'No worries, ladies. Let's get set up.' She opens the door to the hotel spa and salon and sees three beauticians setting up in front of the mirrored wall. The smell of chlorine from the pool hits her nostrils, and the humidity makes her wonder if the bride's hair might turn to frizz.

Someone opens the door at the other end of the room and a woman in her fifties enters with a giggle. She almost falls through the door because her slippers are too big. Madison recognises her as the bride-to-be's mother. Then the rest of the party of women and girls gather around.

Tammy and Orla continue to wheel their trolleys towards the hair station, and Madison can do nothing but stare as Eva walks in.

'Eva, hi,' she says but Eva doesn't reply. The noise around them continues but it's as if Madison can't hear it and that the only two people in the room are her and Eva.

'Hi,' Eva says with a quiver in her voice.

Madison opens her mouth to speak but she can't think of what to say. Last time she saw Eva, the woman had crashed into a fence and Theo was acting oddly; in fact, he hasn't acted normal since that moment. She also knows that Eva's husband Zach came to Theo's cabin to talk business with another woman, and that they were a couple, so what was going on? In the name of female solidarity, she should tell Eva about her husband, but then she thinks about how much she's already upset Eva by mentioning her hair problem. The last thing she'd want to do was speak up and find that she'd got the wrong end of the stick, especially as she had been a bit ditzy lately.

With all the ladies seated, Orla and Tammy start working on the bridal party's hairstyles. Madison turns away from Eva in order to grab five minutes to think. This staring intently at each other isn't doing either of them any good. Madison reaches into the shoulder bag that Orla was carrying. She pulls out the curling tongs and places them on the dressing table. Again, her stare catches Eva's in their reflections. Madison looks down.

It's hot. Madison feels this creeping sensation reaching for her neck, then her chin and cheeks. She fans herself with a hotel flyer and gasps for breath. Why is this happening? She hasn't been this anxious for years, not since breaking up with her ex. The little voice in her head tells her, *you can't trust him. He was out last night and he told you he wasn't. He threw that ring in the bin. He booked a viewing on a house in Scotland and he didn't even run it by you first. He's been lying and you keep forgetting because you have baby brain. Baby brain, baby brain, baby brain.* She wants to yell back at it. She's not even pregnant anymore but she does wake up every five minutes wondering if Emily's okay. She inhales sharply and catches Eva's reflection in the mirror again. This time Eva isn't looking at her; she's talking to Millie and at the same time, she's pulling at her hair and the hairpiece is coming a bit loose.

Theo was looking Eva up on Instagram. Why?

She looks up and Eva is gone. She places her hand on the dressing table to steady herself, but instead of touching the desk, she leans on the curling tongs and yells.

Orla runs over. 'What happened?'

Madison breathes in through her teeth, trying to control the scream that is dying to burst out. In a panic, she looks at her hand. There is a thin red line across her palm, nothing too bad but enough to scare her. 'I burnt myself.'

Orla drags her towards a sink then places her hand under the cold tap and runs it fast. 'Just keep it there for a minute. Doesn't look like you've done any real damage. Why don't you go home? Tammy and I have got this.'

She glances back while still holding her hand under the tap. Everyone else looks a picture of calm. Millie's mother pops a bottle of champagne and the others cheer. 'Actually, I think I will... go home that is. Emily didn't sleep well and I was awake most of the night.' She doesn't tell her it was Theo's fault she didn't sleep, not Emily's. That would lead to a phone call later and Madison doesn't want to chat to Orla or Tammy that evening. She needs to work out what is going on without any distractions.

'I'll text you when we're done, so you know everything is okay.' Orla smiles.

Madison heads out through the door that Eva came through. She leans against the wall and takes a few deep breaths, her hands shaking. Why didn't she say something to Eva, anything? She goes through everything in her mind she wished she'd said. *Eva, can I speak to you for a minute when I've set up? Eva, I need to tell you something, your husband came to Theo's office with another woman and they were holding hands. Eva, I know I upset you when I mentioned your head... Eva, my husband-to-be is not your dead husband. You need to move on...*

She has to find Eva. She doubts she'll say half of what is on her mind, but she has to tell Eva that Zach is a cheat, at the very least. However odd she thinks Eva is, she doesn't deserve to be cheated on. Madison darts from room to room. She's checked out the ceremony room, the function room, the bar, reception. The other assistant, Hallie, is arranging a bunch of roses in a vase. 'Do you know where Eva went?'

Hallie shakes her head. 'No, sorry. I know you, don't I?'

Madison forces a smile, not wanting to discuss her cancelling the Sea Horse. 'I'm the hairdresser. Are you sure you don't know where Eva could be? I just wanted a quick word about Millie and Deepak's wedding arrangements.'

'Have you tried the function room?'

'Yes, she wasn't there, but I'll keep looking.'

She jogs to Eva's office and knocks but no one answers. She nudges the door open and Eva isn't in there. While glancing through the window, she spots Eva on the bridge, picking at her head. Eva stares into the distance before turning and walking away from the building.

Madison runs outside but by the time she reaches the

bridge, Eva is nowhere to be seen. She leans on the wood and stares at her reflection in the pond. The burn on her palm stings a little. A few blonde curls are caught in the wood's grains but there's something more unsettling than that. There is no one else outside, not even a random smoker. The hairs on the back of her neck start to prickle. 'Eva,' she calls, but no one answers. Her phone beeps and she opens the message from the withheld number.

He's a liar. You can't trust him and he's not who you think he is. Don't marry him.

FORTY-TWO

'You're home early,' Theo says as she enters the cabin. 'Emily's asleep.' She glances down at her baby and wants nothing more than a snuggle, but she doesn't want to wake Emily. Theo's phone beeps and he slams it down. He's grinding his teeth so she knows something in that message has upset him. Then again, she can't imagine it was as upsetting as the message she received.

Who would send something so horrible, saying that Theo was a liar and not to marry him? Or does someone know something she doesn't?

Theo turns his phone over. Madison also wants to ask who's messaging him again, especially as he looks tense, but she figures he'll say it's something to do with his mum, or it's a job.

'I burnt myself.' She places her phone on Theo's desk and shows him her hand.

He pulls it close to his mouth and kisses it. 'That looks sore. How did it happen?'

She shrugs. 'I lost concentration for a second. It's okay though. It doesn't hurt that much.'

'Well, I'm glad you're home. Like I said, you're doing too

much which is probably why you had an accident. All this rushing around is no good for you. Drink?'

She nods and he places a decaffeinated coffee pod into his fancy machine and leaves it to hiss and bubble. He draws her to the sofa, and the coffee machine fully growls into action. As soon as she sits, he slips her pumps off and begins massaging her feet. The sounds coming from the coffee machine are almost hypnotic. It stops spluttering. She leans her head back and closes her eyes as he rattles around stirring her drink, getting milk out of the mini fridge and then quickly tapping away on his keyboard.

'Just got to get this quote sent then I'm all yours,' he says.

Tiredness is winning. After the coffee, she promises herself she will have a lie-down but first she needs to speak to Theo. 'Eva was there.' Madison isn't sure what he will say to her random statement, but she needs to see how he reacts so she turns to face him.

He clenches his teeth. The harsh outline of his jaw protrudes through his stubbly face. 'Well, she does work there.'

'I don't know why, but I decided to look for her on Instagram and I found her. Her dead husband looks like you, that's why she was calling you Hugo. I think she's going through something. It's sad really.'

He places her coffee down on the table and continues massaging her feet. It feels so good after the day she's had. 'It's probably best not to get involved. It's not like you're friends and as for me looking a bit like her dead husband, that's not my fault. Can we stay away from her? I don't know what's going on but I feel as though you haven't been yourself since we met her. I personally think she's a bit crazy. I can't put my finger on it but she has this stare, it's intense and it sets me on edge.'

She can't disagree with him on that but she wants to keep him talking, to put her mind at ease if nothing else. 'Theo, you put the wedding ring in the bin. It wasn't me. I feel as though you're trying to convince me I'm crazy.' He lets go of her feet. Her stomach is churning as she waits for him to reply.

'Are you seriously accusing me of gaslighting you?'

Madison looks into her lap, brow creased to match the confusion inside her head. 'You lied about your mum being dead.'

'I know and I'm sorry. She was dead to me and frankly, I wish I'd never decided to find her but I have and now I'm dealing with that problem. That one is on me and if I made you doubt me, I'm sorry. I love you and Emily. I would never gaslight you and I'm appalled you'd even say something like that, but I get it. I should have told you about my mum.'

His eyes look sorry as he shuffles on his knees between her legs, edging closer to her. His lips reach hers and all she wants to do is kiss him back, but she can't, not before mentioning the message she received. With her eyes beginning to well up, she can't hold the tears back.

'What is it, love? I'm worried about you.'

'I...' she chokes out that one word and her nose fills up. She was going to tell him she went looking for Eva earlier, to tell her about Zach cheating on her, but she remembers that she told Theo that she saw Zach at the grocer's. Saying too much will make her look crazy, but then again, she wouldn't have been spying on Eva had she not seen her Instagram page open on Theo's iPad. Instead, she talks about the thing that's upsetting her the most. 'I got this horrible message from a withheld number. It said, he's a liar. Don't marry him, you can't trust him.'

He pulls back a little, lifts his glasses up enough for him to rub his eyes. 'Bloody hell.' He pauses and lets his glasses perch back on the bridge of his nose. 'Who would send something so mean. Can I see?'

'It's withheld but yes.' She nods and gets her phone from the other side of the room. By some miracle, Emily sleeps through her sobbing. She scrolls and scrolls but there is no message. 'It's gone.'

He takes the phone off her and looks. 'You have a message from Camille, apologising for cutting the call off last night. But that was the last one.'

'It was there; I saw it.'

The look in his eyes and his lips pressed together tells her all she needs to know. He doesn't believe her. There was a message and now it's gone. After she'd stood on the bridge, she went back to the salon to say bye. She left her phone and bag there while she popped to the loo. Someone must have come into that room to delete her message, but how? Her phone had been locked – unless they knew the code.

FORTY-THREE

It's as if Emily can sense that the air is thick with tension because she hasn't settled once this evening. Madison yawns, that seems to be her go-to move these days. The baby blanket catches her thin papery skin where she burnt herself earlier and she winces.

She paces through the house and turns on the light to the spare bedroom, also known as yet another junk room. It has even more of Theo's clutter in it. An old pushbike hangs on the wall. The desk she brought with her sits in the middle of the room, just begging to be used once again. This room was meant to be her home office but that never happened. Instead she's been doing the bookkeeping for the salon in the kitchenette there. She bounces Emily but Emily fidgets uncomfortably in her arms, her little legs kicking out of her blanket. Eventually, Emily dozes in her arms so Madison places her in her cot before returning to the spare bedroom. It's dark outside and she has that feeling, the same one as earlier when she'd been standing on the bridge at the Sea Horse. Her skin prickles and she shivers. She hates it here. It's creepy and remote. She thinks of that amazing house in Loch Ness and imagines herself being a part of a community, meeting other parents of young children and dropping in on neighbours for coffee.

Theo barges in, interrupting her thoughts. He's barely spoken to her since they left the cabin earlier. 'I've been thinking.'

'Yes,' she replies.

'About you accusing me of binning that ring. I can tell you still think I did it and you know what?'

She shrugs, wondering if Theo is about to rant at her. If he is, she has no chance of winning. The best thing she can do is let it run its course.

'It's you. I think you've got some sort of postnatal stress or depression, or something that's making you forget things. I feel as though you're barely present when we talk and we haven't...' He puts his glasses on the desk and pauses.

'We haven't what?' She wants to know.

'You never come near me. It's as if I don't exist. I miss you, Madison. I miss feeling close to you and laughing and holding hands when we snuggle on the sofa.'

That is true, they barely cuddle. For a couple about to get married, it is strange but they've only recently had a baby. She definitely needs time to adjust. The medical professionals said sex would be okay when she was ready, but the truth is, she doesn't want anyone to touch her because she is tired, because she's had lots of stitches and they give her the ick because she has Emily and the salon to look after and it is *hard*. She lets out a little hiccupping sob. Maybe something isn't right with her. She can't remember half the things that happened that afternoon. She catches her reflection in the window. Her nightie covers her thin frame and her belly is still slightly puffy from carrying Emily, but her arms are sticklike. Her skin is pale every day, but her make-up expertise gives her a healthy glow, so no one notices. No one sees that underneath all the foundation and blusher, she needs help, or maybe all she needs is a sympathetic ear to listen to her talk. Theo is waiting expectantly for her to say something. 'I don't mean to push you away.'

'I sometimes wonder if you still love me.'

She does love him but receiving that message has planted doubts in her mind. First she doubted Theo and now she doubts herself. That message – it won't leave her mind. Someone is trying to ruin her relationship. 'I do love you, Theo. I love you so much. I just can't get that message out of my mind. Who sent it?'

'I know it was gone when you went to show me, but I believe you about the message. Maybe you accidentally deleted it.' He shrugs.

'Maybe.' She's so grateful he believes her; she wants to throw her arms around him but she holds off.

'Well, the only person I can think would send something like that is Camille.'

'Camille?' She throws her hands in the air, frustrated by him suggesting her sister would do that to her.

'I don't blame her. She doesn't want you to move away. She's trying to drive us apart; she thinks you will stay and I will go. It has to be her.'

'No way. Camille wouldn't do that. I can't believe you even thought that. I haven't even seen her today. What about Eva? She could have deleted it when I went to the loo. I'm always unlocking my phone in front of people. It wouldn't be hard to break into.'

'Really?'

'Yes, really. She thinks you're her dead husband.'

'Whoever it is, we can't let them come between us.' He goes to hug her.

She tries to push him away because she's too wound up to stand there hugging, but he grabs her hard. There's no way out of his embrace, which should feel stifling, but somehow, she wants him close to her, to reassure her that everything's okay.

For the first time since having Emily, she feels the desire that Theo is so desperate for her to have. She feels his hardness press against her as his tongue probes her mouth before flitting gently towards her neck. Her body reacts with little shivers. She reaches down to touch him over his track bottoms, wanting him to take her on the desk that her bottom is about to touch.

Emily's cries extinguish that desire instantly, and Buster begins to bark. Suddenly she feels self-conscious in her ugly nightdress as her reflection stares back at her in the window. 'I best see to Emily.'

He holds her hand as she walks to the door, until their fingers no longer touch. She loves that smile, the one she fell for when they first met. Maybe things are all going to be okay.

While tending to Emily, she listens as Theo heads into their bedroom, then she hears a squeak but dismisses it. It's nothing. He runs downstairs, and as she's feeding Emily, she hears the kitchen drawers open and close. Several minutes of him rummaging passes. 'Have you seen my phone?' he shouts up the stairs.

She takes Emily down with her once she finishes feeding. 'Did you find it?'

'No.' He grimaces before leaving through the back door.

'What are you doing?' She grabs her phone and starts calling his. It can't be far.

'My phone must be in there,' Theo shouts back as he points at the cabin.

Her call ends. 'Did you find it?' she yells out, but he doesn't answer. He's already in the cabin. She grabs a blanket from the back of the settee and throws it around her shoulders and snuggles Emily close to her before heading to the cabin. As she approaches in her slipper socks, she hears him talking.

'... fucking kill you.'

The window frame judders after the loud bang. She wonders if it's his mother again or could it be the person who messaged her? Is his mother even real or is something else going on? Before he catches her loitering, she hurries back to the house. Buster whines, unhappy to be trapped inside while all the action is happening in the back garden.

Theo returns with his phone, and she places Emily in the basket in the living room. She looks at him, wondering who her husband-to-be wants to kill. 'Were you on the phone? I came out but thought I heard you talking, so I headed back in.'

He looks at her for a few seconds and she wonders if he's trying to weigh up how much she'd heard, then his features soften. 'Yes, my mother called again. I think I'm going to have to block her. She's drunk and full of self-pity, and she's blaming me again. It was her fault Emily died, not mine. She could have tried to save Emily and let me die.'

Her doubts start to dissipate. Of course his mother is real. His words stick in her mind as she can't help thinking of their Emily, not his sister. *If our baby had died I'd be distraught. Maybe I'd turn to drink and be full of bitterness, rage and hate.* 'She lost a child, Theo, and she obviously has a drinking problem. Maybe you, or we, should be a bit more understanding.'

He pulls her close again. 'You're such a good person, you know that? You're right. I should be more understanding. I'm so over what I've been through since she let me rot in the system because she couldn't cope, but she's living in the past and her calling me like this isn't on.'

She strokes his hair, knowing that Theo is far from over his past. It has always been hard for her to imagine how having an unhappy childhood could affect a person so badly. 'She's still your mother and whatever she said on the phone, she'll probably regret it tomorrow.'

Buster barks and scratches at the back door. Madison opens it and he darts out into the darkness, probably vexed by a fox that dared to encroach on his territory.

'You're right.' He pulls a curly hair from her face and tilts his head.

Emily sleeps soundly now, and Buster is no longer yapping in the background.

'Where were we?'

She remembers exactly where they were and she thinks they need to feel close again. She needs to believe that he's telling the truth and that the messenger is just Eva thinking that Theo is her dead husband. The woman is delusional, and Madison should feel sorry for her.

Taking his hand, she leads him upstairs and tears his T-shirt over his head. In her haste, she scrapes his skin and he yelps but that doesn't stop him. Nothing will stop either of them now. All their pent-up tension comes out as he touches her, kisses her and finally enters her. Every touch is exactly where it needs to be for her, but with Theo, it always was, and she's reminded why she could never get enough of him. She's missed this and she knows he has too. Her body hasn't popped out of place or bust into a mess as she'd feared.

After minutes of writhing on their messy bed, they lie there, spent and both grateful that Emily isn't awake.

Buster barks at the back door to come in.

'I'll go,' Theo says as he reaches for his track bottoms and pulls them on.

She'd forgotten what he looked like naked. Yes, it has only been a few months but she'd missed his toned thighs and his strong arms.

The dog patters up the stairs and almost jumps on her in bed. She grabs her nursing nightdress and pulls it back over her head before stroking Buster. 'Did you catch that fox, Buster boy?'

He goes to lick her face but she blocks his tongue with her arm. He jumps off the bed and stares at the corner of the room.

She tries to see what he's looking at but it's just her shadow on the back wall. He begins to hack and baulk. 'Buster.'

She jumps out of bed to catch him spewing up a pile of beige goo with a cherry red coloured streak in it. 'What on earth have you been eating out there?'

He whines and comes over to her for some love. She smells something buttery. There is a smear of grease up his snout. She leaves the room to get something to clean the mess up with. That's when she sees through the window of the spare bedroom and shivers. The front gate is open. When she'd been standing there earlier, when they'd come close to making love on her desk, that gate had been closed. The thought that someone has been watching them makes her feel sick. 'Theo,' she yells.

He hurries up with a couple of glasses of juice and a big smile on his face. 'Thought you might want a drink.'

'Theo, that gate was closed earlier and now it's open. Someone has been here, in our garden, maybe in our house, while we were…'

FORTY-FOUR

Madison inhales the fresh morning air at the front door while trying to work out how the gate could have opened. It's too old and stiff to blow open in a breeze. Once again, Theo had put the fact that she had felt watched down to her being forgetful or postnatal, and that she probably left the gate open. The way Buster darted out last night had convinced her even more that someone had been there, and why did he return with butter on his face? The scent of veggie sausages wafts under her nose but her nerves are jangling.

'I've made you breakfast.' Theo stands behind her in the cartoon owl apron she bought him for Christmas. He teases her tangled curls away from her shoulders and kisses her neck. She doesn't even remotely feel the tingle of last night that left her overcome with desire. It's like that button has been switched off, along with her sense of security in this house.

She closes the front door and ambles to the kitchen, wondering if she should have showered first. Like most mornings when she doesn't go to the salon, she feels grotty. Her slippers, leggings and maternity top have become her home uniform, and they are becoming too comfortable.

'I've fed Emily and she's asleep so make the most of this,' he says.

The sandwich is huge. She sits and begins to nibble the edges, trying hard to stop worrying and further making her stomach churn. 'I think making the most of it will mean me putting my feet up.'

'You should. I might head to the cabin. I have a few enquiries to deal with.' He grabs the other half of his sandwich and leaves her alone with her thoughts.

Buster lays his head in her lap under the table, remaining hopeful that she'll throw him some food. She drops a whole sausage into his mouth and he darts away with it.

She leaves the table and heads upstairs. As she enters Emily's bedroom, she hears gurgling. Her baby wriggles in her cot, her little legs outstretched, pushing all her blankets off her.

'Morning, sunshine. It looks like you're starting to teethe.' She strokes Emily's red-cheeked face, then Emily pops her knuckle in her mouth. 'Shall we go for a little walk?' She puts the baby sling on and places Emily in it.

* * *

As they leave the house, Emily gets her hands tangled in Madison's hair but Madison ignores the little tugs.

She leaves the front garden under the arch and begins to nudge the gate back and forth. It's hard to move, like she knew it would be. She tries to recall coming home yesterday. After leaving the Sea Horse Hotel, her mind had been on other things, like the feeling of being watched. Her hand had been sore from the burn – another distraction. She remembers pulling up and getting out of the car with only her handbag over her shoulder. Had she forgotten to close the gate? No. It didn't matter because last night while she was looking out of the upstairs window, the gate was definitely closed.

She walks along the dirt track. On reaching the gate to the woods, she stops. It's closed, but it's never locked. A gust catches the branches. If there were anyone lurking around today, she'd have no chance of hearing them over the tweeting birds and branches slapping against one another. The further she gets into the woods, the bumpier the ground gets which makes her uneasy. If she falls, Emily might get hurt. It's also carpeted with stingers that she's trying hard to avoid, but one catches her ankle.

The shed that Theo built is ahead and it doesn't look like anyone has tampered with it. For a fleeting moment, she imagines someone hiding in there. What if there is a person behind that door? If she were to startle them, would they attack her? Every instinct she has is telling her to run back home. But she can't. She eventually reaches the windowless structure. The only way to see out from inside is to open the flap that Theo positions the camera in to film. It's stuck. Her heart begins to pound as she accidentally kicks a tin feeding bowl towards the edge of the clearing.

Open the door, open the door, her inner voice keeps saying. She walks around the back and tugs at it. Like everything else in the house, it's stiff to budge, but it's not locked. Although the land belongs to them, ramblers very occasionally pass through, and he sometimes leaves a camera in there so she half expected it to be locked. She uses her shoulder to fully open the door. The shed is as big as she remembered. It contains a desk and a chair, a small bookcase filled with tin mugs, animal feed, baby wipes and bowls, all of which are stacked precariously. She sits in his chair and opens the flap then peers outside while wondering how Theo can do this for hours.

Emily tugs her hair again, just to remind Madison that she's still there. As she bows her head to untangle her hair from Emily's soggy fingers, she notices the waste bin. She reaches down, moving aside the crisp wrappers and empty drinks cans to reveal something strange. It's a small raven toy with a sucker stuck to its base. She places it on the desk and wonders why he has it. Shrugging, she cleans it with a wipe and gives it to Emily in the hope that she'll prefer playing with that over pulling Madison's hair.

Rolling backwards in his chair, she spins around to face the desk. She goes to open the drawer, but it's locked. She reaches underneath, feeling for a key, but there isn't one. The bookcase. She checks all the mugs and the animal bowls but again there isn't a key. Emily is starting to gripe. She quickly takes the sling off and places Emily on the floor before kneeling underneath the desk. There is a corner of paper sticking out of the back. However much she tries to pinch it with her fingertips, she can't. That's when she spots another piece of paper stuck against the wall. She grabs it and sits up. It's a newspaper cutting with a picture of a boy on it, but the article isn't included. She stares into the eyes of the smiling kid and she can't think where from, but she recognises him. Her phone rings, making Emily cry. She ignores the call and takes a photo of the clipping on her phone before throwing it back on the floor. She goes to answer the call but Theo has hung up. She pops the sling back on, instantly soothing Emily, then hurries out of the shed. The face in the clipping keeps whirling through her mind but for the life of her, she can't think who it is, and she can't think why Theo would be hiding it away in his shed.

FORTY-FIVE

Madison hurries back to the dirt road, wondering why Theo was calling. She tries to call him back but he doesn't answer. As she's about to reach the gate, something catches her eye. A green that isn't the green of the leaves or shrubs. It's more like an artificial mint colour, like the one she'd used to paint one of the walls in her salon. The piece of material dances to the tune of the breeze. She tugs it but it's stuck to a thorn. After gently teasing it, it becomes free.

Her phone buzzes and rings. 'Theo.'

'Where are you?'

'I'm just out the front. I've been for a walk with Emily.'

'Someone broke into the cabin last night.'

She runs through the gate and in through the front door. He stands in the kitchen, staring out of the back window at the cabin with Buster at his feet. 'Have they taken anything?'

He shakes his head. 'I don't think so.'

'How do you know someone broke in?'

'The toilet window has been pushed out.'

She tries to imagine someone getting through that window.

It's big enough to squeeze through but it's not huge. 'I told you someone was watching us last night.'

'I'm sorry, I should have checked outside.' He huffs out a breath. 'I bet they waited until we were asleep.'

'But they didn't take anything,' she adds.

'I'll board the window up for now. Maybe it was kids camping out in the woods and messing around.'

'Seriously. We need to call the police and not touch anything just in case whoever broke in left their DNA.'

He raises his arms and lets them drop. 'You think they'll send someone out for nothing more than a broken toilet window? Besides, I've already been in there and touched everything. They'll just give me a crime number for the insurance, and there's no point claiming because the excess will cost more. Nothing has been taken.'

She knows the police won't do much but they were broken into. Someone had been watching them, and waiting for them to go to bed. 'It should go on the record. What if they come back?'

'Look, they got nothing. We're looking at selling soon and the last thing we need is any prospective buyers knowing we've been broken into. It'll make the cottage harder to sell. I'm going to board it and then we can forget it.'

She doesn't seem to have a say in the matter. 'I found this caught in the shrubs.' She places the material on the worktop. 'Maybe the intruder was wearing this and they got snagged.'

'Or maybe it's nothing more than a bit of material.'

'I want to call the police,' she says.

'There's no point.'

She feels the battle rising within. Theo hates people coming into their house, and he won't relish police lurking around for half the day. 'But I don't feel safe.'

'It was kids. They won't be back.'

'How do you know?'

His jaw remains locked tight and his cheeks pulse every

time he clenches his teeth. 'If it makes you feel better, I'll set up a little motion camera in the cabin tonight. If anyone dares to enter, I'll be straight out there.' His stare moves to Emily and his jaw slackens. 'What's that?' He points to the toy raven.

'I found it.'

'Have you been in the shed?'

'I, err, I went there for a walk and saw that the door was unlocked.'

'So you just walked in?' His knuckles are white. He begins to breathe in and out, like his therapist showed him.

'I didn't know I wasn't allowed in there.'

'I have a camera set up. The animals won't come if you're there.'

'Don't they come mainly at night?'

'Please don't go in there again.'

'There wasn't a camera set up.' She hadn't disrupted anything and she can't understand why he is hostile.

He snatches the toy raven from Emily and throws it in the bin.

'Theo, what was that for?'

Emily begins to cry again.

He doesn't answer, instead he does what he always does when in one of his moods. He walks out, leaving her frustrated. She knows the raven has hit a nerve but she removes it from the bin regardless, then she hides it at the back of the cupboard.

Theo walks back to the cabin and straight into his office.

She continues to watch him through the kitchen window as he paces back and forth with his phone clasped to his ear and his other arm in the air. He's talking to someone and he looks so angry, Madison feels the creeping sensation of fear at the back of her neck. She's beginning to wonder if she knows Theo at all.

FORTY-SIX

Madison says bye to Orla to end her call to the salon. She's relieved they can cope without her for the week; in fact, Orla insisted that they were more than fine. Deciding to take the week off in the run up to her wedding on Saturday has made her feel lighter. Not only that, but she also needs time to fathom how she feels about the whole wedding and the move.

Theo has been in his cabin since seven in the morning, and Camille is due any moment, ready to go to the dress shop for their ten thirty appointment. She knows she's putting Elisse at Beautiful Brides out by bringing their wedding forward, but Elisse hadn't grumbled when she made the appointment.

A message from Camille pops up. Her sister is waiting for her outside. She rushes out with Emily already strapped into her car seat. She waves at her nephew and niece in the back seat and places Emily's seat next to them. 'Right, dress shop.'

'I can't believe my sis is getting married this week.' Camille does a three-point turn by the gate and the car hops down the drive. So far, Camille hasn't mentioned the move again but Madison suspects she will later.

Once they arrive at the shop, Madison takes a sleeping

Emily out of the car in her seat. Camille grabs a bag of Eden and Francesca's favourite toys and helps them out. She seems calm, not like Madison is when having to take Emily out. 'These should keep this pair happy while you try your dress on. Which dress did you choose in the end?'

'The simple off-the-shoulder wiggle dress. No veil, no fuss, just elegant.'

As they enter, a young woman leads them to a plush room almost filled with a semi-circular couch. Camille sets up the safari animal game on the floor before sitting Eden and Francesca in the middle.

'Can I get you both a drink?' the woman asks.

They both opt for tea and wait for her to leave. 'How have things been?' Camille asks.

Madison doesn't know how much to say. She is still a bit upset that Camille wasn't happy for her when they spoke about the move and bringing the wedding forward, but she understands that Camille was only looking out for her. 'Busy and tiring.' She wonders whether to mention Eva, seeing Zach at the cabin and all the other things, then she thinks, *why bother?* She is moving soon and their new life will be different. Theo will finally chill out and maybe it will put even more distance between him and the current source of his anxiety – the mother that had come from nowhere, or the mystery boy in the newspaper clipping. No, she won't say all that because Camille will use that information to persuade her to stay and, right now, she is weak because she doesn't want to leave her sister and the kids. She glances at them playing nicely and a lump forms in her throat. A tear slips down her cheeks. She loves those kids.

'Madison.' Camille places a hand on her arm and she recoils as she knocks her burn. 'Why are you upset and what happened to your hand?'

'I leaned on a curling iron at work and I'm just emotional, that's all.'

'Is it the move?'

Camille knows which buttons to push. Madison is trying hard to convince herself that she wants the move as much as Theo because she wants him to be happy, but she's slowly waking up to the fact that their relationship doesn't feel right. She can't back out of their wedding, not now. It's too late. 'No, I'm just so happy. I have Emily and I never thought...'

'You have her and look at her; she's amazing, just like her mum.'

The woman walks back in with their teas and places the cups on the table. 'It's lovely to see you, Madison, and I can't imagine how stressful this must be for you getting a dress at such short notice. I have the one you chose in two sizes. Are you ready to try them on?'

'Go do this, sis,' Camille says.

Heading behind the curtain alone, she pulls her loose top over her head and steps out of her baggy jeans. The dress is smooth as it glides over straight into place. 'Can you do it up for me?'

Camille comes in and pulls the zip up. 'It's too big. You've lost weight.' Camille steps back to take in Madison's tiny arms and hollow clavicles.

'I'm here to get it adjusted. It'll be okay.' Madison knows that her new slighter figure, matched with the burn and the sallow-looking skin on her face, is telling a story right now. Camille can't stop staring. 'I've just been busy with Emily. All that running around you do with them... I barely get chance to finish a cuppa.'

'Are you eating?' Camille has her judgemental face on again. It's like when they were teens and Madison stopped eating for a while when she started secondary school and the bullies migrated her way. Food has always made her nauseous when she is on edge. It wasn't an eating disorder, as her parents and sister had suspected; it was her own personal anxiety.

'I'm just busy, that's all. I'll be better when the wedding is over and Emily stops waking me up all night.'

'It's like Theo's constant worrying is wearing off on you. You need to look after yourself for Emily. She needs her mum to be healthy.'

'I am healthy.' She slips out of the dress, her tiny stomach displaying its faded stretchmarks. She places a hand over it, not wanting her sister to focus on what she perceives as her flaws rather than a reminder of how she got her lovely daughter. 'Can you just ask Elisse to come in here and spare me the lecture?'

Camille storms out through the curtain. Madison stares at her figure in the mirror. She wants to eat but she's anxious. Camille is right: Theo and his moods are making her anxious. But she loves him. When he's sweet, he's amazing, and they connected again the other night and it felt so good. He gave her the baby she'd always wanted and he's a good dad. Her mind whirls with the ring, the raven toy, the photo of the babies and the photo of the boy, and the things he's hidden from her and things he is still hiding from her. His reaction to her going into his shed had been a shock that she is only now feeling the impact of.

Elisse enters. 'I'll get it adjusted ASAP for you, love.' She's all smiles with no judgement as she pins the dress and helps Madison out of it before leaving again.

'Camille?'

'What?'

'I'm sorry. You're right. I am anxious at the moment. I'm about to get married, then I'm moving to Scotland and I'll miss you and the kids.' By now she's crying and she can't stop it. 'It churns in my stomach day and night, and I can't eat properly because I feel sick all the time.' She slides down the mirror, onto the floor.

Camille comes in and sits next to her, hugging her closely. 'Sis, please don't go. Don't leave us. I have a bad feeling about all this and I can't shake it off. I'm sorry if that upsets you to hear but you're my sister and I'd hate it if I sat back and said nothing. This doesn't feel right.'

She cries into her sister's top, letting it all out and wondering what she should and shouldn't say. Camille is right. She doesn't want to leave. What Theo said about Camille sending that horrible message to stop her from leaving wasn't true. He was trying to sabotage her relationship with her sister, and maybe he was trying to isolate her. No, no, no – that was her old relationship. Theo isn't trying to isolate her or gaslight her. He needs the move for his own reasons. How could she have allowed her thoughts to go there? She doesn't know what to think, but she can put the brakes on for a while, to give her time to think. She loves Theo and she wants to marry him. He's unwell, not manipulative, but she needs to step up and say what she wants. It's not all about him.

It isn't too late to keep her salon and her life. Theo just needs to be convinced.

FORTY-SEVEN

Madison checks her list.

Cake – tick.

Hair and make-up – tick – Orla is doing it all.

Dress – tick – Orla has collected it. It's still slightly loose but it'll be fine.

Camille's dress – tick – gorgeous.

The bridesmaid and pageboy outfits for Francesca and Eden – tick.

Emily's dress – tick – super cute.

Rings, groom's suit, flowers, celebrant, food and drinks, photographer – tick.

She reads the list again. It's small compared to the original wedding they'd planned to have. In the end, she couldn't convince Theo that they needed a big evening party with more guests. It will be a small soirée in a room that is far too big for their short guestlist so he doesn't feel penned in, and only because the room has double doors that open to the garden. She suspects he'll spend the whole evening with one foot out of the door.

She thinks of her parents who are due to arrive on Friday

and are staying with Camille. Her mum has messaged photos of her fascinator and shoes. Her dad isn't too impressed with his tie but Mum said it's what he's wearing because it matches her dress. She laughs as she thinks of her mum and dad, and how close they've always been. All she hoped for was a relationship like theirs. She takes in her reflection. The dress is still loose but much better. She knows her stress figure will be a shock for her parents, who are used to seeing her a little curvier than this. It seems like wishful thinking to hope that once the wedding is over, she'll feel like a weight has been lifted and will be able to eat properly again.

Her minds flits to Eva. Despite trying to put the woman out of her mind, she can't. She thinks of Eva's husband coming to see Theo with the other woman. It's no good. She feels it's only right to say something even though she wonders if Eva is the one who broke into the cabin. That bit of green material looked like the colour of the jacket she'd been wearing at Deepak and Millie's wedding. Her dead husband does look a lot like Theo, and Madison can see why Eva has been derailed by seeing him. She clicks on Eva's Instagram page and begins to type out a message on her phone.

Eva,

I hope the rest of Millie and Deepak's wedding went well. I had to leave early but I was hoping to be able to speak to you. I'm sorry, I looked on your Insta and saw that I recognised your husband, Zach. He came to see if Theo could do some work for him and his partner's business. I thought they were a couple because they were holding hands, then I saw you and him, and I then knew he was your husband. I also saw that your deceased husband looks a lot like Theo and I know that must be weird for you but…

She takes a deep breath and feels stupid, so she deletes the message. She can't send that. It might be upsetting if Eva gets a message that mentions her dead husband along with Madison accusing her current husband of being a cheat. It is none of Madison's business. She has to stay out of it. In fact, she doesn't know why she is stressing over Eva, her life or the fact that Theo looks like dead Hugo. Her stomach churns again and the thought of lunch makes her want to vomit, but she has to eat because Emily needs her to. She needs to be in a better headspace and to do that, she has to get Eva and all her other worries out of her mind. She wants to be happy Madison – the mother, the beautician, the hairdresser, the entrepreneur, but all she's doing is making herself so small, she's vanishing.

Next week, she'll see her doctor. Maybe they could prescribe some antiemetics; they might help her to eat.

Someone rings the doorbell, and Buster begins barking at the door. She slips out of the dress and grabs her bathrobe before hurrying downstairs. On opening the door, she sees a tall woman with large brown eyes and wild grey-threaded dark hair who looks to be around sixty. 'Hello. Can I help you?'

'Is Theo in?'

'He's working. I can call him for you. Who shall I say is here?'

The woman bites her chapped bottom lip and puts her hands in the pocket of her loose trousers. 'Erica.'

She quickly checks their diaries on her phone. Theo hasn't booked anyone in this morning. She presses his number. 'Theo, I have Erica for you. She's at the front door. Shall I send her round?'

'No. Just stay there. I'm on my way.'

'He's coming.' Emily starts to whimper from inside the cottage.

'Is that your baby?'

Madison nods.

'They're precious, aren't they?' The woman looks down at her feet, exposing her thinning crown and greasy roots. 'Look after her, Madison.'

How did Erica know her name? She hadn't introduced herself.

'Take that little one as far away as possible and never come back.'

Dumbstruck, Madison goes to murmur but Theo has already run around the cottage and is standing at the gate. 'Erica, follow me through to the cabin.'

Erica staggers backwards, her gaze remaining on Madison until she's out of view.

Madison runs through the lounge and kitchen to catch them walking out from alongside of the house to the front of the kitchen window. They follow the path towards the cabin. She runs upstairs and takes Emily out of her cot before heading back downstairs to watch them again. As soon as they enter Theo's office, he closes the blinds. She quietly leaves the house, trapping Buster in the kitchen. He barks at the door, and she hopes that Theo can't hear.

As she walks, she's undoing her maternity top and Emily happily takes her breast. She creeps around the back of the cabin, hoping that the back blind will be open – it is. She watches as Erica almost trips over the coffee table and falls onto the sofa. Madison can't hear what Theo's saying but she does hear what Erica says next.

'I don't know who you are anymore and I can't sit here and say nothing. You're trying to keep me from her and I deserve to be a part of her life. I will accept the' – she clears her throat and emphasises the next word – 'situation. I feel as though I don't know you at all, Theo.'

Emily stops feeding, and Madison notices that there is nothing coming out. Her baby is hungry and her milk has dried up. She wants to cry at her failure. After offering up her other breast, the situation is the same. She is as dry as a desert. Emily lets out regular little shrieks and Madison knows the air will fill with Emily's hungry cries at any moment.

She darts between the cliffside and the cabin in the hope that Theo didn't hear, but she's too late.

Theo opens the cabin door just as she runs around the side and reaches the path. Buster's barks are frantic. She wrestles to button her nursing top back up.

'Madison.'

She can't stop the tears this time. It's obvious to them that she was spying and Theo isn't stupid. 'I heard, Theo. Who is Erica? You need to tell me now or Emily and I are leaving you.'

He runs out and takes her free hand in hers. Erica steps towards the door.

'Madison, meet my mum. Erica.'

FORTY-EIGHT

Later that night, Madison mixes up the formula and offers it to Emily. Her little one feeds until she's milk drunk and falling asleep in her arms. Madison continues talking to Camille on loudspeaker while sitting on the settee. Darkness has fallen so she turns the table lamp on. 'I feel as though I've failed, Camille. I wanted to breastfeed until she was at least six months old.'

'Sis, you're putting too much pressure on yourself. I managed two months with Eden and a whopping eight with Francesca. You did your best and that's more than enough. Not breastfeeding doesn't mean you're a failure. Some people can't breastfeed at all, and it's not their fault either. We women need to stop blaming ourselves for everything. Just be her mum. Love her, cuddle her, and be there for her. That's all you need to do. And stop beating yourself up. Emily is perfect. She's healthy, happy and beautiful. I am, however, worried about her mum.'

'Don't start on me, please. I'm still on edge with Theo's mum turning up like that.'

'I know, what a shock.' Camille clears her throat. 'But if I don't say these things, who will? You need to start eating properly.'

'I'm going to the doctor's on Monday.'

'That makes me happy to hear.'

'Anyway I have to go. Emily needs changing.' She ends the call. Emily doesn't need changing but she needs a moment to think. Overwhelm is threatening to send her into meltdown. If she could lock herself in a cupboard and cry, she would, but she has Emily to be strong for.

She checks the time. Theo has been gone for hours. After explaining that he and his mum needed to talk, he took Erica out for dinner, promising to bring something back for Madison, not that she cared about the food. That wasn't how she hoped to meet her future mother-in-law despite thinking she didn't have one up until recently. She thought of all the problems Theo had been having with Erica. It's good that they've gone out to talk so he can finally deal with them. Deep down, she hopes it will help with his agoraphobia too. Maybe his mother is the root of his problems. That and the loss of his sister.

She looks at the calendar, the one she gives to clients every January that feature all their best hair and make-up photos. In blue sharpie, it tells her she's getting married the day after tomorrow. She texts Theo.

Just wondering how things are going with your mum. Also, do you know when you'll be back as I'm getting hungry?

She isn't hungry but she doesn't want him to think she's hurrying them, even though she is.

He replies instantly.

It's going well actually. We've had a long talk and Mum has agreed to get help for her drinking. I'll tell you more later, and I'm sorry she turned up out the blue. I'll be about an hour.

Mum is just having a dessert. I've booked her into a B&B so she won't be coming back with me.

One hour. That's all the time she has to go to the shed and see if she can discover more of Theo's secrets. She grabs a knife from the kitchen drawer, having no idea how she's going to use it but it's worth a try. She places Emily carefully into her pram and wheels her out of the front door. Buster darts through her legs and stands by the gate, hoping to be let out into the woodland for a run around. She nudges the gate open and pushes Emily over the bumpy terrain. The torch on her phone lights the way. Birds flapping in the trees above make her jump. She doesn't want to go any further. It's creepy and pitch-black but she ignores the sense of unease welling up inside her. She nudges the gate to the woodland open and keeps pushing Emily.

With stingers bunched up around the pushchair wheels, she forces them forward until she eventually reaches the shed. As she presses the handle down, she leans on the door to open it, but it's locked. She grabs the knife from the bottom of the pushchair and begins jabbing at the lock. Nothing she's doing is working and she has no idea how to pick a lock.

She walks around the other side of the shed, leaving the pushchair. Maybe she can try to open the camera flap. Then what? She shines the light at it and pokes the knife into the gap. That's when she sees the camera facing her from behind the glass, the glow of its red light telling her that Theo is recording. She turns around and sees bowls full of cat food and other morsels that the badgers and foxes like.

Her chest tightens. The hairs on the back of her neck prickle as she hears a branch cracking. It was too loud for the gentle step of a fox or a badger.

There's another crack.

This time it's coming from behind the shed, where Emily is.

She darts around the shed, flashing the torch up, down, left and right but she can't see anyone.

Emily lies there, rubbing her eyes. Clasped in her right hand is a clump of brown hair that isn't Madison's. Heart pounding, she pushes Emily back to the cottage, knowing that someone is out there, watching her.

FORTY-NINE

She lies in bed, listening to Theo banging around downstairs as he attends to Emily. She doesn't want to get up. Her mum has tried to phone her several times but she keeps cutting the calls. She sends a message, telling her that she's busy.

Theo eventually came home hours later than he said he would the night before, and he'd brought her some dried-up pasta in a polystyrene box which she'd thrown in the bin. She'd been dreading him looking at the camera footage showing her poking a knife near his camera.

'I've just watched the footage. What's wrong with you, taking Emily into the woods at night with a knife? I think you need help, Madison. There's something wrong. You're not eating, you're forgetting things... I'm thinking postnatal depression.' He shows her a still on his phone, and she looks away. She looks deranged and scary.

Thanks for the diagnosis, Doctor No Qualifications she wants to reply but she bites her tongue. Her stomach gripes, probably because she's hungry and hunger causes nausea and nausea makes her not want to eat. It's a vicious circle and Theo is making it worse.

'What were you doing out there?'

'I told you. Someone was out there. I was checking to see if they'd broken into the shed after what happened at the cabin. I was scared, so I took a knife.'

'And you took Emily. Don't you know how dangerous that could have been if there was someone out there?'

After exhaling slowly to try and calm her jitters down, she replies, 'I should have left Emily in the house but she'd been unsettled. What if something had happened to her? I tried to call you but you wouldn't answer.'

'I told you. Mum knocked back a few shorts and I had to deal with her. I had enough on my plate last night, without you putting yourself and our daughter in danger.' His fists are clenched and she's never felt his breath hot on her face while he shouts at her. That's a first. 'I had a look at that hair by the way, the so-called mystery hair you found in Emily's hand. It's yours.'

'It's not. My hair's red.'

'Do I have to go and get it?'

She sits up in bed, arms folded and bottom lip over her top lip, like a child who's been told off.

He storms down the stairs and comes back up with a small rolled-up clump of hair, then he throws it at her.

It's red. She picks it up and stares with furrowed brows. It had been brown. She'd taken a photo on her phone, knowing how dippy she'd been lately. Reaching around, she grabs the device and scrolls through her photos. It's gone, just like the message. She's going mad and there's nothing she can do about it. Huge ugly sobs escape from her mouth.

Theo sits beside her and pulls her close. 'I'm sorry I shouted. I'm so sorry. I can see that you're not well. You've always been here for me and helped me with my problems. I'm here for you now. I'll do everything I can to get you the help you need.'

His warm kiss reaches her head, and she sinks into him. She

can't believe he's being so understanding after everything she's put him through. There is one thing she can't let lie, though. It doesn't matter how much he hugs and kisses her, and tells her that he'll look after her. 'Theo, I love you and I know I'm going through something but can you humour me and take me to the shed? I need to see inside the locked drawer.'

'Promise me you'll start trusting me if I open the drawer?'

She nods. Theo carries Emily as they trudge back to the shed. He unlocks the door and they enter. He stops the camera from recording, pulls a key from inside a tin on the bookshelf and opens the drawer. 'This is all I keep in it.'

The two lenses make the drawer look almost empty. 'I came in here the other day. There was an old newspaper clipping, a picture of a boy. Who is he?'

He shrugs. 'I used to have a lot of newspapers in here at one point, to line hedgehog houses with. It was probably just torn newspaper.'

'It was cut, not torn.' Without telling Theo that she took a photo of it, she checks her phone to see if it's still there but it's gone.

'Everything okay?'

'Just seeing if Camille has messaged.' She kneels on the wooden floor and peers under the desk. There is no sign of the clipping.

'Can we go now? We have a lot to do and it's our big day tomorrow. I can't wait to marry you, Madison. In sickness and in health. I am yours forever.' He helps her back up onto her feet. From behind his glasses, his brown eyes meet hers. 'I think we both need a new start. Being here isn't good for you so I put the deposit on that house. I had a word with Orla and Tammy and they're happy to keep everything ticking along at the salon until the sale goes through. This place is playing with your mind, Madison. You need to be on a lovely estate with other parents and neighbours. We're too isolated here. I'm going to take you away from all this and I'm going to look after you.'

She goes to protest but she can't speak. Her chest tightens and she can't breathe. It's all too much. It's moving too fast and she doesn't even know her own mind anymore. As she collapses, he's there to catch her fall with his spare arm. She looks up at him, mouth gaping. She's never noticed the faint blue rim of his iris. The person she's seeing isn't the man she met. She doesn't know Theo anymore.

FIFTY

Panic had overwhelmed her last night, so Theo had given her something he'd been prescribed for his anxiety, and she'd fallen into a deep nightmarish sleep. She now found herself staring at her made-up face and wedding hair in a mirror at the Clifton House Hotel with not much recollection of how she arrived.

She was getting married. Her heart juddered away.

'It's okay to be nervous...' Orla places the hairspray down. 'You look beautiful.'

The dress gapes under the arms but who cares? She might as well get married in the slip she's wearing, the one that's meant to go underneath her clothes. Her head is woozy, like she's had too much to drink. The wedding planner takes her from Orla and leads her to the bridal suite. It's as if everything is just happening and she has no say in it. As she enters, everyone cheers and a glass of champagne is thrust into her hand. She thinks of Emily and the fact that she can no longer feed her, then she gulps the drink down. Camille holds Emily. Instead of a joyful look on her face, Camille looks worried, like she's pasting a smile on. Madison knows she shouldn't have mentioned the deposit on the other house.

Her three cousins and her mother begin to pop another bottle. One of them starts playing a Black Eyed Peas song at full blast, which almost knocks Madison off her feet. Soon she is swept into the frivolity as Francesca starts doing a cute dance while holding Madison's hand. She holds the tears back, knowing that if she goes along with what Theo wants, she might only see her little niece once a year.

There is a knock at the door.

'Must be the wedding planner again.' Camille rolls her eyes as she opens the door.

'Who is it?' Madison calls, barely able to think or hear. A wave of giddiness comes over her. She makes her way to the door, glass in hand. It can't be... she clicks her fingers, hoping that Eva will magically disappear, but she doesn't. 'Er, Eva from the Sea Horse?' Eva shouldn't be here.

'I need to talk to you. It's important,' she yells.

The base thuds through Madison's feet. She's confused enough without Eva turning up. Madison's hair is coming slightly loose and dangling around her shoulders.

Madison calls back to the party. 'Carry on. I'll just be a moment.' What she needs to do is get rid of Eva. Her life has felt like it's unravelling since Eva came into it.

'Theo isn't who you think he is. He's my husband, I mean my dead husband Hugo. Look.' Eva enlarges a photo on her phone. It's of her dead husband and her son, who Madison recognises from her Instagram account. Then she shows her the photo of the babies, one like the photos Madison found in Theo's cabin. 'See this, this is our son, Caiden, and our daughter, Emily, a short while after they were born.'

'Where did you get that photo?' Madison knows that's a photo of Theo and his sister Emily. 'You broke into our house. It was you the other night.' Madison feels rage building up inside her. It's radiating from her core and needs to escape, and the fact that Eva hasn't denied breaking into the cabin makes it worse. Had she been at the cottage again the other night? Brownish roots, red hair? Had anyone been at the cottage? She can't cope with her mind full of unanswered questions, and she needs everyone to shut up so she can think. Heart thudding, she rests her hand on the doorframe to stop herself toppling.

'He's not Theo. You have to believe me. I need to prove it to you and everyone. I'm not going mad. I've just been speaking to his mum, Cynthia.'

'His mum is not called Cynthia. Seriously, Eva, get out now or I'm calling the police. In fact, I'm going to call them anyway, just not today because you're already ruining my big day. It's as if that bump into the fence the other week has fried your brain. You want to know why we cancelled to come here? Theo had a bad feeling about you and now I can see why.'

'He's going to kill me.'

She's being melodramatic now and Madison can't cope anymore. Theo may be a liar but a killer – seriously? She slams the door in Eva's face – and instantly regrets it. She wishes the floor would swallow her up and take her to a quiet room away from the chaos.

There is a knock at the door, again. Madison's cousin opens it and swears, getting rid of whoever it was. Madison assumes it was Eva again. Her older cousin puts another song on and turns the volume up even more.

'We need to get your dress on.' Camille feeds it over her head. One of the others has already placed her shoes in front of her to step into. Once again, she's being carried along with no way back, down a one-way road to hell with no brakes.

Her thoughts swell as she's taken down in the lift, her bridal party there waiting and cheering. Emily whimpers and Francesca sings a nursery rhyme to Eden. The noise filling her head needs a release. She's hot and her breaths are coming short and sharp. Her stomach churns even worse now as she's delivered to the back of the ceremony room. Ed Sheeran starts to play. She peers through the door at the back, and a bouquet is thrust into her hands. Of course she takes it. She's become the person who has forgotten how to say no, the person who is doubting her own sanity. Is this what madness feels like? If it is, it's the noise in the brain that feels like a humming colony of insects that are trying to find a way out. It's the sight of a swaying room when you know there hasn't been an earthquake and it's the sickness in the pit of your stomach that is telling you to run as fast as you can and never come back.

'I need a minute. I can't breathe. Stay with Emily.' She doesn't want Camille to follow her. She needs to be all alone. After almost tripping over her own feet, she darts past reception and through the main doors where she drinks in a lungful of air and tunes into the singing birds and the gentle breeze. Everything flashes through her mind. The feeling of being watched. The ring. The raven toy. The photos. Her sanity. The move. Her business. Theo's eyes. Theo's lies. What Eva said!

She paces around the car park until she spots a weeping willow, then she sits under it and wipes her damp eyes.

'Madison.' It's Camille calling.

'I'm here.' She stands up and staggers towards her sister, the champagne on an empty stomach taking full effect. As she passes a row of cars, she stops to pick up the blood-tinged hairpiece. It's Eva's. Why didn't she leave the bridal suite and talk to Eva? Madison had been horrible to her. She should have at least listened but she's not herself.

'What's that?'

'The woman who came to the bridal suite, it's her hairpiece.'

Camille takes it off her. 'If you have a single doubt right now, don't marry him, Madison. You and Emily can stay with us. We'll work this out.'

She can't fight the sobs, and the thought of having to explain everything to her mum and dad makes everything worse. 'I don't want to move away and I want to keep my salon. I'm losing my mind.'

'You are not losing your mind. You're the sanest person I know, Maddie. It's him. I can't put my finger on it but I've never trusted him, and him trying to isolate you from us was the last straw.'

* * *

Madison walks to the ceremony room, knowing what she has to do. As the music starts again, she leaves her bridesmaids behind and walks up the aisle. Her make-up has run down her face and there's a grass stain on her white dress. Her mother gasps out loud. As soon as she reaches the front, she leans into Theo's ear and whispers. 'I'm on to you. I'm leaving you and I will never marry you. We're over.' Then she runs out of the room, the guests aghast. For the first time in months, she can hear herself think.

Camille is close behind with Emily in her arms. 'Get in the car, sis. I am so proud of you. Let's get you out of here.'

FIFTY-ONE
EVA

As I rouse from a weird, feverish sleep, I reach for my bedside table but instead of my glass of water, I press my fingertips into wood, and then I remember: I'm trapped in a box and I can't get out. I'm dopey and disorientated like I've been drugged but I don't want to lose consciousness again. If I do, I might not wake up. This could be my punishment. I'm trying to wake up but I can't stop thinking about what I did, how Hugo had covered for me back then and how I couldn't bear for the truth to come out. I slip into unconsciousness again and I'm taken to a place I want to forget...

I'm back in that hot June day. I'm in the cupboard under the stairs where the cries of our twins fill my head. While sitting on the floor rocking back and forth, I'm screaming along with them. Hugo opens the cupboard door with Caiden in his arms, anger written across his face. I left my baby boy in our boiling hot car to die and I can't even remember how I got in the cupboard...

Wake up... My body trembles. I nearly killed my son. I so deserve this. I'm cold – so cold, and my mouth is so dry my tongue needs prising from the roof of my mouth. My head pounds like I've been whacked, then I remember: my poor head was smashed into a rock. I reach up and touch the sticky mess on my forehead and flinch as a shot of pain goes through me.

'Nicole,' I yell, in the hope that she at least answers me. The last thing I saw before I blacked out was a flash of her T-shirt. Once again, no one replies. I think of Caiden and all I want to do is be snuggled up with him, watching *Despicable Me*. 'Why, Nicole?' This time I scream and start to hit the sides of the box again. The wood is hard. My knuckles are sore and full of splinters where I've already tried to punch my way out. Where could Nicole have taken me? She lives with her dad and I can't imagine her keeping me in his tiny house and no one being able to hear me screaming. *Keep thinking.*

She could have brought me to Theo's cottage. It's isolated. I remember when I came here, there was a small structure, a bit like a large shed, which was a short walk away from where I left my car that night. Panic rises up again and I can't catch my breath. I'm trapped and I just want to get out. My heart feels as though it's blocking my trachea.

Nicole doesn't know Theo or Hugo. I hit the walls again. She wants me out of the way so she can have Zach all to herself. What's happening here is not a delusion of any kind. I hurt all over and I can't escape. It's real. I'm trapped in a box.

'Nicole, let me out.'

I need to think outside the box. I cry and laugh at the same time. The box – the bloody box. If only I could think outside of this box and not be trapped in it. What am I missing? Nicole, Zach, Theo, Hugo, Madison... Cynthia? Maybe I'm looking at this situation wrong. What do I think about what Cynthia said? She and her husband adopted Hugo because they believed they could help him, but as Cynthia put it to me, you can't change a psychopath; their daughter will never walk again or know who she is, all because of him. He has to be behind it if she's to be believed. He's a psycho and he's come for me and he's got Nicole involved – somehow. Poor Cynthia. Their fear kept them away from Caiden and me. They were even mean to us to make us stay away. The only person I blame for that now is Hugo.

I let out a manic laugh that turns into a whimper. I married a monster. Like any monster, self-preservation will win. I can't breathe as I think of Cynthia's daughter and poor Cynthia, who can never tell anyone what had happened to her. On the day of our wedding, Cynthia had wanted to tell me what he was like, but she chose to remain silent to save her family from his threats.

I let out a roar and kick the box again. What I still can't work out is what Nicole has to do with any of this. I definitely saw Nicole just before I was attacked. I yell again and again until I hyperventilate, because I know that Theo and Nicole are going to bury me in those woods and no one will ever find me. Then something more terrifying hits me: what if I'm already buried in the woods?

FIFTY-TWO

MADISON

It's late afternoon and Madison sits in Camille's garden, watching her wedding dress burn on the barbeque. She has no idea if she did the right thing by running out on Theo at the altar, and she can't stop thinking about how hurt he must be. He'll want to see Emily, and she feels awful for not responding to all his calls and messages.

'Shall we have a marshmallow toast to new beginnings?' Camille passes her a skewer of pink marshmallows, just like when they were kids. Whenever they achieved something at school, they would always have a marshmallow toast. 'I sent Mum and Dad out for some dinner. They've taken Emily with them. Neil has taken our two to the park. I said we needed a bit of alone time to talk.'

Madison doesn't know what she'd do without Camille. She takes the mallow kebab and starts toasting it on the flickering flames. The leggings and hoodie she borrowed from Camille swamp her but they're comforting. 'He keeps trying to call me. He says he doesn't know what he's done.'

'Don't answer. You need time to think without him going on at you.'

'When we were in the bridal suite, a woman knocked at the door.'

Camille frowns. 'The wedding planner from the other hotel. You didn't look too happy with her.'

Madison exhales slowly as she removes her browning marshmallows from the flames. 'She was real?'

'Of course she was real. You spoke to her. What's going on?'

Madison shakes her head. 'Where to start?' She pauses while trying to process the events of the past few weeks. 'I haven't been right. I've been throwing things in the bin and not remembering. I thought I'd received a horrible message and I also thought I'd taken photos of things, but when I checked my phone, neither were there. Theo thinks I'm stressed; maybe all this is stress and I'm slowly losing my mind.' Madison tells her about the photos of the twin babies, the raven toy, the newspaper clipping in the shed, the horrible message and the wedding ring magically appearing in the bin.

Camille places a hand on her arm. 'It's him. You are not ill, Madison. He's doing this to you and you see it, don't you? That's why you didn't marry him today.'

She bites into a marshmallow and swallows, despite the lump in her throat. It tastes so good. It's the best thing she's eaten in weeks. It reminds her of happier times with her family, and those feelings are filling her heart as she tears each one off with her teeth and gobbles them up. She reaches into the bag and eats more of them, enjoying the sugar on her tongue.

'I have to see Eva.'

'Really? Shouldn't you think on this overnight?'

'No, I was horrible to her earlier. Those things I said weren't me, and what if she's right?'

'What, that Theo is her supposedly dead husband?'

'Only Theo can make someone look that crazy. Look at me. I need you to take me to the cottage to get my car. Would you mind? I don't want to go inside; I can't face him. I just want my car. I can't manage without it around here.'

'Okay, but I'm waiting for you to pull away first. Can I come to Eva's with you?'

Madison shakes her head. 'No, I should do this alone.'

'How do you know where she lives?'

'She posts her life on Instagram and there are a lot of photos of her house and the view. There's only one spot where you get that exact view, and there's only one house on that stretch of road.'

On arriving at the cottage half an hour later, Madison looks for Theo's car but she can't see it parked anywhere on their land. She shivers. It's dusky and she'd rather leave before it gets any darker. 'He must be out. Maybe I should pop in and grab a few things.'

'I wouldn't. He could come back at any moment. I'll come back with you tomorrow.'

Camille is right. Madison feels far too delicate for any form of confrontation. She needs to get away from the cottage and any hold that Theo has over her. He lied. He made her think she was losing her mind and the worst of it is, she misses him like mad. She can't picture bringing up Emily without him, and she can't imagine never lying next to him, laughing with him or hugging him. She swallows as she gets into her car and drives away with Camille following close behind her. As they reach the main road, Camille turns left to go back home, and Madison turns right and drives straight to Eva's house.

She pulls up on the main road and starts walking towards the gate – and gasps. That's when she spots a police car parked up on Eva's drive. Two PCs are standing at the door, and Zach is talking to them on the doorstep. She discreetly passes the gate and loiters behind the treeline to listen to what is being said, but she can't hear a thing. Why are the police there? A flutter grows in her chest. The police never turn up with good news. Something bad has happened and Madison needs to know what that is.

All she does know is that she doesn't trust anyone anymore.

FIFTY-THREE

Madison turns around and hurries back to her car. Her phone rings again. It's Theo. She turns it onto silent. Eventually the two PCs walk away from the house and drive away. She steps out of the car again, and a shiver runs through her as a few drops of rain dot her face. As she reaches for the gate catch, her hands start to tremble.

She enters the beautifully landscaped drive and garden. Eva's West Highland terrier yaps as it charges at her. She reaches down and pats its head. Zach opens the door, curiosity written all over his face. The man in front of her is definitely the man who came to see Theo. There's no doubt in her mind. She makes a promise to herself that after she's spoken to Eva about Theo, she will tell Eva about Zach and the brown-haired woman.

'Hi, is Eva around?'

His Adam's apple bobs as he swallows, and his eyes are dark underneath as if he's been rubbing them. 'Who are you?' His brows furrow as he waits for her to answer.

She wonders if he recognises her, but he barely looked at

her when he came to see Theo all those months ago. With no make-up, and wearing Camille's clothes, she doubts that anyone would recognise her today, but his gaze lingers on her face.

'Do I know you?'

'Err, no. I cut Eva's hair. We're friends.'

The dog darts through his legs into the house. She pulls her damp frizzy curls around her face to further disguise who she is.

'Come in.'

He didn't say if Eva was in and she doesn't want to be alone in the house with Zach. As she steps into the hallway, she's reassured to see Eva's son sitting in the snug with a woman who looks like she could be Eva's mother. She spots the back of another boy's head.

'Come through to the kitchen.' He leads her into a huge family room. She pauses to take in the spectacular view of the sea. She could only dream of owning a house like this; spacious, modern and clutter free. 'Can I get you a drink?'

She shakes her head. He gestures for her to take a seat on one of the couches then he sits opposite her. 'So, is Eva here?' she asks.

'We can't get hold of Eva and we're worried. We've been calling her all afternoon. She said she was working today.' He pauses and rubs his stubbly chin. 'We've called the hotel she works at and they haven't seen her all day. They said it was her day off, but she told us she was working. You just missed the police, though a fat lot of good they were.' He sits back and blows out a breath. 'I don't know what to do. I don't know where to look. We haven't lived here long. She doesn't have many friends and one thing she doesn't do is vanish for hours on end. She'd never leave us worrying like this. People talk to hairdressers. Did she say anything to you?'

Her whole body is now jittery. Eva is missing. Madison thinks of Zach having an affair and wonders if her being missing is down to him. He looks upset but then again, people are good at lying; she has first-hand experience of how good people are at lying. She'd fallen deeply in love with two liars.

One of the boys starts to cry. 'Do you need to see to him?'

'It's okay. Eva's mum can handle it. He's worried about Eva.'

She listens as Eva's mum comforts the boy, saying that his mother will be home soon. All Zach can do is nervously tap his fingers on the coffee table. Eva's mum tells the boys they can have the chocolate milk from the fridge. The boys run into the kitchen, and the one Madison recognises as Caiden pours two drinks as he wipes his teary face with his other hand. The other boy turns to smile at them, and Madison recognises him instantly. It's the boy she thought was Zach and the brown-haired woman's son. He must be her son. The boys leave the room as quickly as they arrived. A prickle forms at the nape of Madison's neck and it's not just from the cold rain that has soaked through her clothes. Confused, Madison goes to make her excuses to leave, but Zach interjects.

'Well did she?'

'Did she what?'

'Did Eva say anything to you?'

'I, err.' She looks at Zach and she can't trust him. She doesn't know who to trust. 'No, she didn't say much.' She remembers Eva's Instagram posts. 'She has some friends she meets for coffee, I think they might be other mums from the school. Do you know them?'

He shakes his head. 'Had you and Eva planned to do something tonight? She didn't mention that anyone was coming over.'

She pulls the hairpiece out of her bag. She'd tried her hardest to clean the blood off it for Eva. 'She accidentally left this. I just wanted to give it back to her.' She thinks back to where she found it: the Clifton House Hotel car park. She needs to go back to see if Eva's car is still there. Maybe she's drinking in the bar because she knows her husband is a cheat and because she's certain Theo is Hugo.

'What is it?'

'A clip-in hairpiece.'

He takes it and places it on the coffee table. 'Can I give you my number? If you see her, can you tell her to call me or drop me a message to let me know that she's okay? I just want to know she's safe.'

'Of course.' She hands her phone to him so he can pop his number in her contacts. As he's about to pass her phone back, it silently buzzes and Theo's name pops up on the screen. Zach stares at her.

She snatches her phone from his hands and walks towards the door. 'I need to go. I have to get back to my baby.' What she really needs to do is head straight to the Clifton House Hotel and look for Eva, then she has to speak to Theo. Camille will be upset with her for going to the cottage but it can't wait until tomorrow.

'Wait,' Zach shouts as she runs out of the house and gets into her car. Before she can start the car, he's trying to open the door. 'I know who you are. I came to your house to speak to your husband,' he yells. 'Theo has her, doesn't he? You know where she is, don't you?'

'No,' Madison replies, but she can tell he doesn't believe her.

'Where is she? Where's my wife?'

Madison wants to know where Eva is too. She goes to reply, but he interrupts.

'You don't know him at all, do you?'

He stares through the glass, and Madison is trembling so hard; she needs to get away. He's scaring her.

'Where is she?' He slams both hands on the window.

She needs to get away now. Zach seems to think she has

something to do with Eva being missing and she doesn't know what he'll do. All she can see is rage in his face.

As she pulls away, he bangs on the side doors and the rear window but she doesn't stop. Her throat feels like it's closing up as she processes what he said. *Theo has her*. No, it can't be true. Eva is at the hotel, and Madison is going to prove it and bring her home to Zach. Maybe then he'll stop accusing her. Eva has to be at the hotel. Theo is a liar, not a monster... or is he?

FIFTY-FOUR
EVA

I'm all cried out and what good did that do me? I'm buried alive, and panicking makes everything worse. Soon I won't be able to breathe. I'll suffocate. I begin to hyperventilate, then I remember that if I keep on like this, the air will run out faster. Running my hands through my hair, I reach for the back of my head and begin to pick. If nothing else, my horrible compulsion helps me to think. Maybe Mum was right about Zach. My current situation could actually be down to Zach and Nicole. Theo, Hugo – whoever he is, might not be the reason I'm in this box. If Zach has been having an affair with Nicole, it stands to reason they might want me out of the way. All my money in the house would belong to Zach if I went missing and was eventually presumed dead. Is he playing his part nicely in the outside world? Maybe he's reported me missing, and he and Mum are pacing around the house – him pretending to be worried.

I kick and punch the sides of the box again. Is it Theo? Is it Zach? Which one of them is Nicole helping? What will happen to my son if I never come home? That's the question that tears me apart. I don't care about the house or any of them. If I survive this, I'm taking Caiden away from here to stay with

Mum. Is Caiden safe with me? I need Mum and I need to tell her how much I love her. That day in the car keeps flashing into my mind, and all I can hear are Caiden's cries. Why has that come back to haunt me now?

'Help,' I cry as I kick out at the end of the box. That's when I hear an almighty break, and I yelp in pain. My ankle has gone right through the end, getting caught in wood. I can't help but laugh manically. There's nothing at the end of the box. No soil, at least. I fling my legs out again and again, ignoring the searing pain every time the wood gashes my skin. One final kick and the end is out. I lean up a little but I can't see anything. I'm not outside, as there isn't a breeze. I'm in darkness. There's a slight tapping sound, so I withdraw my foot and hold my breath. It's the sound of rain pattering against a roof and maybe there's an electrical hum in the background. I can't hear anyone around, so I begin to shuffle on my back until my feet kick a wall. There's not enough room for me to get out. I beat the sides of the box again but the rest of it is sturdier than the end.

I stop when I hear a cough. My breaths quicken and cold sweat starts gathering on my forehead.

Someone is out there and they're watching my every move.

'Eva?'

'Nicole?'

FIFTY-FIVE

MADISON

As Madison pulls up at the Clifton House Hotel, the car park is virtually empty. She swallows the lump in her throat as she takes a moment. She and Theo should have been cutting their cake and soon would have been thinking of slipping off to the honeymoon suite to make love while Emily shared a room with Camille, Neil and the kids; but that dream is over. For the first time that day, she allows herself to sob for the loss of her future. She heads back over to the weeping willow to escape the rain and leans against the tree trunk. Her engagement ring glints in the moonlight – another reminder of what she's lost. She pulls it off and throws it in the bushes.

After wiping her eyes on the sleeve of Camille's hoodie, she stands and jogs across the car park. She hasn't seen Eva's car, which means that Eva didn't go missing at the mess of her wedding that never happened. There's more parking space alongside the building. As she walks towards it on the pea-gravelled surface, she catches sight of a car that looks like Eva's. She uses the torch on her phone to peer through the window. A keyring containing a photo of Eva's son lies on the passenger seat. Eva never left the hotel. She has to be inside.

Madison peers in through the windows, searching the bar. A woman sits alone but it's not Eva. She turns around, her bag in her hand as if she's about to leave, then she frowns as she catches sight of Madison. Tammy has spotted her. A long chat about the disaster of her big day is the last thing Madison needs, but maybe Tammy has seen Eva.

'Madison?' Tammy appears at the end of the road holding her tiny bag over her head. She struggles to balance in her stilettos. 'You look...'

'Like crap, I know.'

'I'm so sorry. Orla and I have been worried about you.'

'You're both at the hotel?'

Tammy nods. 'Orla went to bed and I was just about to go up. We'd both had a drink earlier so decided to stay. How have you been? Actually, don't answer that. What a stupid question.'

'It's fine. I'm okay, honestly.'

Tammy raises her brows. The rain starts to pour down. 'Why don't we go inside. You're soaked through.'

Madison is so used to looking after Orla and Tammy, it feels odd for Tammy to be looking out for her. She gently leads Madison into the reception area. 'Have you seen Eva?'

'Eva?' Tammy shrugs. 'Do I know her?'

'The woman who came in for a haircut the other week. You booked her in.' Tammy looks blank so Madison calls up Eva's Instagram. 'She came here to speak to me earlier. She's the wedding planner at the Sea Horse Hotel, the place we cancelled to come here.' She holds a photo of Eva up for Tammy to see as they both sit on a couch.

'Ah, I saw her earlier. She dashed in while we were having canapes. What was she doing here?'

'I haven't got time to explain. You've been here all day, haven't you? Have you seen her since?'

Tammy shakes her head, her wonky fascinator falling into her lap. 'No.'

'I saw her.' The receptionist pipes up from behind them, coat in arms as she was just about to leave. 'Sorry. I didn't mean to interrupt.'

'It's okay.' Madison stands and thrusts her phone at the receptionist.

'Some angry, drunken woman came in, knocking the flowers over earlier.'

'Was this before the wedding?'

'You mean the wedding that wasn't?' The receptionist suddenly recognises Madison and clears her throat. 'I'm sorry, that was your wedding. Err, the woman in that photo told your wedding planner that she was your sister and that she had something for you. Next thing, the other woman, long brown hair down to her waist, knocked the flowers over. We told her to leave. She clearly wasn't dressed for a wedding, and you had the place booked out for the day. The woman in your photo went outside looking for her. I didn't see either of them after that. I assumed they'd left.'

'And you haven't seen either of them since?'

'I've been here since this morning and they haven't been back.'

Madison holds the photo up. 'This woman is called Eva. Her car is still in the car park and the police are looking for her. Do you have CCTV on the car park?'

The woman frowns. 'The camera out the front only reaches the terraces. It doesn't cover the car parks. There is another camera alongside the building but it's out of action. You could ask the day staff a few questions if you come back tomorrow. They might remember more. Could the woman in your photo have got a taxi? She might have had a drink while she was here. That's what normally happens when people leave their cars overnight.'

'I guess. Do you know why the woman with the brown hair was here? You said she was angry.'

The receptionist swallows. 'I feel really awful having to say this.'

'Please, I walked out on my wedding today. Whatever you have to say, say it.' Madison's stomach begins to turn.

'She said she had to stop your wedding. Your partner was angry at her presence, and he asked us to get rid of her. He said she'd been stalking him. He also asked us not to say anything to you as he didn't want the day ruined, then he left us to deal with her. I nearly called the police to get her off the premises, but she left. When you ran out at the altar, we thought that someone else had told you about the incident and that you were upset or that maybe he was having an affair with her.' The receptionist pauses. 'Sorry, I shouldn't have said that. You've had a horrible day.'

'It's okay.'

Tammy places a loving arm around Madison's shoulder.

'Again, I'm sorry,' the receptionist says.

'It's okay. It's not your fault.'

The receptionist flashes a sympathetic smile and leaves.

Madison thinks back to the day that the brown-haired woman and Zach had their meeting with Theo. She stared at Theo, and Madison remembered thinking that it was strange at the time. What if all this time, Theo had been stalked? She thinks of all the phone calls, the messages, his rising stress levels. Theo said it was all down to his mother, but now Madison doesn't believe him. She thinks back to that night she was checking out the shed, when someone had been watching them. Emily did have brown hair clasped in her tiny hand, not Madison's red locks like Theo had claimed. He'd tried to cover for his stalker, but why? He should have told her if she and Emily were under threat.

Primal anger rises within her, the type of anger that would definitely result in an explosion – and there is only one person in the world she wants to release that bomb on. Theo.

FIFTY-SIX
MADISON

Before turning onto their bumpy drive to the cottage, Madison spots a small empty van set back from the main road. It's parked up against the hedge, almost hidden from view. After pulling up, she steps out of her car and sees that Theo's still not home. Both she and Theo arrived at the hotel in a wedding car that morning so he had to have come back for his car – and gone where?

The hairs on Madison's neck prickle again. It's dark and creepy now, and she doesn't have Camille with her for backup. She tries to ignore her pounding heart. The anger that brought her here is now swirling in her stomach as fear. It would be so easy to get back in her car and drive away. Buster barks from behind the door. With Theo being AWOL, there's no way she can leave her little dog behind. She pulls her door key from her bag and heads through the creaky gate towards the front door.

An owl hoots which adds to her sense of unease. She feels its piercing yellow eyes on her but when she looks up, all she can see is the moon. Buster barks again. 'It's okay, Buster. Mummy's here.' She turns her key in the lock and gently pushes the door. Buster dashes past her feet, into the woods. 'Buster'.

He's gone. She steps into a puddle of urine by the door. His harness is usually hung on the coat hook by the door but it's not there.

She turns the light on and gasps at the mess. Sofa cushions have been strewn across the carpet. The coffee table has been smashed into chunks of wood, and Emily's baby basket is broken. What has Theo done? She thinks of her poor little dog. He must have been terrified.

She hurries to the kitchen to look for the lead, which isn't in any of its usual places like on the back of the chair or flung over the kitchen door. The wedding ring she found glints on the worktop. She rustles through the kitchen cupboard, searching for the raven toy but that's also gone. As she steps back, she kicks Buster's harness. Grabbing it, she hurries to the front door.

'Buster,' she calls from the doorstep. Her heart bangs harder.

Frantic barks echo through the woods.

'Buster. Why are you doing this to me,' she whispers, her voice quivering as she turns the light off and hurries out of the house. She thinks of her brown-haired stalker and Theo's mother. Maybe one of them messed the cottage up in a temper. The van had to belong to one of them. Buster whines. She runs in the rain, crashing through several puddles on her way to the gate. As soon as she arrives at the shed, she calls out to Buster, who barks frantically. Hands shaking, she nudges the shed door open and lets out a shriek. There's a panel under the hatch and it's open. In the gap, she spots boxes upon boxes of disposable brown-eyed contact lenses. She drops the harness and touches some of the boxes in disbelief.

She can't breathe. It's as if her throat is closing. Buster's barking stops. She runs out of the shed and accidentally kicks an animal feeding bowl. He's gone. She spins in every direction, trying to spot her beloved dog. The police – she needs to call them now. Her phone isn't in her pocket. She left it in the side of the door of her car.

'Buster,' she whispers as she hears the crack of a branch followed by footsteps approaching from behind. She turns her head but can't see anyone so she sprints. After stumbling into her car, she locks herself in and prays that Buster will come to her. Someone was out there, following her. The police. She reaches for her phone but it's gone. She goes to turn the keys in the ignition but they're also gone. Then she spots a note on the passenger seat. Thick marker print on white paper that she can just about read.

> Madison. We need to talk. Please go into the house and don't leave until I get back. I will explain everything in a short while but lock the door and wait for me. I won't be long. Trust me. I love you. Stay inside and don't answer the door to anyone. Theo. X

Explain everything! She wants to leave with her dog but he's taken her keys and phone, and now Buster is missing. How dare he tell her not to leave the house. Every worry she's had over the past few weeks swirls around in her head. She has no choice but to step out of the car. There is no way she's going to wait in the house for who knows what to happen. As soon as she has Buster, she'll leave on foot without her phone if she has to. One thing she now knows for sure is that Theo is close by. It must have been him creeping around in the woods. She takes a deep breath to try to control her nerves. Buster. She thinks of what Camille had been saying to her. Theo has isolated her; she isn't losing her mind – it was Theo playing her. Is she walking into a well-planned trap? She thought of the mess in the house. Nothing about today had been planned which is why he'd lost it.

Buster whines again. As she steps into the messy hallway

and lounge, she hears him scratching an upstairs door. She creeps up the stairs, one by one, not turning a single light then she finally reaches their bedroom. When she opens the door, Buster crashes through her legs and darts around in the dark. She goes to pick him up but he wriggles out of her grip. His lead – she left it in the shed. Buster runs downstairs into the kitchen. Without calling him, Madison follows and steps into the darkness. The moon's light shines through the kitchen window and she can see that the ring has gone. Buster barks at the back door. 'Buster, shush,' she whispers, but she can't get him to stop barking and scratching at the back door.

Her phone lights up on the windowsill. She runs across the kitchen and grabs it. It's Camille. She presses to answer but Theo snatches it from her hand and stamps on it.

'You couldn't just wait for another minute. I told you we had to talk,' he yells.

All she can focus on are the whites of his eyes as he stares. She steps back into one of his shoes, nearly tripping over it. 'Theo...'

'You're just like the others and I thought you were different. I love you and look what you did to me today. We were going to move away and start a new life but no, shit just follows me around.'

He's crying. Madison doesn't know whether to reach out and try to comfort him, but he smashed her phone and he never mentioned having a stalker. She wants the truth, about Eva, about the brown-haired woman and the fact that she hasn't got baby brain or whatever he liked to call it. Camille would call it gaslighting. 'What are you talking about, Theo?' Theo. She'd seen the contact lenses – the lie. 'You're Hugo, aren't you?'

'No, no, no, no, no...'

Madison flinches as he slams his hand on the worktop.

'Tell me about the ring, Hugo.' She has to push him for answers even though she's on the verge of hyperventilating. She loved him, or still loves him – it's complicated, but she needs the truth. 'Tell me about your mother, tell me about Eva, Caiden and the woman with the brown hair who tried to crash our wedding earlier. Tell me about her and Zach, and why they were at our house.' She won't stop, not now she's revealing her hand. There's no going back now. 'Tell me about the contact lenses in the shed. Tell me about the photo of you and your sister, Emily. Is it even you and Emily in the photo? Who's the boy in the newspaper cutting?' The room is silent. 'Tell me,' Madison yells as Buster barks relentlessly.

'No.' His raises his arms then runs towards her roaring, his eyes wide open.

She opens the back door and runs into the rain as fast as she can.

'Stop. You have to come back.'

She glances over her shoulder. She can't get around the side of the house. He's standing on the path, blocking it off. She might be able to use one of his devices in the cabin to call the police, but she has to get there first and she has to lock him out. The door's jammed. She shoulder-barges it and stumbles into the small hallway. As his hand is about to grab her hoodie, she regains her balance and slams the door in his face, then she locks it.

'Open it now,' he shouts as he pounds against the wood. 'Open the door or I will smash it down.'

A bang from behind the store room door makes Madison shriek. She needs to get away from whoever is in there, so she runs around his office looking for something to make a call on, but there isn't anything. His computer would take a while to turn on – but it was worth a try. Her hand falls onto one of the twin photos as she reaches for the mouse then a mighty crash leads to glass spraying underneath the closed blinds. Theo forces a foot through. She sees his iPad on the floor and grabs it.

The store room. She hurries out and closes the office door

before placing a hand on the store room door handle. Another bang comes from behind the door. She doesn't want to go in there, but she can't leave through the front door and Theo is in the office, swearing under his breath. The office goes silent and that silence is scarier than any noise. She presses the handle and gasps. The brown-haired woman is slumped over a desk and her eyes are almost closed and she's slurring her words. On the table behind her is a bottle of vodka and there are tablets scattered on the floor by her feet.

Madison turns Theo's iPad on but there's no internet connection. She turns her head to the half-battered wooden crate with splintered wood sticking out of the back end, and the woman mutters some quiet words.

'Eva's gone. He took her.'

FIFTY-SEVEN
NICOLE

What had Nicole been thinking? She hadn't intended to drink but as soon as she arrived at the Clifton House Hotel earlier, she'd downed a few gulps of vodka from her travel mug while contemplating what to do from the safety of her van. She'd needed it to be able to face Theo and stop the wedding, but being tipsy and angry had made her look unhinged. And now she is tied up in a weird room full of computer things and he has taken Eva. If she gets out of this nightmare, she's never going to drink again. She hasn't quite come around yet. Her mind drifts and she can't fight the dreamworld that keeps drawing her back in.

The argument she'd had with her dad still rings through her head. She'd only asked if he could look after Aaron for a while, but he said no. He'd called her a fantasist and blamed her for ruining her marriage to Will. Yes, she had made a mistake. A big mistake but it was one she had come to not regret, regardless of how shit her dad made her feel about herself. At least Susan had been accommodating, which meant Aaron was safe.

She prises her eyes open again. A tear drizzles down her cheek as she sees the fear and worry on Madison's face. She has to properly think about what to say to her, and how to say it, and she has to stop herself from drifting off again. Theo could come back to kill them both at any moment.

The banging has stopped but the thumps in Nicole's head continue. 'Has he gone?' she manages to ask Madison with a slur. She knows she sounds drunk; Hugo forced vodka down her neck until she'd passed out.

'I think so. I can't hear him. Have you taken any of those tablets?'

Nicole shakes her head. She'd fought him off, despite being so sleepy. He'd forced a few into her mouth but she spat them in his face. Eva had been banging as she came out of the box which then distracted him.

Madison's dog barks from outside the door. 'I'll just be a minute. We need to find a phone. I'll call the police.'

'No.' Nicole doesn't want to be left alone. He took Eva away when she escaped from the box, and now Nicole is alone again because Madison has left to chase that yapping rat. She understands though. If that rat were hers, she'd love it enough to risk life and limb. She thinks of Aaron and all she wants to do is cuddle up to him and tell him how sorry she is because his whole life is a lie.

'Madison.' Nicole tries to stand but her legs are like jelly and she's seeing double. She grips onto the doorframe to steady herself. Her legs work, that's a start. The kitchen is lit up. Madison is throwing everything out of the drawers looking for what Nicole presumes is a phone. Whatever she does, she can't let go of the doorframe yet, or she'll fall.

Madison runs back to her with her dog in a harness. 'Do you know where he took Eva? We have to find her.'

'No.' The fresh air and rain are helping to sober Nicole up a little.

'I can't find a phone and he's hidden my car keys. We're

going to have to walk to the road. I saw a van parked up. Maybe there is someone close by who can help.'

Nicole shakes her head and laughs manically. 'There's no one else. That's my van,' she replies, struggling to get her words out clearly.

'Is that how you got here?'

'Yes. I was just about to warn Eva that he was there, in the hotel car park, but he pushed her into a rock. He forced me into my van with her and drove us here. He drugged me and made me drink vodka. He was going to force me to take those tablets...' She begins to sob as she realises how close she'd come to dying and never seeing her son again. 'He was going to make my death look like suicide because he said no one would miss an unhinged drunk.' She forces a laugh through her tears.

Madison places her arms around her and it feels nice to be cared for, especially because it must be a shock for Madison too. 'We're going to get help, okay? Can you lean on me and walk with me to the main road?'

Nicole nods. She doesn't know if she can but she has to try. She wants to get past all this. She wants to tell Eva everything including how she and Zach really met. She also needs to prove herself to her dad and get her act together. Her dad hates her for the big lie she told, and he hates the fact that she can't get her life together and she keeps losing houses and ending up with him. When she gets out of this mess, there will be no more drinking. No more secrets, no more lies and no more self-sabotage. She's made some massive mistakes and she needs to own them. She's going to make things up to her dad, Will and Aaron, and most of all she hopes that Eva will forgive her for what she doesn't yet know.

As they limp down the road, the mud path underneath gets more and more slippy with the falling rain but Madison keeps encouraging her to keep going.

'Why did you come to our house with Eva's husband all

those months ago? You came with your little boy. I have to know so please don't lie.'

'We needed to know if Theo was Hugo.' There, she had said it. It was time to let go of the secrets. Everything was coming out after tonight. 'One of them died. Theo and Hugo were twins.'

'Twins? Theo had a twin sister.'

'There's no sister. It was Theo and Hugo. They killed Zach's brother, Justin. When he was a little boy, Zach saw them with a knife. He hid and watched his brother get killed.' Nicole swallows down the acid at the back of her throat. The truth is hard to share but Madison needs to know what kind of a man she nearly married. 'The twins' mother, Erica, claimed they were both at home at the time Justin was murdered, giving them an alibi. The murder weapon was never found.' She pauses to gather her confused thoughts. 'Zach had been looking for the twins for years and he finally found Hugo.' Nicole shakes her head and lets out a puff of air. 'He spotted his photo in the obituary section of a newspaper in Worcestershire.'

Madison's brows crease. 'There was a boy in a newspaper clipping and I recognised him. Theo kept it in his shed. The boy looked just like Zach. He must have been Zach's brother.' Rain runs down her face but she keeps helping Nicole and holding her dog with the other hand. 'And Eva married Hugo, knowing what he was capable of?'

'From what Zach told me, Eva doesn't know about any of this. She thinks that Hugo's mother is Cynthia, the woman who adopted him in his teens. I wanted to tell her everything, but Zach said he needed to be the one to tell her.' Nicole lets out a little sob, knowing that her lies will make it difficult for Eva to forgive her.

Nicole can see what Madison is thinking. Is Theo Hugo?

Madison presses her lips together in thought before speaking again. 'But I thought Eva's husband was dead.'

As they head around a bend, they stop. Nicole can't help but stare at the car in the middle of the road, obviously left there to block them from leaving in Madison's car, had she managed to find her keys.

'Bastard,' Madison screams into the night air. They glance through the window as they pass. It was too much to expect that Theo had accidentally left the keys in the ignition. 'We're nearly there. Do you have your van keys?'

After reaching into her pocket, she pulls out the spares. When she drinks, she loses keys so she has spares of them all. 'Yep.'

They reach the end of the road, soaked through to the skin. Nicole's teeth start to chatter. A breeze picks up and she wishes she had a coat, but it's okay, they'll soon be in the van and they can turn the heating up on their way to the police station; that's until they both stop and stare. 'Where did he leave the van?' Nicole asks.

'It was here.' Madison lets go of Nicole and passes the dog lead to her.

That's when Nicole knows they won't be getting into a nice warm van to go to the police station because Theo has taken it.

Madison falls to her knees and pounds the ground with her fists. 'I hate you,' she yells, her tears mingling with the rain.

Nicole leads the dog to the roadside where she stands. She'll stand here until someone passes or until she falls over, which could happen soon. Madison joins her and lays her head on Nicole's shoulders. They sit on the kerb. It's too far to walk either way. Madison is limping and Nicole knows she can't go any further.

Madison sighs. 'So, tell me everything from the beginning, not missing anything out.'

How to begin? Nicole settles on this line. 'The man you were about to marry is Hugo. I had sex with him in a car almost eleven years ago.'

FIFTY-EIGHT
EVA

He's tied me to the passenger seat; and we haven't come across a single car for ages. These roads are quiet and I don't know where he's taking me, but I can tell we're on the coastal path heading towards Combe Martin. I'm shaking. He's going to kill me. It's the only way he gets to keep his secret. It's obvious to me now. Theo *is* Hugo.

'Caiden needs me,' I blurt out in a teary mess. I think of Caiden and that day I left him in the car, and only now can I see what happened. As I reframe the events of my past, it's like a light has been switched on. The window wipers swish back and forth as the rain buckets down.

'And all you had to do was to be a fucking mother and forget about me,' he yells.

My heart judders. I thought he was going to reach over and hit me. His knuckles are white as they grip the wheel of Nicole's van. I try to focus on the raven toy that he's stuck to the dashboard. 'I have been a good mother. I love Caiden more than anything in the whole world, and he'll be missing me. He needs me. He's already lost you.' I have to play this well or he could drive us both off a cliff edge. If anyone is unhinged right now, it's him. I pause and wonder if I should ask my next question, but I don't think I have much to lose right now. 'How did you do it, Hugo? The DNA of the body in the car matched yours.'

He swerves into a car park, making my stomach sink as he pulls right up to a cliff edge. 'This time I'll do a better job.'

I think of my son but I can't beg this man for my life. I hate what he's put me through. I don't want to sit here and do nothing but cry. If we're going to die, I want the truth. 'How did you do it? I actually think I know but I want to hear it from you.'

'You're so stupid, Eva. You always were. You couldn't possibly know anything.'

That hurts. Trusting maybe. Loving, definitely, but stupid – that was cruel. Then again, anyone that could do what Hugo has done is cruel so why would I expect anything less? I keep thinking over our years together and the night my psychosis came out to play, a totally unexpected event but it happened nonetheless. Or did it? DNA is unique, the police kept telling me. My mother said the same thing but I've been researching and my theory makes sense. I had plenty of time to think things through in that box. 'I broke into your office and found photos of Caiden and Emily. At least, I thought the babies in the photo were Caiden and Emily, but one of those babies was you, wasn't it? You had a twin brother, didn't you, Hugo? His name was Theo. That night I came downstairs and saw a body on our living room floor, it was him, not you. This is where I had to really think.'

'You, think? Don't make me laugh.'

I ignore his swipe at me. 'He wasn't dead, was he? You kept him against his will... let me guess... in our shed, and just before I came back with Mum after our theatre trip, you killed him, then you sent the car through that flimsy excuse of a wall and made it look like suicide before vanishing into your new life, the life you'd prepared with the savings I thought we had. You couldn't have killed him when he was unconscious on our living room floor because the police would have known by the state of his body that he hadn't just died. Anyway, if we're going to die, I just wanted to tell you that I figured it out.' I pause. 'And you were happy for me to think I was crazy.'

'You think you know it all.'

I shake my head while trying to subtly untie my binds. I need to keep him talking but I'm fast giving up hope of getting any purchase in this knotted mess. 'I spoke to your mum.'

He slams a fist into the steering wheel.

'She told me how she and your dad adopted you, wanted to give you the best life ever and take you away from your violent past. Theo had kept running away from various homes to be with your real mother. I don't know why you never told me you were adopted, but I guess you'd have to reveal the real you. Cynthia told me how you startled her daughter's horse and caused her accident. She told me how you called her to tell her I was mad too. You made me out to be crazy when you told her about me thinking you were dead one minute and alive the next. Poor woman was scared of us all but most of all, she was scared of you, Hugo, and the threats to her life should she ever try to expose you. She was mean to me because she thought it best that I drop it when I called her to tell her you were here. You'd been out of her life for five whole years and she wanted to keep it that way but me, I needed the truth. I heard the fear in her voice, Hugo.'

'That bitch doesn't fear anyone.'

I inhale, wondering whether to continue but for the first time in my life, I feel my anxiety melting away. I've never felt this sense of being unburdened and the consequences don't even matter. I just want the noise in my head to leave and talking to Hugo is helping. I had a hard time at university. I struggled as a new mother but I am not as bad as he caused me to be. It's taken this situation to make me realise how strong I really am. 'She told me everything. You said that if she kept going on saying that her daughter's tragic accident was down to you, she'd have a tragic accident too. You warned her to stay away from me and Caiden, and at the same time, you told me how cruel they were in not wanting to have anything to do with you or us. You made me hate Cynthia because of what you said.' I pause, not knowing what to say next. None of this was planned. 'Madison told me she'd met your mother. Did she even know if you were Theo or Hugo? I bet she didn't.'

'My mother doesn't deserve to know. She chose a life of drugs and abusive men over me and Theo.'

There's a sadness in his eyes and, for a moment, I see the Hugo I used to love. He removes the glasses he doesn't need. It's my Hugo and my heart almost bursts on seeing him. I still love the man he was but I hate the man he is now. I spent all those years in counselling, missing him. I moved on and managed to love again. Confusion fills my heart. 'It really is you, Hugo.'

He doesn't reply.

Something changes within me. I'm back in the understairs cupboard and Hugo is looking at me in that exact way. It's only now I see the extent of his lies. He was the architect of my downfall because I'd shared the tiniest bit of my past with him. Granted, he never got the details but he knew about my breakdown at uni.

'I never left Caiden in that blistering hot car that day, did I? You told me I'd left him in the car and I believed you because I was ill.' I'm shaking. All these years I've lived with that guilt and I hated myself so much.

'That's not true. I covered for you, Eva. We both know I did. Come away with me. Let's get Caiden and leave right now. I didn't abandon you but you have to understand, I had to leave. Theo was threatening to expose me over something we did as kids. It was an accident. I didn't mean to hurt anyone but things went too far and there was no going back. I couldn't go to prison. Think of how much worse things would have been for you and Caiden if I had.'

'What was Theo threatening to expose?'

'I can't talk about it. I don't ever want to talk about it. It hurts too much. Please come away with me. We don't have to go over this cliff. This doesn't have to be our end. Let's leave. We don't ever have to come back. I know how to get us new identities. I have money stashed away. Please, Eva. I'm sorry I said all those things just now; I was angry, that's all. I love you. It was always you.'

'What about Madison?'

'She's nothing.'

'Emily?'

'I have choices to make and she'll be better off with Madison.'

My thoughts move towards Emily, our twin girl that we lost. 'You called her Emily because we lost our Emily, didn't you?'

He shrugs. 'My heart ached for her too.'

I pick up the raven toy. 'Did you leave one of these in our new house in the hope that Caiden would find it and remember you?'

'I've never been in your new house. It wasn't me. I came over once and I swear, I only went in your garden to look through the windows. I just wanted to see Caiden, that's all.'

'Why do you have this then?'

'I don't know. It was left outside my shed. Someone came over and left your wedding ring in the fruit bowl.' He points to the centre console and there it is, the wedding ring I buried beside our tree.

'Do you know who?'

He nods. 'Nicole.'

'Nicole? Why would she do that?'

He turns to me. I stop fiddling with the rope and he grips my hands. 'Forget about her and Madison. Please say we can go away together. We need to go to yours now, get Caiden and leave. Please, Eva. I've changed.'

I shake my head, and he lets go of my hands. Probing away, I push a finger through a loop and the binds get a little looser. For the first time in an hour, I feel as though I might have a chance.

'You know Zach is a liar; you can't trust him. If you're sitting there thinking about how hurt Zach will be, don't. His whole existence in your life is a lie.'

That has thrown me. It's the last thing I'd have expected Hugo to say. 'What...? I don't believe you.'

'He's not who he says he is, and he and Nicole, you've suspected them for ages, haven't you?'

Mum was right. I feel like such a fool. A part of me wonders if Hugo is saying this to manipulate me, but another part of me has suspected that Zach and Nicole are having an affair. I think of Nicole and the state she was left in back in the store room. She needs help. I wonder if I should even contemplate helping her if she's trying to steal Zach off me, but then again, I'm not Hugo. I don't know what Hugo was trying to stop Theo from telling everyone. My head is filling up with chaos again. I'm angry at Nicole and I'm livid with Zach, but I won't leave her to die.

'You shut me in a box and made me believe I was buried alive. I had to kick my way out.' I wiggle my wounded ankle and it stings. 'I don't trust anything you say. I will never trust you again. I don't trust Zach and I don't trust anyone. Happy now? You have made me into this person.'

One of the knots has unravelled. I start on the next one.

'I could never be with you again. You're only saying all this to get yourself out of this mess.'

Another knot unravels.

He looks at what I'm doing. 'Then you leave me with no choice.'

Sweat prickles across my forehead as he turns the engine on. He revs it up and releases the handbrake. I can't undo the last knot.

'Are you leaving with me?'

'No,' I yell.

'Then it's over.'

FIFTY-NINE

I close my eyes and hope that I die fast. I imagine the van hurtling down the cliff side. My life flashes through my mind. Growing up. Mum. Nan. Happy memories. I met Hugo and it was love at first sight. When I thought I couldn't love anymore, I gave birth to Caiden. I lost Emily. Letting out a cry, I wait for the clutch to be released – but it doesn't happen. I open my eyes. Hugo pulls the handbrake back on.

'I'm sorry about everything I put you through. I wish things could have been different but the cards weren't mine to play. I did what I had to do to survive but you'll never understand. I can see that now. I'm going to make it up to you, okay?'

'I don't want anything from you. I just want to be with Caiden.' Tears fall down my face. The thought of going over that cliff has made me feel more alive than ever. I don't want to die.

He leans over and kisses me on the lips, like he used to do all those years ago. In another life I'd have melted and told him how much I love him, but that life is over. He opens the driver's door.

'I can't live this life anymore. You and Caiden deserve more.

Emily deserves more. I'm no good to anyone. You were right about everything. I killed Theo and took his life as my own. I threatened Cynthia and I did everything she said I did. All because of one stupid mistake as a kid. There's no place in this world for me after what I've done.' Tears form in the corners of his eyes. 'Goodbye, Eva.'

He slams the door and begins to walk to the top of the stone steps that lead to the small shingly beach below.

I hate him, I really do but I can't let him take his own life. Yes, he's evil, calculating, manipulative and a murderer, and he needs to pay for what he's done. I wonder how Caiden would feel if he ever found out that I let his father die. I'm not like Hugo; I can't carry on as normal and pretend that none of this happened and move on, and I doubt that Nicole or Madison can either. After one final struggle, I manage to free my hands. I reach over and untie the binds that are fixing my body to the passenger seat and I fling the van door open.

Limping towards the top of the steep stone steps, I carefully walk down them one by one while holding onto the rail. With each step, the wound on my ankle stings. The moon is reflected in the sea. The wind almost sends me flying, and the rain pelts at my face, making it almost impossible to see too far ahead. A huge cloud starts to block the moon's light. I'm in the dark, but I can hear the crashing of breakers on the pebbly shore.

'Hugo?'

As I reach the bottom, I step onto the stones and keep calling his name. I'm soaked through and my hair is plastered to my face, including that bloody fringe. I struggle as my feet sink into sand and stone with every step, then I eventually reach the shoreline. With one of my hands shielding my eyes from the torrential downpour, I scan the ground. That's when I see a shadowy lump ahead. I limp over to it and kneel beside it and I begin feeling my way through Hugo's coat and boots.

'Hugo,' I call out, hoping that if he's in the sea, he'll hear me and come back. I glance back at the rock face. It looks like it wants to swallow me up. Hugo is nowhere to be seen. I spot his top crashing to shore on a wave, and I yell at the sea, 'Hugo.'

I cry into his coat before I slip it over my shoulders, then I hear something jangling from the pocket – the van keys. I glance once more at the sea and I know that Hugo is gone forever. It's over.

SIXTY

EVA

Two days later

I'm sitting at our table. Zach has packed his bags, and Mum is respectfully waiting in the kitchen. I'll pack once he's gone and maybe I'll move back in with Mum for a bit, once I've worked my notice at the Sea Horse. The house is going to have to go. Hugo didn't die by suicide when we lived in Malvern, and the insurance money isn't mine; the investigation will bring all that up. All I'll get to keep is the equity Hugo and I had in our house at Malvern before he died, which I'm not scoffing at. I'm going to need every penny. Of course, I am a victim in all this. I had no idea Hugo had lied all these years, or that he murdered his brother. Mum and I haven't explained any of this to Caiden, but I will have to say something soon because the newspapers are already reporting some of our story.

'I love you, Eva. That wasn't a lie.' Zach picks up his bag.

Caiden will miss him and I will too, but I've had enough. Is it so hard to find genuine love? I thought I had, twice, but each time was a lie. 'You inserted yourself into my life when I was vulnerable. I believed you.'

'I was vulnerable too, Eva. I was genuinely grieving for my brother.'

'You never did tell me how you found me.'

'You want me to tell you?' He throws his bag down, not in a temper, more in frustration.

'Yes. It creeps me out that you targeted me, got to know me and worked your way into my bed, my life, my son's life. I even married you!'

'I'd spent years looking for Hugo and Theo. Years.' He runs his fingers through his hair and paces towards me. 'After the incident, they both ended up in care, so it made it impossible to find them. Of course, they were never convicted of my Justin's murder; and it was their abusive homelife that got them taken off their mother.' He shakes his head and swallows. 'When my mum died, I found Justin's old school photos and I recognised one of the kids. It was Hugo. He was the boy who I saw stabbing Justin from inside that wooden playhouse. I searched online for him by name and his obituary came up, the obituary that you sent to the paper.' He paused and looked out at the sea below. 'I searched for you and I found you. After that, I put the feelers out, sharing Hugo's school photo and his obituary photo online in the hope of finding his twin, and some people had said there was a man in Devon with similar features so I spent more time targeting this area. That's how I met Nicole.'

'How could you lie all that time?'

'Because I love you, I fell in love with you. Yes, I started coming to your bereavement group to get to know you better. I thought you might know more about Hugo's brother, though I soon found out that you didn't know he existed at all. By that time, I was already in love with you. I knew if I told you that I'd inserted myself into your life to investigate your husband's brother, you'd dump me.'

'And look how that worked out for you.'

'If you're going to be like this, there's no point talking to you.

I'm being honest here. I fell in love with you. I didn't want to lose you. I love Caiden. What I did was wrong. You have every right to hate me.'

'It was wrong, and for the record, I don't hate you. I just don't trust you and I'm sorry about what happened to your brother. I can't imagine what you went through seeing him killed like that.'

'But you're casting me aside.'

I lean on the worktop. 'I can't do this. I need a fresh start – and then there's Nicole.'

'I know and I'm sorry. Nothing happened between us, she just helped me look for Hugo.'

'How did she know him?'

He shrugs. 'I don't know. Maybe I should have asked but I was so fixated on my own needs. I didn't get into it with her.'

My hands clench together and I slam one on the worktop. 'You both lied to me. She owes me nothing so I can forgive her.'

'She found Hugo and we were investigating him together. When I saw her in our house that day, it was a shock. I made up some rubbish about her mooching through drawers...'

'Then you had to call her to make sure she said the same thing?'

He nods. 'She was helping me. It's not her fault and she was upset because she really liked you; and I made you think she was up to no good. Nothing went on between us.'

'How did we end up right here, right where you needed to be, to look for Hugo?' I'm angry. I feel so played by Zach. I know why but I want to hear him say it.

'When we spoke about moving, I went on about how wonderful it would be to live here. You had that photo of Caiden on the beach, and I knew Combe Martin held a special place in your heart. I knew that being here would help me find Hugo and get justice for my brother.'

'Then you must have known that I might see Hugo, too, and

my world might be blown apart. You also must have known that for you to get justice, the truth had to come out and it would affect me too.'

'I didn't think. I'm sorry.'

'Then you and Nicole just happened to meet up all the time at the pub to talk about your past and your loss, the same loss you didn't want to share with me.'

'You were still in Malvern and, as I said, Nicole was helping me to find Hugo. I'd had a few drinks at the pub on a couple of occasions and I shared a bit too much with her, but we never had a one-night stand, an affair, a kiss or anything.'

I don't know if I believe him but what I do see is genuine sadness in his eyes. He loved his brother, that was real. 'You say that they killed your brother, that it was Hugo. Was it definitely him and not Theo?'

I have to know if I was married to a man who could murder a child. I'm prepared for him to say he doesn't know; after all, he was a scared little boy when he saw his brother being murdered. He swallows again and dips his head. I can tell it's upsetting for him to talk about this so I walk over and give him a friendly hug. I'm disappointed in Zach but I still care for him.

He tries to kiss me, but I turn my face away from him.

'The boy who killed Justin had a large birthmark on his neck. Other people who knew them both told me that Theo didn't have a birthmark, that's how they could be identified. Since I've been here investigating, he kept it covered up, but Nicole had seen it, she knew.'

That sends me almost sick. In my head, I'm picturing young Hugo chasing an innocent boy down with a knife. That's what Theo must have been threatening to expose on the night Hugo killed him. I'll never know what Theo wanted. Maybe it was money in exchange for his silence or maybe he wanted the truth to finally come out.

I wish that everything had been different as I drink in the

musky, woody smell that is Zach through and through. When we first met, I wish he'd knocked at my door enquiring about Hugo and Theo. He could have told me the truth about them from the start. It would have been a shock but I still think I'd have fallen in love with him. He didn't need to follow me around, get to know where I hung out before joining my bereavement group. He didn't need to lie to insert himself into my life. I'm sad for what he's been through but I can't get past this.

From now on, it's just me and Caiden. I hug Zach again. I'm not even angry anymore but I think he can tell by the way I'm only lightly hugging him that we're over.

SIXTY-ONE

MADISON

Two weeks later

Nicole enters Madison's salon, her hair all tangled down to her waist. Tammy and Orla aren't due in for a couple of hours. Camille is looking after Emily; she's taken them in until Madison can find somewhere to rent. She never wants to go back to that cottage, even though the police said she can go over to get her things now that they've released it as a crime scene. She's also since found out that the cottage never belonged to Theo; it was rented. That's why he'd never allowed her to knock a wall down or decorate. His whole life was a lie.

She still misses the Theo she knew, even though she now knows she was living with Hugo and that Hugo had murdered his brother years before. Their poor mother had been confused at everything, and Madison doesn't believe she'll ever stop blaming herself for what happened in the past. Erica had expressed a lot of regrets for letting her boys down, but her problems had made it impossible for her to be the parent she wanted to be. She'll keep in touch with her, let her know how Emily is doing and maybe send photos.

Madison still can't believe she was living with a murderer. She's ignored several emails from journalists asking to be the first to break her story. She's not up for an exposé. She, Nicole and Eva have decided to try as hard as they can to keep out of the public eye for the sake of their children. She thinks of Emily and she knows that's the right thing to do. She also knows that she has a secret of her own, and the last thing she needs is journalists fishing through her past mistakes.

'I'm glad you came, Nicole. It's lovely to see you even though I wish we'd met under better circumstances. Sit and tell me what you want.'

'A very big transformation. I'm thinking shoulder length. Two weeks off the booze so I'm celebrating a new me.'

Madison throws the cape around Nicole's neck. 'You're looking well for it. How's Aaron?'

'He's okay. He's actually staying with Will for a few days. I know he's not Aaron's biological father but he's been the only father that Aaron has ever known. That counts for a lot. He's finally come round and Aaron is thrilled to spend time with him.'

'You're lucky you have him.'

'I know.' Nicole pauses and looks down, stopping Madison from continuing to comb her hair. 'I have to tell you something.'

Madison frowns and looks at Nicole in the mirror.

'I sent you a text message, telling you that Theo was a liar and not to marry him. That must have been worrying for you but I wanted to warn you about him, that's all. I thought you should know. I tried to warn Eva too, but as usual it came out all wrong. She thought I'd been sleeping with Zach, instead of taking what I said as a drunken rant about Theo.'

Madison lets out a long breath. 'I knew I received that message. It was gone when I went back to look for it.'

'I messaged Theo after, telling him that I'd messaged you. I couldn't help myself. I know by doing that I was adding fuel to the fire, but I was happily being reckless in the moment. He must have deleted your message,' Nicole says.

Madison thinks back to when she was sitting in his office on the couch while he tapped away at his computer. He could have easily deleted the message.

'I came to the cottage several times to speak to you, tell you what he was like, but when it came to it, I chickened out. I was in the woods one night, trying to psych myself up and you came out with Emily. When you were walking around the shed, you left her asleep but she woke up. I couldn't help but take a look at her. She grabbed my hair, and I ran. I'm sorry if I scared you but I couldn't do it. He'd threatened to kill me, and if you ran in screaming, telling him I was outside, I don't know what he'd have done.'

Madison's hands are shaking. 'Sorry, I need a break. Can't cut your hair with these hands.' She wipes a tear away. 'Have you spoken to Eva?'

'I called her and told her everything. She said she needs time to think so I thought I should at least respect that.'

'You told her how you and Hugo met?'

'Yep, warts and all. She was owed the full truth; after all; we are all connected forever now. Our children are half siblings. I don't know about you, but I want Emily and Caiden to be a part of Aaron's life. I feel as though we have a really special family, and I weirdly love you both, and the kids. I just hope Eva comes round because I miss her.'

Madison feels fuzzy at the idea of them all being one family, connected by their kids, and she doesn't want to let them go. She swallows. The burden of a lie – her lie – runs deep. Madison thinks back to her ex, the man who kept drawing her back into his life. Like an addict, she tried to get away but when he came calling, she'd crave him. It was easy for Camille to tell her to walk away, never speak to him again, but it wasn't that easy. Being with Theo had helped her to start moving on.

She thinks back to the night she and Nicole sat in the rain with Buster, waiting to be rescued, and she realises that friendships like theirs are special, which is why she will never tell them that Hugo is not Emily's father. She can never tell her ex the truth either because he'd want to be in her life again. Like an addict, she needs to stay away from him forever.

SIXTY-TWO
NICOLE

Madison has stopped shaking so she snips away at Nicole's hair. Nicole can't help but think of Eva and how she now knows most of the truth.

She didn't spare a second thought for Eva when she met Hugo all those years ago. One five-minute quickie in a layby with him had resulted in her finding the real love of her life, Aaron. At the time, she hadn't cared that Hugo had a wife waiting for him back at their holiday rental. She only cared that the stupid raven had unstuck itself from the dashboard and that it kept getting caught under her buttocks as they had sex in the driver's seat of his car. She and Will had argued that night, mostly because of her drinking again. Will had left her in the pub, and she and Hugo had got on well, too well. She left his car fifteen minutes later with only the raven as a reminder, that's until she found out she was pregnant with Aaron.

She knew that Will wasn't Aaron's father but keeping that information to herself had seemed like the right thing to do at the time.

Madison gathers up about twenty centimetres in length of Nicole's hair. 'Are you ready to say goodbye to it?'

Nicole smiles and nods. It's time to move on.

As Madison continues, Nicole closes her eyes and thinks back to after Aaron was born. Nicole had tracked Hugo down online. She knew his name and found out that his wife had a baby before she'd had Aaron. There was one particular post on Instagram that had been removed as fast as it was posted, but Nicole would never forget it. It was a baby scan of twins; and Eva had called one of the babies Caiden and the other one Emily.

Eventually, she stopped looking on Instagram at Eva's posts, that was until five years ago. Nicole had the shock of her life when she spotted Hugo walking along the beach in Combe Martin. She feared he'd come to blow her life apart. She went online and saw that his wife, Eva, was sad at his passing. Her obsession with him and Eva became more in real life instead of online, after that day. Nicole had travelled up to Malvern many times just to watch Eva and Caiden. Her dad, bless him, always looked after Aaron. It had been his way of trying to make it up to her after leaving her when she was three. While watching Eva, Nicole saw how sad she was and she wanted to tell her that Hugo was alive, but she still couldn't be sure it was him. Being wrong wasn't an option. Instead she stayed a while that day, watching how Eva tended to the tree she'd planted in Hugo's honour. As soon as Eva had left it, Nicole had dug up the letter that Eva wrote to him. She dug up the wedding ring just after Eva moved to Combe Martin, knowing that it could be used to unnerve Theo, or Hugo – whoever he was.

She thinks back to the nights she spent checking up on Eva after Hugo had died, wondering if she should contact her and deciding not to. Eva has been a part of her life for such a long time and she didn't know it. Nicole's fingers had typed out message after message, only to delete them after. What if she was wrong about Hugo being alive? The last thing she ever wanted to do was upset the poor bereaved widow, and she'd also have to upset her more when she told her about Aaron.

By then, her own marriage had been falling apart. She and Will had been bickering for months but Will still thought Aaron was his son, despite moving back to Kent. Nicole lost their house, then she struggled to pay the rent on the house next door to her father's, so her poor dad had no choice but to take them in.

'Your hair is amazing,' Madison says as she begins a bit of fine tuning.

'You're making it amazing.' Nicole thinks back to the moment when everything changed, the moment Zach came into her life. While scrolling through social media in the middle of the night, she saw a missing person photo pop up – a man who was known to have been seen in the area – and she knew it was Hugo from the obituary photo. There was no name attached. The nose and the slightly horsey look about him were two things that gave him away. The mole sealed the deal for her. It was Hugo. She replied, telling Zach that she knew where Hugo lived. Ever since then, she'd helped Zach to try to expose Hugo; but the closer they got to Hugo, the more she took it upon herself to rile him up.

She wanted him to feel that his past was catching up on him. Those raven sucker toys were easy to find online. She ordered another and left it outside Hugo's shed, then she left the wedding ring in their house. She wanted him to know that he was about to be exposed, though she had never wanted to put Madison and Eva in harm's way.

She'll never tell Eva that she watched her for years, that's just weird. And she'll never tell her that she left the raven toy in her new house while Zach was at the DIY shop.

Nicole had wanted to trigger Caiden's memory, which is why she'd left a little sticker on the toy saying, 'My name is Emily'. Whenever Caiden and Aaron played, she did her best to bring them together in the hope that when they found out they were half-brothers, they would also get to know about the sister they'd lost. In her mind, the toy would start the conversation. Looking back on that move, it wasn't her finest but she couldn't go back in time and do things differently.

When the boys played, Caiden often said that he wished he and Aaron were brothers and Aaron kept saying the same. That is how she knew she'd done the right thing in messing with Hugo's new life. Operation 'unravelling Hugo' had been a success.

EPILOGUE
EVA

One year after Hugo's death

The sea is a little choppy, it's breezy, but the sun is out.

It's taken a lot out of me to get this far but I'm finally ready to move on, and I want to move on with Madison and Nicole, my two best friends. Our children are happy together. Emily is a beautiful toddler now. Caiden and Aaron adore her and they all know that they're half siblings. They took it well. It's amazing how children get on with things. Aaron and Emily are the reasons I won't leave Combe Martin. I want to stay for the children, so that they can all grow up together, which is why I've bought a small terraced house in Ilfracombe and decided to stay working at the Sea Horse Hotel. I keep in touch with Zach and we spend a lot of time talking on the phone and neither of us has initiated a divorce as yet. Maybe we might get close again – one day – who knows? I still can't get over how he deceived me, though knowing about the pain he was in does help a little. Cynthia has started to visit Caiden and I really like her. She's not his blood grandmother but she's amazing with him. I'm happy that she no longer has to live in fear of what Hugo might do to her.

Madison has set up a marshmallow toast on the beach. Apparently, it's what her family do on any occasion, and I think it's lovely. We all have a skewer and she's trying hard to get the small barbeque to light, but given the windy weather, I admire that she's even trying. Sea spray catches my cheeks and it takes me back to the night I was standing here looking into the sea for Hugo. Despite how bad he was, I hope he died fast and it wasn't painful. I've spent many nights since then trying to imagine what it would feel like to drown and it's what nightmares are made of. I shiver at the thought.

'I give up,' Madison says. 'I think we'll just eat them as they are. Who needs to toast?'

I'm proud of her. We spoke a lot in the weeks after Hugo's death. Since Emily's birth, she'd struggled to eat and her family had been worried, but after the truth came out, she's been happier and has put on weight. As a big family, we all eat out together regularly so things are looking up. She's even hoping to move her salon to larger premises with a spa. I know she'll do well, and Nicole and I will be there to cheer her on.

Nicole sits on a rock, hugging Aaron. I admire how she's turned her life around. I look after Aaron while she attends regular AA meetings. She's been throwing herself into her gardening business and even has a contract with the Sea Horse, where I still work. She comes over to me and smiles. 'Well, one year has passed. It's weird thinking we're here. I don't know if I'm meant to feel sad or happy.'

I shrug as I watch a boat bobbing around in the distance. 'I feel more at peace than ever.' I don't want to go into the details but knowing that Hugo was instrumental in me thinking I'd lost my mind, and that it was the same for Madison too, I can't help but feel relieved that Hugo is gone. I'm here to celebrate but I won't shout about it.

'I guess I do too. I'm happy,' Nicole says.

'Me too.' Madison holds Emily in one arm and puts her other arm around me. 'Without Hugo, we wouldn't have each other. We nearly all died but hey-ho. Things worked out well in the end.' She holds her marshmallow stick up. 'Let's toast – without the toast bit – to friendship and family.'

'Friendship and family,' Nicole repeats.

I throw my arms around them. Caiden and Aaron join us. All one big happy, unconventional family. 'Friendship and family,' I say as I look over Nicole's head at the exact spot where I thought Hugo was going to drive me over the cliff's edge. That's when I catch sight of a man wearing an anorak and a beanie hat. A chill runs through me as his eyes meet mine. I'm not close enough to see his features but I know it's Hugo. I release the others and step back to look again, but he's gone, and I wonder, was it really him?

A LETTER FROM CARLA KOVACH

Dear Reader,

Thank you so much for choosing to read *My Husband's Wife*.

I hope you enjoyed reading it as much as I enjoyed writing it. The situation of a widow coming face-to-face with her 'dead' husband on a very normal day was a fun premise for me to explore. I loved delving into Eva's, Nicole's and Madison's lives. Also, the location I chose to set the story in, Combe Martin, is special to me. My husband and I have had many holidays there. It's an amazing place with the most beautiful rockpools and beach.

If you enjoyed *My Husband's Wife* and would like to keep up-to-date with all my latest releases, just sign up at the following link. Your email address will never be shared and you can unsubscribe at any time. You'll also get a free story.

www.bookouture.com/carla-kovach

I'm on BlueSky, Facebook, Instagram and TikTok as I enjoy being part of the online writer/reader communities.

As an author, this is where I hope you'll leave me a review or say a few words about my book.

Thank you,

Carla Kovach

KEEP IN TOUCH WITH CARLA

facebook.com/CKovachAuthor
x.com/CKovachAuthor
instagram.com/carla_kovach

ACKNOWLEDGEMENTS

I'd like to say a massive thank you to everyone who helped create *My Husband's Wife*. Editors, cover designers, people working in every aspect of publishing from admin to management – you're amazing. I'm so grateful and happy to be a part of team Bookouture.

My editor, Helen Jenner, is super and I couldn't have created this book without her.

Thank you, Lisa Brewster. I absolutely love the book cover.

Everyone on the Bookouture publicity team is fabulous. As always, they ensure that publication day is made brilliant.

Sending mahoosive thanks to the blogger and reviewer community. I'm always grateful to those who chose my book from a sea of books available.

Thank you to the Fiction Café Book Club. If you're not in this Facebook group and you're a reader, check it out. This group is awesome.

As always, I love being a member of the Bookouture author family. Huge thanks to them. They show the most amazing levels of support to me and each other. My other author friends are lovely too. Authors are wonderful.

Big appreciation to my beta readers, Derek Coleman, Su Biela, Abigail Osborne, Jamie-Lee Brooke and Vanessa Morgan. Anna Wallace helps me at the proofread stage so great big thanks to her too.

Lots of gratitude to Jamie-Lee Brooke, Julia Sutton and

Abigail Osborne. I love our 'Hot Dog Cringey Crew' support group. This is an in-joke, sorry.

Lastly, special thanks to my husband, Nigel Buckley, for the coffee, the admin, dealing with my website, photography at events, and a whole host of other jobs I'm useless at, and mostly for being with me throughout.

PUBLISHING TEAM

Turning a manuscript into a book requires the efforts of many people. The publishing team at Bookouture would like to acknowledge everyone who contributed to this publication.

Audio
Alba Proko
Sinead O'Connor
Melissa Tran

Commercial
Lauren Morrissette
Hannah Richmond
Imogen Allport

Cover design
The Brewster Project

Data and analysis
Mark Alder
Mohamed Bussuri

Editorial
Helen Jenner
Ria Clare

Copyeditor
Janette Currie

Proofreader
John Romans

Marketing
Alex Crow
Melanie Price
Occy Carr
Ciara Rosney
Martyna Młynarska

Operations and distribution
Marina Valles
Stephanie Straub
Joe Morris

Production
Hannah Snetsinger
Mandy Kullar
Nadia Michael

Publicity
Kim Nash
Noelle Holten
Jess Readett
Sarah Hardy

Rights and contracts
Peta Nightingale
Richard King
Saidah Graham

RAISING READERS
Books Build Bright Futures

Dear Reader,

We'd love your attention for one more page to tell you about the crisis in children's reading, and what we can all do.

Studies have shown that reading for fun is the **single biggest predictor of a child's future life chances** – more than family circumstance, parents' educational background or income. It improves academic results, mental health, wealth, communication skills, ambition and happiness.

The number of children reading for fun is in rapid decline. Young people have a lot of competition for their time, and a worryingly high number do not have a single book at home.

Hachette works extensively with schools, libraries and literacy charities, but here are some ways we can all raise more readers:

- Reading to children for just 10 minutes a day makes a difference
- Don't give up if children aren't regular readers – there will be books for them!

- Visit bookshops and libraries to get recommendations
- Encourage them to listen to audiobooks
- Support school libraries
- Give books as gifts

There's a lot more information about how to encourage children to read on our websites: **www.RaisingReaders.co.uk** and **www.JoinRaisingReaders.com**.

Thank you for reading.

Printed in Dunstable, United Kingdom